UNEXPECTED

THE HENRY BROTHERS

AMY KNUPP

CHAPTER 1

KNOX

This was it.

This was the opportunity I'd been waiting months for. Maybe a lifetime.

Even though my timing sucked, if I didn't level with these people now, I didn't know when I'd get a better chance. It was random luck that I'd ended up on the Rusty Anchor beer patio at the same time as the entire Henry family in the first place, and now all the other customers had cleared out, so it was just the Henrys, their significant others, and me.

I glanced around at each person, all of them jovial about Cash and Ava's engagement announcement. None of them suspecting there could be more to their family.

Simon Henry, with his wife, Faye, at his side, glowed with happiness now that the four children he'd raised had found their life partners—Hayden with Zane, Holden with Chloe, Seth with Everly, and Cash with Ava.

I stepped up to the group, between Ava and Hayden and across from Simon Henry, my heart about to hammer right out of my chest.

"Hey, everyone," I said above their conversations. "I'm sorry to intrude on a private family moment, but I have something I need to say."

The Henry family quieted relatively quickly, expectant smiles and welcome expressions focused on me.

That would change in a heartbeat.

I cleared my throat. "I know this isn't the best time, but I need to level with you all about the reason I came to this small town in the first place."

I was semi-aware of Ava clasping on to my wrist. "What's going on, Knox?"

Focusing fully on the patriarch of the group, with his gray-brown hair and warm eyes, who stood mere feet from me for the first time, I said, "I found out a few months ago that you, sir, are my biological father."

For three full seconds, there wasn't a sound other than a frog or two in the distance. I wasn't sure anyone in the group of ten had breathed.

Then Ava, my closest friend in town as well as my writing partner, squeezed my wrist tighter and breathed out, "Wow."

I kept my eyes locked on Simon Henry, my father, holding my own breath as I waited for his reaction. There was confusion, then shock. Then he glanced toward his wife, who wrapped herself around his arm supportively.

"Holy shit," Holden said from somewhere to my right.

I didn't divert my attention from the sixty-eight-year-old man in front of me, my heart pounding harder with every second he remained silent.

Finally, with the slightest tilt of his head, he said calmly, "Who is your mother?"

"Janet Breckenridge."

Simon blew out a sharp breath, and his gaze became unfocused, his eyes widening. "I didn't think anything of it when I heard your last name..."

"It's a common name," I said.

"You know this Janet Breckenridge, Dad?" Seth asked.

Seth was the second oldest of my half-siblings. I'd gotten to know him over the past three months and considered Holden, the third oldest, a friend. I was older than all of them, even Cash, who'd only recently become civil toward me. He stood on the other side of Ava, and I didn't have to turn my head in his direction to sense the antipathy emanating from him.

"I did," Simon answered. "How old are you, Knox?"

"I turned forty-two in February."

I could see him doing the math in his head. I knew it would work out. I didn't have anything to go on except my mother's revelation after her death, but I trusted her. She didn't have any reason to make this up.

"I…" Simon blew out another breath.

I didn't know him, hadn't laid eyes on him in person until this evening, but I could tell he was shaken.

"I guess I don't understand," he finally said. "Your mother…never told me. I never knew I had another son…"

"You still don't know that," Seth said.

"My mother died in December," I explained, steamrolling right over any sadness that threatened to seep in. My grief had no place in tonight's discussion. "She left a letter for me that revealed the secret she'd kept for my entire life—the name of my father." I nodded once at Simon.

"Why would she keep that from you?" Hayden asked, her voice teeming with emotion.

I inhaled slowly, gathering my composure, because even with several months to work through this, even after reading her reasons, I still hadn't made peace with my mother's decision all those years ago.

"I only know what she said in her letter," I said quietly, hoping we were indeed alone on this patio. The news would travel through town fast enough as it was, but I'd prefer that didn't happen until the Henrys were ready to talk about it.

"Tell us," Hayden said. "What did her letter say?"

I did my best to keep my voice neutral, like a narrator talking about someone else's crazy background. "She said she met you"—again, I nodded to Simon—"at a convention for the company she worked for. The company *you* worked for."

"In Houston," Simon said. "It was early summer, already sweltering there." He frowned. "Nita and I were going through a rough patch. We'd broken up that spring," he explained in a rush with a glance around the circle. Nita was the late mother of my four younger half-siblings.

"My mom mentioned that," I said, "so you must have told her."

Simon nodded. "We…connected for that short interval of time. Spent the weekend together."

"We don't need details of that, Dad," Hayden said with a plea in her voice.

He let out a halfhearted chuckle and shook his head. "Details will not be offered. I told Janet about Nita, not because she needed to know but because I was confused about her. At the end of our weekend, Janet and I agreed not to stay in touch. There was no point. She lived in Texas, and I lived in Tennessee. We didn't have email back then. No cell phones. You had to really want to stay in touch with someone…"

His story matched what my mom had told me.

I continued, "She found out she was pregnant and hired an investigator to track you down."

"They couldn't find him?" Holden asked. His wife, Chloe, held his hand. "Henry's a pretty common name, I guess."

"They found him," I said. "Through his and Nita's engagement announcement in the newspaper."

Someone, maybe Everly, gasped.

"My mom made the decision to keep the news to herself. She didn't want to shake up your future with your fiancée," I said to Simon. "She moved to a management position at a competitor, so she made good money and didn't have to travel much anymore. She decided to be a single mom, and that's what she did."

"She never got married?" Hayden asked.

"It was always just the two of us," I answered.

"And she never told you who your father was?" Ava asked.

I shook my head. "When I was young, she told me some kids had two parents and some had one, and our family worked out that I had one parent. Eventually I wanted to know more, of course, and she told me she only ever knew my father's first name and that there was no way to track him down."

There was a collective silence again, and I could feel people judging my mother. I could understand it. I'd felt more than a little anger myself since finding out the truth, but that was mixed in with compassion and love and grief, because my history was her and me against the world. We were all the other had, as my grandparents had died when I was a toddler, and my mom had no siblings.

"But she decided to tell you everything in a letter?" Seth asked. I could hear the skepticism in his tone.

"That's right," I said. "She explained she went through periods of doubt my whole life, when she felt guilty that I didn't have a father figure like other kids. When she realized she wasn't going to beat the cancer, she knew she had to tell me the truth. She acknowledged in her letter she took the coward's way out."

"I'll say," Cash said. It was the first thing he'd uttered, and his tone wasn't kind or understanding.

I couldn't say I disagreed with him, but again the emotions I felt about my mom were a quagmire. She'd been a good mother, sacrificed a lot for me, so nothing was as clear-cut in my heart.

"Anyway, I found out, like I said, a couple of weeks after

she died. I sat on it for a few months, trying to figure out what to do. I searched for you online"—I nodded to Simon again—"and learned you'd retired recently from the same company. I didn't find much other information on you, but I did find Henry's Restaurant and realized it was run by your sons. My half-brothers." I swallowed hard, because emotion surged in my throat despite all my months of imagining this moment. "I've never had a family, ever. Just my mom. So while a part of me acknowledged it might be smart not to shake things up, a bigger part of me needed to at least meet you."

"To hell with not shaking things up, I guess," Cash muttered.

"Cash," Ava said, running a soothing hand over his back.

"I'm reeling more than a little," Simon said. "It's going to take time to wrap my head around everything."

"I understand," I said. His words gave me hope that he had every intention of doing just that.

"Do you have any proof of what you're claiming?" Seth asked.

I shook my head. "Only my mother's word, but I'm willing to do a test. Whatever you want." Again, I looked at Simon because that was up to him, not his son.

"Maybe. I don't know. I'm not thinking straight." Simon rubbed his forehead.

"It's okay, Dad," Hayden said. "You don't have to figure out everything tonight."

"None of us do," Faye said. "I, for one, am glad you told us, Knox. I won't put words into my husband's mouth, but he's one of the most caring men I've ever known. I suspect you have some of that in you too."

"Remains to be seen," Cash said. "He's been lying to us for months."

"Cash," Simon said sharply.

"It's okay," I said. "He's right. I want to apologize for that.

You might not believe me, but it's been keeping me up at night. You all have been so welcoming, and I hated not leveling with you, but I thought your dad—*our* dad— shouldn't be the last to find out. I thought I'd run into him long before this. And while I'm apologizing, I'm sorry for raining on your happy news tonight. I hesitated, but I didn't know when I would get this opportunity again, where you were all together."

"That's fair," Hayden said. "I just have one question. How the hell am I getting stuck with yet another older brother?"

There was halfhearted laughter, mostly from the women and Holden, and I sensed it would take a while for Seth and Cash to accept me—if they ever did.

"Welcome to the family, Knox," Hayden said as she gave me a quick hug, and a small portion of my tension dissipated as I let it sink in that I was hugging my half-sister. Family.

"Thanks, Hayden."

Before I could say more, Simon spoke up. "Like Faye said, I'm glad you told us. I hope we can get to know each other. Faye and I are leaving town for a long weekend. That'll give me a chance to start to absorb this news. Let me get your phone number. I don't know much, but I do know, if you're my son, I'd like to know you better."

"Thank you. I'd like that." I exhaled, feeling the beginnings of relief that he hadn't rejected me or taken the news badly. A chance was all I wanted.

When he held out his phone with my name typed into a contact, I entered my phone number.

"Let's go, Ava. See if we can get back to our celebratory mood," Cash snapped. He stormed toward the patio exit without saying goodbye to anyone.

"Are we still on for tomorrow?" Ava asked me, half-turned to watch her fiancé leave.

"If you're up for it, hell yes." I needed to bury my brain back in fiction writing as soon as possible.

"It's my job. Cash isn't going to like it, but you and I are working together. I'm still totally in. I'll be there." She squeezed my arm again. "I gotta go. Night, everyone."

"Night, Ava. Good luck with him," Hayden called after her. Others said their goodbyes to her as well.

There was nothing else I could say tonight to win anyone over. I'd known this going in, but I couldn't help feeling empty. Worried. "It's getting late," I said. "I'm going to take off. I'm probably not the most welcome guy right now. Again, I'm sorry for the inopportune timing. Thanks for hearing me out."

Simon—my father—stepped forward, his hand extended. We shook as he said, "I'll be in touch soon, Knox. You have a good night."

"Good night." I nodded at the group in general and headed to the exit, noting only a couple of them said goodbye.

As I walked toward the house I'd just bought down the road, I couldn't help but wonder if purchasing real estate here in Dragonfly Lake, Tennessee, had been premature and overly optimistic. If moving to the same small town as my only biological family was a giant mistake.

What if my only living family never accepted me?

The thought of them had given me hope for the past few months. Getting to know my half-brothers—even though they hadn't realized we were related—had given me a taste of what it would be like to be part of a family, to not be so alone. In the process, I'd fallen in love with this close-knit community, the scenic town situated on the shore of Dragonfly Lake.

Now I wondered if I'd ever truly be accepted here as a member of the Henry family or if I'd just made the biggest miscalculation of my life.

CHAPTER 2

QUINCY

The apartment was quiet as I pulled on my new super-cute jean capris with my Henry's Restaurant T-shirt, yesterday's buzz of excitement spilling into today in spite of a medium-sized hangover from the celebration. The capris would probably be my last unnecessary clothing purchase for the next few months as I needed to save up as much money as I could. I wasn't going to feel bad about buying these though.

They *were* cute. They had bling on the pockets.

I smiled at myself in the bathroom mirror even though I had shadows under my eyes from the late night, popped some acetaminophen to remedy the dull headache, then accidentally dropped the bottle of pills on the floor before I'd gotten the lid screwed on. I crouched down and played fifty-two pickup—or more like a hundred fifty-two pickup—not letting a minor thing like my chronic clumsiness get me down today.

My headache would go away soon enough, but maybe I was getting too old to stay out drinking until the bars closed, at least on nights when I worked the next day. Was twenty-eight too old? I'd definitely have to make a lot of changes in January when I went back to college. Coincidentally that was one of the things we'd been celebrating—my acceptance letter.

I swept my hair up in a messy bun, then grinned again, savoring the relief at finally finding a direction for my life. Better late than never, right? Funny how a breakup could help a girl get her shit together.

I walked out of the bathroom, pulled on my lime-green work shoes, and noted Jewel's door was still closed, which told me she hadn't woken up for the day yet. Probably for the best, as she'd been overserved last night, even more so than I. She didn't have to work today.

We'd gone out to the Fly by Night and then the Barn Bar to celebrate Jewel's promotion to management at Humble's Pizza Pie and my acceptance letter to go back to school. It seemed like everyone who'd been out on a Tuesday evening had bought us a celebratory shot. I'd handed more than a few of mine over to my roomie, knowing I'd struggle with my work shift if I didn't. She absolutely deserved the fun times—and the promotion, of course. She was great at her job.

I was not so great at my job as a server, but it was only for three more months. Normally my inadequacy at my full-time job would make my gut tighten, but having an end date and a plan made everything more tolerable. I just hoped the Henrys' patience with me and my clumsy self would last that long.

I searched the trinket tray on top of my dresser for my cartoon dinosaur earrings that hung off my lobes by their mouths, making it look like they were biting me. They drew a genuine grin from me, like they always did, and were usually good for conversation—and higher tips—at work, especially on tables with kids. Since I wore my hair up, the dinos would be impossible to ignore.

I put them on, then went out to the kitchen to fill my water bottle.

The apartment door burst open, and Piper, my other roommate, breezed in, her caramel-colored hair draping over her shoulders and her eyes lit with happiness.

"Okay, what are *you* up to?" I asked, raising a brow. No one should be *that* cheery and bright-eyed after staying out till two a.m. on a weeknight. "Where've you been?"

"Downstairs working."

"It's Wednesday. You don't usually start so early on Tansy's day off."

"I was catching up on paperwork and orders before I open." Her tone reminded me she, too, loved her job as the owner of Oopsie Daisies, an admittedly adorable flower shop.

"You need your office back," I said.

When Mitchell and I had broken up a few months ago, my entire world had been turned upside down. I'd been living with him, so I'd needed a new place to stay stat. Piper had cleared out the third bedroom in her apartment. She and her cousin Jewel had helped move me out of his apartment and in with them.

Finding myself suddenly single had messed with my head, made my server job seem less like a life plan and more like a stepping stone to…something. I hadn't known what at the time. But ultimately, the breakup had led to the decision to finally go back to school, something my dad had been encouraging me to do since I'd dropped out at age nineteen.

"I can work just fine in the shop, so hush. Anyway, I have news." Piper bounced up and down in her daisy-print sneakers.

"Tell me."

"I heard from the Marks Resort. They're signing the contract."

I shed my gloom faster than a stripper could shed a Velcro

dress, rushed over to her, and hugged her. "Oh, my God, that's awesome, Piper! For the weekly service?"

"For the weekly service!"

We jumped up and down together, laughing and still hugging. I gave her a big smackeroo kiss on her cheek and squeezed her tight before ending the hug.

"I'm so stinking happy for you," I said, my grin as wide as hers.

"Thank you. I can hardly believe it. First delivery is next week, which means this weekend is going to be double crazy what with the homecoming dance Saturday."

"You know I'll be helping you Saturday. I took the day off for you."

"I couldn't do it without you and Jewel and Tansy. I wish I could give you more frequent shifts."

I laughed. "But do you really? Think of the vases I could break in a week."

"There is that," she said lightly, as if it didn't matter that I was the actual clumsiest person alive. "What time do you work?"

"Ten. I guess I better get going."

Piper laughed. "Wouldn't want to be less than twenty minutes early."

"Fifteen minutes early is late," I said with a shrug and a grin. I got a lot of lighthearted teasing from my roomies about my need to be early everywhere. I checked the forecast on my phone. "Suddenly jacket weather is here, huh?"

"Happy fall," Piper said. "I swear the trees started changing color overnight."

I ducked back into my room, dug through the closet, and located my cropped denim jacket and my dark blue scarf. Yesterday the weather had been beautiful, but we'd been warned a cold front was coming through.

On my way out, I hugged Piper and told her congrats again, then rushed down the flight of stairs to the sidewalk level, hitting the final step wrong and nearly stumbling. But I didn't, and I congratulated myself on the save.

The pavement was wet, though it wasn't raining at the moment. The clouds were heavy and looked like they could open again soon. I should've grabbed an umbrella, but I was banking on the hope I could make it the three blocks to work without getting soaked. I had a car, but I walked whenever I could because it was stupid to drive three blocks.

Our apartment was directly above Oopsie Daisies, and I couldn't help but notice the display window as I walked by. Piper had done more than paperwork this morning.

The window was awash with golds and oranges from an array of chrysanthemums, sunflowers, and pumpkins. She'd created a farmhouse-style display, with an old wooden ladder, metal buckets, an antique chair, and rustic-looking crocks. She'd added three wooden signs—something Piper both collected and created—"Pumpkin kisses and harvest wishes," "In a world where you can be anything, be kind," and "The earth laughs in flowers."

My roommate had such a knack for making things beautiful. There was no question she was doing exactly what she was meant to be doing.

As I reached the sidewalk in front of the gym, my phone rang. I pulled it out.

Cynthia. My stepmother. My friends had a litany of not-so-nice names for her, but I tried not to use them. I babysat my younger half-siblings often, had cared for them since they were born, and I'd hate to slip up around them.

As I crossed to the hardware store, I sucked in a breath for fortitude and answered the call.

"Hi, Cynthia."

"Quincy. You remember the annual awards ceremony for your father's company is next Thursday evening, right? The one where he's receiving an award?"

I'm doing well, thanks. How 'bout you?

The lack of warmth between us was the status quo. It could be exhausting, so I mostly tried to ignore it.

I tried to recall mention of a ceremony. "I don't think you told me about a ceremony," I said, actually certain she hadn't. An award would be a big deal for my dad, and I would've remembered it.

"I'm sure I did a few weeks ago."

"If you did, I don't remember it," I said, keeping my tone light, making an effort to get along. She was the type of person you couldn't win an argument with.

She expelled a disappointed sigh. "Fall sports season is extra busy for us, so maybe I forgot. At any rate, the dinner is at seven in Nashville, and we'll need you to be here to watch Molly by five thirty."

I tried to remember my schedule for next week. "I'll have to check whether I work."

"If you do, you need to switch shifts with someone, Quincy. You know I can't find anyone else this late."

Which was why she should've asked me about two weeks ago instead of assuming I could stay with my half-siblings.

"This is an important night for your father."

I rolled my eyes and bit my tongue. I loved my father, everything about him except his choice of second wife. He deserved the recognition, deserved to bask in the spotlight for his normally unspotlighted job in insurance. But I resented her using that to manipulate me.

"It's just a server shift," she pressed. "Surely you can find someone to trade with. They do that all the time in the food industry."

That wasn't false, but I ground my molars together because Cynthia knew exactly nothing about being in food service. She had never worked in the industry. She'd had her job as the office manager at Dr. Julian's medical practice for as long as I'd known her, and her self-importance because of it was off the charts. It reeked of insecurity, but even knowing that didn't make her easier to deal with.

"Please, Quincy," my stepmother said, her tone suddenly warmer, a sure sign my dad had entered the room she was in.

"Hey, honey," he said in the background, confirming my suspicion.

My dad had a good heart and worked his butt off. His main fault was that he'd fallen in love with Cynthia.

"If I have to work, I'll find someone to trade with," I said, not for Cynthia but for my dad and for Molly, my youngest half-sibling, who was eleven and still legitimately needed someone to stay with her when her parents were gone.

"Oh, thank you, honey. Hannah's got a cross-country meet, so it'll just be Molly and Brayden. They'll be so happy to see you."

Brayden loved me, but I could promise her, at fourteen, he hated having a babysitter, even me. "I'll be happy to see them too," I said, even though I'd just seen Molly earlier this week.

Cynthia repeated what time she needed me. Then we said goodbye—without a thank-you from her—and hung up as I crossed the street and turned the corner to Main.

I tried to force my annoyance with Cynthia out of my mind. It was so tiring. I wished I knew how to get along better with her, but this was our pattern, and I had no idea how to change it. It would take two to fix it, wouldn't it? And working together wasn't something my stepmom and I did well.

Thankfully, before I had time to get too absorbed in my irritation, a familiar face down the way distracted me.

"Oh, my goodness, is that the cutest girl in the world?" I called out.

Two-year-old Aster and her parents, Tansy and Reggie, were coming toward me.

"Do you see Quincy?" Tansy asked her daughter, who she was carrying.

They were still about two stores down when Tansy let Aster down, took her hand, and rushed toward me, with Reggie grinning and following at a more normal pace.

"Heeeey," I said, holding my arms out for Aster.

"Kissssy!" the little girl yelled, which was how she pronounced my name.

When she reached me, I swept her up into my arms and gave her a big hug.

"Look at you," I said, making a point of checking her out in detail. She wore a long-sleeved black cotton dress with horizontal, rainbow-colored stripes, a denim jacket, and black leggings with a heart print in rainbow colors. Her black hair was pulled up into two balls on top of her head and held up with pink-beaded elastics. "Did you get a new dress?"

Nodding, her irresistible brown eyes earnest, she said, "'Cause it's cold!"

"Yes, it is. What are you guys doing out and about today?" I asked Aster's parents.

"We're going to the Dragonfly Diner. Little miss, here, used the potty for the very first time," Tansy said.

"Good for you," I told Aster, holding out my hand and receiving a high five.

"At this rate, potty training's going to get expensive," Reggie said, grinning, a proud sparkle in his eyes.

"Hey, congratulations on your school news," Tansy said.

"Yeah, congrats," Reggie added.

"Thanks! It feels weird to go back at twenty-eight, but I'm happy to finally have a plan."

"Teaching, right?"

I nodded. "Elementary ed."

"You hear that, Aster? Miss Quincy's going to be a teacher. Maybe she'll be your teacher when you go to school."

Aster didn't appear to know what to say to that. She just grinned big and clapped her hands together once as she stared at me with her earnest eyes.

"I'd love to be your teacher, Aster."

"Bet your dad is happy for you," Tansy said.

Tansy and I weren't super close, mostly just knew each other through Piper's shop, but it was common knowledge that my dad had wanted me to go back to school for ages. I knew he was only trying to help, and he wasn't too bad about the pressure. I just hadn't been ready until finding myself suddenly single. Waiting tables wasn't right for my lifelong plan, and I guess I'd been completely invested in the belief that Mitchell and I would marry someday and have a family.

"Where are you heading on this gloomy day?" Tansy asked.

"Work, which reminds me I should probably get going." I planted a noisy kiss on Aster's chubby cheek, eliciting a giggle. "But I'm so happy I got to see you."

"Me too," Aster said as I set her on the sidewalk.

After telling Reggie and Tansy goodbye, I headed off to work, tripping a bit up the curb but keeping a genuine smile on my face. It might be crummy, chilly weather, I might not adore my job, but my future was looking up. Finally.

CHAPTER 3

KNOX

I was all screwed up on Wednesday.

I hadn't slept for shit last night after my spontaneous "big reveal." I'd thought once I spilled the beans, my stress might ease some. At least I wouldn't be keeping a secret from people I had become friends with.

The scene had been less than reassuring though, and I'd been fixated on it for hours on end. Had there been a better way to tell them? Should I have told Simon first, in private, then fessed up to my half-siblings separately?

I'd decided I'd done what I had to do, when I had to do it, for the sake of my conscience and my mental health, but in the end, that hadn't calmed my mind at all.

When I'd come to Dragonfly Lake for a two-week stay back in June, my goal had been to meet the Henrys and explain our connection. I'd never thought it would be easy. In fact, multiple times, I'd argued with myself that I should let it go. Forget about meeting my family. Forget about trying to connect with my only living relatives.

Turned out I hadn't been able to. Once I'd been aware of

their existence, I was compelled to meet them. The world could seem like a lonely place when you didn't have any family to speak of.

So I'd come here for that short vacation, run into my half-brothers at Henry's as I'd hoped, fallen in love with the town and the lake, and decided to make this my home.

Now, months later, I'd just relocated from Texas and bought and moved into a lakefront property—for better or worse.

After my restless night, I'd attempted to work on the chapter I owed Ava for our work in progress, but between being sleep-deprived and preoccupied with real life, I hadn't made much headway.

Then Simon had called.

He'd apologized for how he'd handled last night—apologized, for God's sake—and invited me to dinner at his and Faye's home in Nashville next week. I'd snapped up that invitation immediately, and we had a date for a week from Sunday.

Hearing from my father, being reassured that he hadn't done a one eighty and decided I could fuck right off, had settled me down some. I'd finally gotten some words down on the story, but I'd lost track of time in the process.

Now I was late for my two-o'clock plotting meeting with Ava.

I was uneasy about meeting at Henry's because chances were decent I'd run into Seth or Cash, but I refused to hide. And maybe one or both had calmed down overnight, Seth from his suspicions and Cash from his anger.

I rushed out to my car, deciding to drive even though my house was only a block and a half away. Then I'd be less late.

My garage was full of moving boxes, so my SUV was parked in the driveway. I clicked the fob to unlock it, started to get in, then realized I'd forgotten my writing bag with my notebooks and laptop. Swearing to myself, I left the driver's door open and jogged back inside to get it. I grabbed the bag, then noticed my computer was still plugged in and sitting, open but asleep, on the kitchen island where I'd been reading over my work.

"Son of a bitch," I muttered, shaking my head and wondering if Ava and I would get anywhere with my head so far up my ass I could see my throat. I might be better off staying home and taking a nap. Too bad I'd never been a napper.

I unplugged the cord, then took the time to wind it neatly and stuffed it and the laptop in my bag. With a glance at the clock on the stove, I noted I was now fifteen minutes late. I pulled out my phone and clicked on Ava's name to text her.

> On my way. Sorry I'm late.

Without waiting for a response, I stuffed my phone in my pocket, picked up my bag, hurried to the door, and went outside.

A car took off from in front of my house as I exited. I only half noticed it and only noticed it that much because it was a no-parking zone, so there weren't normally cars parked along Lake Road. As I walked to my gaping driver's-side door, I wondered if Cash, who was the executive chef at Henry's, was working today—

I stopped short because there was something sitting on the driver's seat. Something of considerable size wedged in between the steering wheel and the seat back.

I frowned and went closer, wondering who the fuck was messing with me when I was running so late. Glancing around, I did a quick search for someone watching me, taking video of me, paying any bit of attention to me, but fall had shown up in a chilly, unpleasant bluster overnight, and there wasn't a soul in sight.

With a couple more steps, it hit me that that was a car seat thing for a kid—maybe? It was bulky and had an awning facing me and a handle—

Then I saw two tiny feet in baggy socks with rabbits on them, jutting out from beneath a blanket, and the breath came gasping out of me as my heart thundered.

Those feet looked real.

I peeked over the awning to see more, and…those feet were attached to…

Fuck me running, there was a baby in there.

I dared to crane my head over the edge of the seat to confirm that it was a living, breathing tiny human, holding out hope I'd discover a plastic doll head with realistic legs and body.

It was real as real could be. *She*, judging by the pink blanket wrapped over everything except the feet. The baby appeared to be sleeping peacefully.

I took a step back, feeling the exact opposite of peaceful.

There was a baby in a car seat in my car.

There was no one around to take care of or claim this baby. Another more careful look around the area confirmed that.

The car that had driven off…

Had someone intentionally stuffed this baby into my front seat and left?

I rubbed my hands up and down my face, wondering what the ever-loving fuck to do.

I didn't know the first thing about babies. I'd never held one. Never gotten one out of a car seat. Wouldn't know how to care for one if I did.

I had to do something. Call the cops? I didn't even know what to tell them.

I stepped close again, working up my courage, as if there was a venomous snake in that bucket-like seat instead of a bundle of pink human. My angle on the baby's face was awkward, as she was facing the passenger door with her back to me, but I peered down at her. Her tiny bottom lip quivered, and I stiffened.

Definitely a live baby.

In my car.

As I straightened and tried to back out of my hunched position over her, I knocked my head on the doorframe, held in a swear word, and simultaneously noticed a piece of paper tucked in at the baby's side.

Swallowing, I grabbed the paper and carefully stepped back without hitting my head again. I straightened and unfolded it, my hands shaking.

> Knox,
>
> This is your daughter, Juniper Grace. I wanted to tell you in May when she was born, but you didn't want to talk to me. I never signed up for this. I can't do it anymore. Sorry.
>
> Gina

I read it three times, then glanced around for someone laughing, ha ha, joke's on me.

I was still alone on the quiet street. Excruciatingly alone with a...five-month-old baby, I guessed...

My daughter?

Running another calculation in my head, I figured a May baby would be conceived in August, maybe early September.

Gina and I broke up last October.

It was mathematically feasible, I guess, but...a baby?

I wasn't a father. I couldn't be.

My phone buzzed in my back pocket, and I knew without looking it was Ava. Shit. Ava. She was still waiting, and there was a baby in my front seat, and what the hell was a person supposed to do with a spare baby?

I couldn't think straight, but I knew I was in way over my head. I'd take her to Ava, and she'd help me figure out what to do.

I went back to the door and leaned in over the carrier— over the *baby*—and stopped short. A handle jutted up, so I grabbed it and carefully tugged the carrier out enough to flip it around so I could really see the infant.

She slept on, not noticing she'd been moved, having no idea that her life had just been gigantically altered when her mother had deserted her.

As I studied her fuzzy patch of light hair, chubby cheeks, and doll-like eyelashes, my chest contracted with sadness for this tiny girl. Sadness for her and a stirring of anger at Gina. What the hell was she thinking? She *hadn't signed up for this?* Welcome to life, honey.

Anger wouldn't solve my problem, wouldn't solve this baby's problems. I didn't have the first clue what would, but standing here in my driveway wasn't the answer.

Slamming down on my emotions, I went into practical mode.

Babies rode in the backseat. I knew that much.

I pulled the carrier out, opened the back door, and tried to figure out how to install it. I didn't have a clue. I glanced to the east, toward Henry's. If I took a few steps to the end of my driveway, I'd be able to see the sign. It was that close.

I set the carrier on the seat with the baby facing forward, so I could keep an eye on her in the mirror, and got in. There was undoubtedly a way to belt her in, but I had no idea how. I'd drive the block and a half slowly, carefully. There was almost no traffic anyway on this gloomy Wednesday after-noon in the off-season. I knew it wasn't ideal, but I needed a class in car seat 101.

When I climbed into the driver's seat, I checked the baby

—Juniper—in the mirror and saw she was still sleeping, so peacefully, so naively.

My whole body felt shaky, nervous as fuck that something would happen between my house and Henry's that would endanger the helpless baby. With a breath that did nothing to settle me, I backed out and drove the block and a half to the parking lot, relieved to see it was only partly full, the lunch crowd mostly gone.

I pulled into a spot near the door, put the car in park, and exhaled. My gaze went to the mirror again in time to see the baby turn her head, her eyes still closed.

Okay. I'd gotten her here, and she appeared to still be okay.

What now?

I couldn't walk into Henry's with a baby. Word would be all over town before I could settle in at a table. There'd probably be speculation that I kidnapped her or stole her, because I was the least likely to actually *have* a baby.

Except you might have a baby.

Yeah, I couldn't process that right now. Not even close.

I took my phone out and saw that Ava had indeed messaged me not to rush, that she had coffee and was fine, watching her fiancé run the kitchen.

With a quiet, semihysterical laugh to myself, I wished coffee would make me fine, but I wasn't sure anything could, maybe not ever again.

My hands were shaking so badly I could barely type, but I finally got a text to her.

> I'm in the parking lot. I need you to come out to my SUV, please.

CHAPTER 4

KNOX

I spent the next five minutes—which seemed like an hour —flipping my gaze between the door Ava would come out, as if she could singlehandedly save me and fix my problem, and the baby in the mirror.

Finally the restaurant door opened, and Ava emerged. She smiled as she spotted me. I couldn't seem to smile back.

I rolled my window down as she approached.

"Hey, partner. What's going on?" Her brows went from raised in greeting to puzzled.

"Something happened," I said, "and I don't know what the fuck to do." I pointed over my shoulder to the backseat.

Ava's gaze shot behind me. Then she looked back at me and tilted her head. "What happened?"

"There's a baby. In my backseat."

She stepped to the door, leaned in closer, and peered into the backseat. "Whose baby?"

I let out a laughing scoff. "Mine supposedly."

Ava's head popped back in front of my window, her eyes wide. "Come again?"

"Right?" I leaned my head against the headrest. "I was running late. Went out to my SUV, realized I'd forgotten my writing stuff. Went in to get it. It took me no more than two or three minutes. When I came back out, the baby carrier was in my driver's seat."

Her mouth gaped for a couple seconds before she spoke. "How did it get there?"

"I noticed a car pulling away when I came out. Didn't think much of it at the time, but that's all I can figure out. Whoever was in that car stuck the baby in my front seat."

She stared at me for another few seconds. "And you have no clue who?"

"There was a note tucked in. It's from my ex, Gina." I swallowed hard and said, "She claims this is my child."

"Wow." Ava peered at the baby again. "Is it— Do you think it's true?"

A crazed laugh escaped me. "I'd like to say no, but…" I shook my head, wondered what twilight zone I'd stepped into. "On the surface, the math could work."

"Hold on." Ava hurried around the front of my SUV and climbed into the passenger seat. "Less conspicuous this way. So your ex never mentioned she was pregnant?"

I shook my head. "We broke up in October. Juniper— that's the baby's name—"

"Adorable," Ava said, turning back to check out the infant again with one of those baby-crazy grins women sometimes got.

"Juniper was supposedly born in May," I continued. "So she would've been conceived before we broke up. If the dates are true."

"I'm not an expert on babies by any stretch of the imagination, but she could be five months old."

"I have no idea how to find out the truth, but in the meantime, what the fuck do I do with this tiny baby in my car?"

With a sympathetic grin and a supportive hand on my arm, Ava said, "I'm not sure, other than try to stop swearing."

With my elbow propped on the console between us, I rubbed my fingers over my forehead.

"Do I take her to the cops?" I asked.

"I'm pretty sure they'd take the baby to social services. What if it *is* yours? You don't want that, right?"

I let out a desperate laugh. "I don't have the slightest idea what I want. I've not given any thought to having an insta-baby."

"Understandable," she said. She turned to watch the baby. "We're not going to solve anything sitting here. Why don't we take her inside, get a drink and some food if you're hungry, and figure out the next step. Seth's in his office, and Cash is in the kitchen. Maybe one of them will know what to do."

"Have they had someone leave a baby in their car?"

"Not to my knowledge, but they're pretty resourceful."

"What are people going to think if I walk in with a baby?"

She paused from opening the door. "People will talk. No matter what. They haven't had a story this rich since Everly Ash hid away in Seth's apartment. But their talk is harmless, and maybe someone will have an idea what to do. This town is pretty helpful when someone's facing tough times."

I thought over the options. I suspected she was right about law enforcement getting children's services involved, and while I wasn't convinced that would be the worst thing, I wasn't convinced it wouldn't be either.

"I don't like it, but let's go," I said.

We both got out of the car and met at the door by the baby. "Should I take her out of the seat?" I asked.

Ava shook her head. "I think leave her in. She's sleeping peacefully right now. Why disturb her? She'll probably wake up hungry at some point—"

"Fuck. Then what'll we do?"

With a gentle laugh, Ava said, "Language. We'll feed her. Somehow. Someone in there has to know more than we do."

"Most likely everyone in there knows more than I do."

"Was there any kind of bag with her?"

I shook my head. "Just the carrier shoved into my driver's seat and the note tucked into the blanket."

Ava reached in and grabbed the carrier. "We need to figure out how to hook her in."

"And how to feed her. And diaper her. And clothe her…" I swayed with a wave of dizziness and grabbed on to the car door. Thankfully it passed within two seconds.

As Ava hefted the carrier out, she grunted. "You're heavier than you look, little lady."

Feeling shell-shocked, I reached for the handle, noting gratefully that the baby slept on. "I'll carry her. You get the doors."

I followed Ava to the main entrance.

To think, when I'd woken up this morning, I'd believed my life was rife with complications. God or whoever was in charge had apparently been peering in on my existence and had thrown out a big, fat *hold my beer*.

CHAPTER 5

UINCY

or some reason, today's lunch shift at Henry's had
been chaotic and crowded.

Even though it was technically the town's slow
Henry's didn't appear to be affected by any downturn
ss. Which was good, of course. Though filming for
Town Smorgasbord episode hadn't begun yet, word
People were excited to support the Henrys.

ppy for them, especially Cash, who'd made
show his sole goal for months on end. No one
w good the food was here. I was happy for
se a full house meant more tips for me. If the
dn't spark me, I just played a game with
ed to predict what familiar faces would
shift. There were always several. Always.
one of my lunch tables remained occu-
no one else would come in before the
between lunch and dinner service. I
prepping for the dinner shift, but it
o and from tables and balancing

trays, which was not my strong point. So far today, I hadn't dropped anything, so that was a win.

I was bussing a table when I noticed Cash's fiancée, Ava, coming back in the door with her writing partner, Knox. Our host, Elijah, had left early, and the rest of us were covering the host stand, so I headed over to greet them.

"You're back," I said to Ava, smiling. I didn't know her well yet, but what I knew I really liked. She was so easygoing, the opposite of Cash. I liked him too, but I knew my record of breaking dishes bothered him, and I couldn't really blame him. It bothered me too, but it was what it was. I tried hard not to be a klutz.

"We've had a wrinkle crop up," Ava said, then glanced behind her.

"Oh!" I said, noticing Knox had an adorable baby with him. "Who does this precious girl belong to?"

"Question of the hour," Knox muttered, or at least I thought that's what he said.

I knew him even less than I knew Ava. I'd waited on his table a few times, and he was always friendly and a good tipper, but we didn't chat much outside of his order and the requisite small talk. He was older, maybe early forties, but he was one of those men who looked good enough you didn't really care about his age. After the morning's news—that he was the half-brother of the Henrys—it all made sense. G apparently didn't make ugly Henrys...or Breckenridges, that matter.

"We..." Ava looked around me, toward the dining sec on the other side of the bar. "Could we get that corner by the window? Tucked out of the way?"

"Of course," I said. It was in my section, so I'd been about no one else coming, but I didn't mind. Particula meant I could coo over that sweet baby.

I picked up menus, then lost my grip on one of

bent over to retrieve it and asked, "Do you need a high chair?"

Ava and Knox paused and looked at each other, then looked at me.

"I have no idea, honestly," Ava finally said. "I don't think she's old enough to sit in one. We'll just let her sleep in her carrier for as long as possible."

I led them to the table, puzzled by Ava's lack of familiarity with the baby. Puzzled by so much. "Are you two babysitting?" I couldn't hold the question in.

There was a tense pause before Ava said, "No." She and Knox exchanged a look. "It's going to get out," she said quietly.

Knox set the carrier on the floor to the right of one of the chairs, out of the way and out of sight of most of the restaurant. He lowered himself to the chair and seemed defeated.

"Quincy won't talk," Ava said.

Bursting with curiosity, I studied him. When he finally turned his gaze on me, I was taken aback by the intensity in his expression. I hadn't noticed how gorgeous his blue eyes were before.

"Someone left this baby in my driver's seat while I ran inside my house," he said. "So if it seems like I don't have any idea what to do with a baby, that's accurate."

My eyes popped wide open, and I craned my head to look beyond him at the bundle in the carrier. "Oooh," I gushed sympathetically, either for the baby or for him or…probably both. "My goodness." I went around his chair and bent down to look at her. "Who would do such a thing?"

"We're trying to figure out what to do," Ava explained.

"I bet," I said, forgetting my job completely as I gazed at the sleeping baby with angelic features. "It's like a movie plot."

Cash made his way from the kitchen on the opposite end

of the building, toward the table, wearing his whites and looking stormy.

I straightened. "Oops. I guess I should get your drink orders."

Before anyone could tell me what they wanted, Cash came up to the table with a scowl.

"Cash," Knox said.

Cash's response was a growl. "You left your coffee in the kitchen," he said to Ava, setting a half-full mug down in front of her.

"Thanks, handsome," Ava said, smiling. "Be nice."

"You two planning to eat something?" Cash asked gruffly, ignoring me, which was fine. He could be intimidating when he was grouchy. Lately, since he and Ava had gotten involved, he'd been happier, but maybe his unfriendliness had something to do with Knox's revelation that they were related.

"Um…" Ava angled her head to look at the baby on the other side of Knox.

"Who the hell is that?" Cash said.

Ava touched his arm with affection, and it seemed to have a calming effect on Cash. "Do you have five minutes to sit down?"

I hovered in the background, feeling like an intruder, but I still needed to get Knox's drink order and find out whether they wanted food.

Cash glanced at the other dining sections behind him, scowled again. "What's going on?"

"I'll tell you if you sit down," Ava said.

"Fine."

"Can I get you something to drink while you talk?" I managed to slip in.

Looking sidetracked, understandably, Knox said, "Water's fine."

"Anything else for you, Ava?"

"I'm good," she answered.

"Thanks, Quincy," Cash said, and I went to grab a single glass plus the coffee carafe.

When I approached their table, I overheard Cash saying, "How's that for irony? The guy who sprung a family secret on us last night has a surprise baby dropped on him today."

"Which means you should be more sympathetic," Ava said.

Knox let out a half laugh. "Fair enough. Maybe it's karma. Doesn't really matter what it is. I need to make a game plan."

"Any ideas what he should do?" Ava asked.

"Get Seth out here. He might know something. I sure as hell don't," Cash said. He leaned over to glance at the baby again, looking as if she was a dangerous predator who might pounce at any second.

I pressed my lips together against a grin. These guys were ridiculous with babies.

I set the water down in front of Knox, then held out the coffee toward Ava. "Refill?"

"Please. Maybe spiked with some Bailey's." She muttered the last part, telling me she wasn't quite serious.

As I filled her cup, there was a tiny sneeze from the carrier. Knox stiffened and swore quietly.

"I'll go tell Seth what's going on," Cash said, jumping up as if he was afraid he'd get stuck with baby duty.

I took the coffee back to the warmer, determined to mind my business but also tuned in to whether the baby fussed. My heart went out to her. Who, seriously, could desert that beautiful, innocent child? Her little sleeping face was irresistible. I wanted to squeeze those chubby cheeks and touch the tip of her perfect nose and watch her tiny mouth break into a baby laugh.

I checked in with my lunch table in a different section from Cash's group. They were ready for their bill, so I got that to them quickly, noticing that Seth and Cash had both joined Ava and Knox and the baby. Seth stood along the windowed wall that faced the lake, leaving the chair next to the infant empty. There was hushed discussion going on, none of it lighthearted.

When I began restocking the sugar packets at the empty tables, I heard the first baby squawk of discontentment from the Henrys' table. I glanced that way and saw four adults in varying states of panic. As I went to the next table to add a few packets to the sweetener container, Ava stood, went tentatively around Knox, and squatted in front of the carrier. I couldn't see more from here, but what she didn't do was take the baby out of the carrier.

I tried hard to stay on task, but a few cries later, I couldn't ignore them.

"Can I pick her up? See if I can soothe her?" I asked.

"Yes," Ava said instantly, popping up to make way for me.

"Please," Knox said, leaning toward the baby, his expression concerned and fearful.

"We thought maybe she'd just settle back down and go to sleep," Ava said as she returned to her place at the four-topper.

These people really didn't know anything about babies. They'd learn soon enough, as their sister-in-law Chloe was expecting in a few months.

"She probably needs to be fed or changed." I pulled the pink blanket away, unfastened the straps, and freed her arms.

"We don't have any supplies," Ava explained.

I pulled the baby into my arms. She paused her fussing and peered at me for a moment with wide, blue eyes.

"It's okay, sweet girl. We'll figure out what you need." To the adults, I asked, "Do you know her name?"

"It's Juniper," Knox said. He was watching us closely, either to make sure he was safe from the scary baby or to learn how to handle her. I wasn't sure which.

"You seem to have experience with babies," Ava said.

As I stood, I pulled Juniper into my chest and hugged her.

She quieted and grabbed my shirt with her fist. I pressed a kiss to her fuzzy head and said, "I practically raised my three younger siblings from birth."

Knox exhaled in what sounded like relief. "Can you tell us what we need to get through the next few hours?"

"Sure. I'd be happy to," I said.

"Thank God," Cash said. "Someone who knows babies. I need to get back to the kitchen. You can sit here, Quincy." He rose, leaned over to kiss Ava's temple, frowned at Knox, then hurried away.

I went around the table, tracing gentle circles on Juniper's back. Though she wasn't crying exactly, she was fussing as if she was about to start.

"Tell you what, Quincy," Seth said. "I'll handle your tables so you can help Knox."

"There's only the one left," I said. "Table twelve. I just dropped off their check."

"I'll take care of them. Let me know if I can help somehow —aside from babysitting. Good luck," Seth said and walked away.

"Okay," Ava said to me as she pulled up a blank note page on her phone. "I'm hoping we can get what we need at the Country Market. Although, if you need me to, I can drive into Nashville."

I sat Juniper's tush on the table, holding her with both my hands around her middle, and tried to distract her with goofy faces and silly sounds. She stared at me with big eyes, curious enough to stop fussing for a few seconds.

"I bet you're hungry," I said to her in a cooing voice, then switched to my adult tone to tell Ava and Knox, "You'll need formula, first and foremost. There wasn't any information with her? Like what brand she takes? Whether she's on solids?"

"None of that. Just her name and that she's about five

months old." Knox didn't take his eyes off Juniper's back, as if he'd never seen a baby close-up.

"She'll need diapers," I said. "Are you wet right now, sweet pea?" I touched my nose to hers. "I'd be surprised if she wasn't, so we'll need those ASAP too. You'll have to guess the size, but there should be some guidance on the package."

As I racked my brain for other necessities they'd need short-term, Juniper lost interest in my goofy faces and remembered she wasn't happy. She ramped up into a full-on cry, and as soon as I pulled her back against me, the stink emanating from her told me why.

"Uh-oh. How soon can you get diapers?" I asked.

Ava and Knox both shot me looks of horror.

"We'll need to get this one off her as soon as we can," I said. "Phew. Toxic. We don't want her to get a rash."

Ava pushed out from the table. "I'll go now. Give me your number in case I have questions."

I recited it, and she headed out in a hurry.

"Are you taking her to your house?" I asked Knox, who also stood.

"Uh, I guess I am." He swallowed, looking panicked.

As he put the carrier on top of the table, I said, "Oh, you still have the base attached. That's the part that stays belted into the car."

"The base?" He looked at the carrier, then stuck both hands up in surrender. "I'm out of my element here. Is there any way I can convince you to come with me and help? I'm totally safe, not a serial killer. Ava will vouch for me. I'll pay you double for whatever you miss out on by leaving your shift early. I'll even bribe Seth to let you go if necessary."

His desperation was impossible to miss.

I would've done it for free, but who was I to argue? The one thing I didn't want was to be the one to ask Seth. "If you can convince Seth, I'd be happy to."

"I'll go track him down."

"I'll have her fastened in by the time you come back," I told him.

Knox might be in a perpetual panic, but my Wednesday afternoon had taken a turn for the better. It had nothing to do with his gorgeous eyes and everything to do with his tiny, adorable "wrinkle." This darling baby was too much to resist.

CHAPTER 6

KNOX

Seth might've questioned my character last night, but any lingering doubts were apparently superseded today by approximately twenty pounds of baby. He'd readily agreed to let Quincy leave early to help me.

Thank fuck.

A half hour ago, I'd barely known who Quincy was. Now I didn't have a goddamn clue what I'd do without her.

"This is home," I said loudly, so Quincy could hear me over the crying in the back seat, as I pulled the SUV into my driveway.

"The Sanderson place," she said, referring to the elderly woman I'd bought the house from.

"I just moved in. You'll have to excuse the mess. I've got boxes everywhere."

We both got out and shut our doors. I breathed in the fresh air and appreciated the momentary muffling of the crying. Quincy hadn't been kidding when she said that bundle smelled toxic. The whole interior of my vehicle would need to be fumigated.

Quincy met me at the door where the car seat and baby were.

She'd taught me how to attach the base and make sure the carrier was secured inside it—also that the baby should face backward. Whoops. She'd explained it was for safety reasons, and that made sense, but it seemed counterintuitive not to be able to see the infant by looking in the rearview mirror.

"Here we go. Brace yourself," I said as I opened the door. The baby's face was screwed up in an angry cry, still going at full volume. "How do I get the carrier out?" I had to raise my voice to be heard.

"There's a release lever on the back, right under where Juniper's head is," Quincy said.

I leaned in, nearly choked on the stench, and felt around for the lever. It was easy to find now that I knew it was there. When I lifted it, the carrier loosened and I raised it out.

"Fast learner," she said with a smile.

"I like to think I'm not stupid, just completely inexperienced." Truth be told, I'd never felt so incompetent in my life.

I led Quincy to the front door, unlocked it, and let her precede me inside.

She gave a cursory glance around and then turned her attention to the bundle in my hand. "Let's get her stripped down and washed up. I hope Ava gets here soon."

"Where do you want to do this?" I asked.

She looked around again and apparently realized the open living, dining, and kitchen area wasn't the place, as half-unpacked boxes were everywhere.

"Since we don't have baby wipes, we'll need some water and a washcloth. Where's your bathroom?"

"Right there." I pointed at the first doorway in the hall.

"Do you think you can take her out of the carrier?"

"I think I can manage that," I said. Surely I could do that.

I set the carrier down on the floor and squatted in front of it as Quincy disappeared into the bathroom. "You're having a rough day, aren't you?" I said to the baby as she gulped in a breath between cries.

I'd been absorbed in the immediate panic of what to do with this baby—Juniper—and hadn't had a real chance to wonder what the fuck Gina was thinking. Leaving her baby? With me? Whether I was the father or not—and that was a question I couldn't begin to wrap my head around—you didn't just drop an infant off and disappear.

There was no more time to ruminate on Gina, not with this squalling, intimidating little bundle depending on me to figure shit out—fast.

I unfastened the straps holding her in, then worked her flailing arms out so I could pick her up. Copying what I'd seen Quincy do, I pulled the baby to my chest, bracing myself against the smell and the noise.

"Shh, it's gonna be okay," I said into her ear, even though I wasn't sure of that at all.

Tense as hell, I kept murmuring into the baby's ear what I hoped were soothing things. I could hear Quincy in the bathroom, presumably setting things up for Project Clean Juniper, so I stood there and waited for her to tell me what to do next.

And then I felt it...moisture soaking through my shirt. Damn. Somehow she'd peed on me.

"Quincy? I've got a bit of a problem."

My savior popped her pretty blond head out of the bathroom with a questioning expression. "What's wrong?"

"My shirt's wet."

As she walked toward me, her gaze on the infant, Quincy's eyes widened. "Oooh, no." She grimaced. "Welcome to blowout city. Wow. You've landed right in baptism-by-fire territory."

"Yeah," I said. "Trust me, when I woke up this morning, one thought I *didn't* have was that I'd get peed on today."

"Oh, that's not pee," she said, holding her hands out for the baby.

I stopped short as her meaning sank in. "This is stench?"

Quincy smiled sympathetically. "Pretty much."

"Does she not have a diaper on?"

"She does. A blowout is when they poop so much that it literally blows out of the diaper, up their back, sometimes even up their front. They're disgusting, but they happen."

I held Juniper, still crying, away from me, toward Quincy, and noted the mustard-brown streaks up and down the front of her formerly white-with-pink-bunnies one-piece outfit.

"Hell," I finally said.

"You go shower," Quincy said. "I'll get her out of this outfit and… You don't have other clothes for her, do you?"

"She showed up with the clothes on her back, the car seat, and the blanket, which I'm betting is toast now too."

"Likely." Quincy held Juniper at eye level, and the baby stared at her between cries. "You're gonna need some new outfits, aren't you, sweet pea?" Switching from her baby tone to her normal one, she asked me, "Ava said she'd go to Nashville, right? I don't know of anyplace in town that has baby clothes. We can wash these, but she could have another blowout an hour later."

Jesus. "I'll text Ava."

"Have her bring the diapers and formula here first. Emergency. Come on, sweetie. Let's get you cleaned up."

"I'll be out to help in five minutes," I said, texting Ava as I headed toward the master suite on the opposite side of the living room.

I'd pulled my shirt over my head by the time I hit the door to the bathroom and tossed it to the floor, disgusted.

After shutting the door behind me, I set my phone on the counter, stripped down, then started the water, feeling shellshocked and like the day was surreal.

I was in and out of the shower quickly, though I scrubbed like crazy with soap to get the smell off. I dried and dressed in clean clothes—sweats and a tee because who knew what I'd be getting myself into for the rest of the day.

And then what?

I didn't have a place for a baby to sleep. I didn't have a high chair. I didn't have one bit of confidence that I could even make it through the next hour with an infant, let alone until tomorrow.

Once I was dressed, I hurried back out to Quincy to see what I needed to do next. I found her in the hall bathroom with a naked pink baby in the sink, splashing her hands in the shallow water, no longer screaming.

"You got her quieted down," I said, grateful but scared she'd tune up again at any moment.

"She loves the water. Don't you, sweet pea?" Quincy had a hand around the baby's middle, supporting her, even though it appeared she could sit on her own. "This is our third round of clean water. Juniper was a mess. Can you hold on to her for a second while I grab the towels? We're going to dry her off with one and swaddle her with another until we get diapers, ointment, and clothes."

"Swaddle," I repeated, probably sounding like a moron taking mental notes—because I was.

"I'll show you how."

I put my hand around Juniper's tiny, pudgy torso the way Quincy had. Quincy stepped to the towel rack near the tub and grabbed the clean towels. When she returned to the sink, she edged in close so she could reach Juniper, and I caught the scent of Quincy's hair. It was sweet, something I couldn't quite place, but it somehow reminded me of sunshine.

As soon as she had a secure hold on the baby, I stepped back. The bathroom was small enough I couldn't go far, but I did my best to give her space. I needed every ounce of my focus to go on what the baby needed, not how good Quincy smelled.

She had Juniper dried off in no time, with me watching

every move. We moved to the spare bedroom next, where she spread a dry towel on the bed and taught me how to swaddle Juniper into burrito form. Halfway through the process, the crying started again.

"She's hungry, I'm sure," Quincy said.

"Ava should be here any minute."

"Good. You want to pick her up, maybe pace? Sometimes that will help them calm down, although when they're hungry, not much besides food will settle them."

I picked up the bundle, the incessant crying skyrocketing my stress level, but at least she smelled clean now. And who could blame her for screaming her head off? She was having a hell of a day, one that would likely be formative in her whole life. You didn't get deserted by your mother and not come out unscathed.

My chest constricted at that thought. My own mother had done the opposite of Gina and made every effort to make up for me only having one parent. She'd handled all of this and more. A crying, stinky baby for a couple of hours? Take that times a million and that was what my mom and all the other single parents out there did to raise children.

What I wouldn't give to be able to hug my mom one more time and tell her a heartfelt-more-than-ever thank-you. I swallowed hard on the sadness that rolled through me.

It struck me that I was in the position to be for this baby what my mom had been for me. A rock and a provider, at least until I figured out a long-term plan.

"Knock, knock." Ava's voice rang out from the living room, and though I didn't know if I'd ever relax for as long as this baby was in my care, I did breathe out some relief as I strode to the living room with Quincy trailing me.

"The holy saint of baby food is here," I told Juniper, even though she was hollering too loudly to hear a thing. "I owe you for life," I told Ava.

She smiled on her way to the kitchen counter, and I was pretty sure I saw the smile turn to a grimace at the racket.

"I got the very last four-pack of baby bottles on the shelves at the Country Market," Ava said as Quincy and I gathered around her and the grocery bags. "Formula, diapers, burp cloths, pacifiers, ointment…"

"You're a lifesaver," I said to Ava as Quincy started unpacking the bottles and washing them. "Both of you."

"Hey, I'm just doing what I'm told," Ava said. "I'm as clueless as you."

Quincy moved at high speed, washing and drying a bottle, mixing up formula, heating it, explaining to me all the steps and how to test the temperature.

"You'll probably want to find a comfortable place to sit while you feed her," Quincy said. "It might take a while."

If those weren't daunting words…

Shaking it off, I went to the living room, still holding Juniper, with Quincy following me, bottle and cloth in hand. The sectional had two open boxes on it.

"I'll get those," Ava said since my hands were full of a still-squalling baby. She pulled the boxes to the floor, and I sat down stiffly. "I'm running to a big-box store in Nashville now. I've got the things you mentioned on a list, Quincy, and I'll call Chloe on the way and see if she has anything to add."

My pregnant sister-in-law would likely be on top of that.

"Thank you, Ava. You want to take my card?" I asked.

"You can pay me back. I need to go so I can get back in good time."

She grabbed her wrist wallet and keys from the kitchen, then hurried out the door.

Quincy helped me situate Juniper so she was propped up on my arm.

"Depending on how long you're going to have her in your care, you might consider getting a pillow for feeding time."

I ignored all of that because I had no idea of anything

beyond this minute. If we could get the crying stopped, my chances of thinking straight would be better.

Quincy leaned over me, bottle in hand, and showed me the basics of bottle-feeding a baby. Juniper took the nipple in her mouth right away and went after the formula as if she hadn't eaten for a week.

Frowning, I asked, "How often do babies eat?"

With her eyes locked on Juniper, Quincy sat next to me and adjusted the burp cloth on the baby's chest. "It varies. She'll let you know."

"Oof," I said, not liking that answer at all.

"How long will she be here, if you don't mind me asking?" Quincy asked.

"I wish I knew," I muttered, my gaze glued to the baby as she drank avidly, her eyes wide and focused on me.

When I glanced back at Quincy, her expression was one of confusion, and I realized she probably had even more questions than I did.

"The baby's mother is my ex-girlfriend," I said. "She left a note that says this is my child, and she's done playing mama."

Quincy gasped, and her mouth gaped as she stared at me with stunned eyes. Several seconds ticked by before she said, "That's a lot."

"Yeah. I'm still processing."

Her gaze veered back to the baby, then to me again, as if she was looking for some resemblance. "Do you think it could be true?"

I exhaled and noted the shakiness of it. "Mathematically, it could be."

"And that's why you haven't called authorities."

"Seth said he'd have Holden talk to the sheriff, let him know what's going on. Even if she's not mine, I don't like the idea of her going into the system. I don't know much about it, but it can't be good for a baby. I figure I'll see about a paternity test tomorrow."

"Was it your ex who dropped her off?"

"I don't know. I saw a car take off, but I didn't think much of it. All I can tell you is that it was a gray sedan. That's not what she was driving when we broke up last October, but apparently a lot of things have changed since then." I looked back at Juniper, whose lids were getting heavy.

"I can't imagine," Quincy said. "I'm sorry to talk bad about a woman I've never met, but that's so selfish it makes me feel sick."

"Gina has…problems. Her mental health isn't stable," I said. "I'm not defending what she did, just saying she makes bad decisions. A lot. There's a part of me that thinks this baby could be better off without Gina, at least until Gina makes some changes."

Quincy frowned and nodded. "A baby is better off with her mother…except when she's not."

"Exactly. I'm just not sure I'm the best answer for this one."

We both turned our attention to Juniper, who seemed to have stopped sucking on the bottle, and her eyes were completely closed.

"Is she asleep?" I whispered, afraid to rock the boat.

Quincy leaned across my lap and gently grasped the bottle. She eased it out of Juniper's mouth, but the baby didn't stir. Quincy nodded. "She got her belly full. She'll probably sleep for quite a while."

"Doesn't she need pajamas?"

With a musical laugh, Quincy said, "Do you have something she could borrow?"

I tried to smile, but I wasn't sure I succeeded. "You put pj's on Ava's list, right?"

"Yes, and I promise, if she's anything like me, she'll come back with a handful of adorable baby outfits."

"What do we do in the meantime?"

"She's okay in her towel for now. We'll sneak a diaper on." Quincy leaned over me and eased her hands under Juniper.

I caught another hint of Quincy's sweet scent. As she stood, settling the baby against her chest, I was struck by how pretty she was, with blond hair pulled back, blue-green eyes, and smooth, young, suntanned skin. Emphasis on the young. She had to be no more than mid to late twenties. I was practically old enough to be her father. I had no room to think about how attractive anyone was, not with this baby in my care anyway. Besides, Gina had soured me on relationships.

What seemed like a hint of attraction was just gratitude— Quincy had saved my ass today, and fuck did I appreciate her for doing that. She had absolutely no reason to help me other than an obviously good heart.

"Why don't we put a couple of blankets down on the floor in the bedroom," she said. "I don't know if she's rolling over yet, but we can't leave her on the bed, just in case. She'll be safe on the floor. Grab a diaper and the ointment. We need to get one on before dinner goes through her."

I went to the kitchen, ripped open the diaper packaging, and pulled one out. Then I followed Quincy to the spare bedroom, which had a bed, a dresser, a nightstand, and not much else. It wasn't a big room and didn't have a lot of space, but you could easily fit a baby on the floor at the foot of the bed.

My gut had sunk with what she'd said, because without her guidance, I probably would've laid the baby on the bed, thinking it was a good, soft place for her to sleep, and what would that have done? Endangered Juniper, apparently. Fuck me.

Quincy settled the baby on the floor on a blanket I'd folded into quarters. The room was dim, with only the light coming in from the hallway. She took the diaper from me and kneeled in front of Juniper. "I'll show you how," she whispered.

I nodded, bending next to her so I could watch as she unswaddled the baby, spread ointment all over her bum, between her legs, anywhere the poop-splosion had reached. Then she lifted the baby's legs enough to slide the diaper under her rear and put it on. When she was done, she glanced around the room. "We should have Ava grab outlet covers too," she whispered. "I doubt she's crawling yet, but it could be close."

"Got it." We both stood and left the room. Quincy pulled the door shut most of the way, and I took my phone out and texted Ava again, then stuffed it back in my pocket, distracted. Distressed.

Back in the living room, Quincy said, "Do you want me to stay until—"

"Yes," I said in a rush, panic rolling through me like a tidal wave. "Please."

"Okay," she said easily, and gratitude seeped in around the edges of my panic, helping it recede.

What the fuck was I going to do when she left? Ava wouldn't be in Nashville more than a couple of hours. Once she dropped off supplies, though, she'd need to get home to Cash. I'd be left alone with this helpless baby.

I'd held her bottle for her, but I wasn't even sure I could remember the steps to mixing a new one that Quincy had so patiently gone over.

And that was just feeding. Diapers? I'd watched just now but never done it. And if there was another blowout, God forbid, what then? Ointment, I assumed, but how often? How much? And what else? What the holy hell else did I need to know? There had to be scores and scores, but I was so clueless I didn't even know what I didn't know.

"Quincy," I said once we were in the kitchen and she'd started taking everything out of bags and packaging. "I know you don't know me from Adam, but is there any way you'd consider staying here tonight? I'll pay you well, provide your dinner and breakfast, and we can find a different place for the baby so you can have the guest bed. It's brand-new and…" I shook my head. "If it sounds like I'm desperate, it's because I am. Please. I need help."

She set the extra bottles on the counter and met my gaze. "I'd be happy to, Knox. Whatever I can do to help." She smiled as if it was no big deal, even though to me, it was a big, giant deal.

I exhaled. "Thank you."

I was so damn relieved I could kiss her.

And I meant that only in a manner of speaking, of course. Nothing else.

CHAPTER 7

QUINCY

E ven though I was sure Juniper would sleep for at least a couple of hours, maybe more, I could tell Knox was terrified of being alone with her, so I waited with him until Ava returned.

He baked us a frozen pizza, and we ate it with a beer as we got to know each other better. Nothing too deep, just the basics, almost like a first date except it wasn't. At all. I told myself that several times, because the more I got to know about him, the more I liked him. He seemed smart and thoughtful, concerned for the baby in his care, and determined to succeed at his new fiction career with Ava.

As we finished tidying up the kitchen, Ava returned with a trunk full of baby gear.

"I don't even know what half of this is," Knox said as he and Ava hauled everything into the house.

"You'll learn soon enough," Ava said lightly.

"Are you sure I'll need all of this? I don't even know how long she'll be here."

"What are the odds of Gina driving up and asking for her

daughter back?" Ava asked. "And on the off chance she did, would you let her take her?"

Knox frowned but didn't answer. I shared a look of concern with Ava because both points were valid.

"I'm sorry to bolt so fast, but I should get home before Cash does," Ava said once the car was unloaded.

From what I gathered, she was in a difficult place, trying to keep peace between Knox and Cash, who was upset that Knox had lied to everyone about his identity. I knew Cash's temper well enough to understand Ava would have to balance carefully between her writing partner and her life partner.

"He's cooking for me when he gets home from work," she continued. "Kind of our private celebration of getting engaged."

"You've gone above and beyond," Knox acknowledged. "I appreciate your help more than you know, particularly in light of your fiancé's opinion of me."

"He'll get over it." Ava blew out a breath. "It just might take some time."

"Lucky for me, Quincy's here to save me. Or really, to save Juniper *from* me." Knox laughed uneasily.

"You're going to do fine," I said confidently. "We'll get you comfortable with her."

His brows shot up, as if he didn't know if that was possible. I found it endearing that this competent guy, who had to be so super smart to be a technical writer and a fiction writer, could be so insecure around a small human.

"Quincy will get you whipped into shape," Ava said. "Thank God for you, Quincy, because I'm as out of my element as Knox."

"Most of this is just experience," I told them. "I was twelve when my sister Hannah was born. Then Brayden and then Molly. I've changed a lot of diapers."

As Ava opened the front door, a cry sounded from the guest room.

"Shit," Knox said, visibly tensing.

"I'll go get her while you see Ava out. Good night," I said to Ava. "Have a happy celebration dinner with your fiancé."

As she said goodbye, Juniper's volume increased to a full-out, I'm-hungry howl.

I went into the dim bedroom to find she'd worked her way out of the swaddle and was lying on her tummy, screaming her lungs out. So she was capable of rolling over then. Good thing Ava had picked up a playpen for her to sleep in tonight.

"Come here, sweet pea," I said as I picked her up. "Shh. It's okay. We'll get you a bottle." I laid her on the bed and checked her diaper. "And a dry diaper and some brand-new pajamas."

"Another blowout?" Knox asked as he entered the room behind me.

"Just wet, I think. Could you flip on that lamp?"

He went to the nightstand and turned it on.

"Are you ready to change your first diaper?" I asked him.

"I don't know if I'll ever be ready, but let's do this." He rubbed his hands together as he came closer to Juniper, who'd paused in her crying to watch him, her head tilted and eyes curious.

I stepped aside so he was front and center and handed him a fresh diaper. I talked him through the steps, watching his every tentative move, resisting the urge to reach in and help him get the ointment rubbed in and show him how to fasten the tape tightly enough. The more he did on his own, the more his confidence would grow.

I handed him the pajamas with the pastel rainbow llamas on them and talked him through putting them on, holding back a grin at the inexperienced fumbling of his large hands that I was sure were competent at lots of other things—just not dressing a baby. Yet. Eventually Juniper was fully suited up in her new pajamas, and Knox exhaled as if he'd thought he'd never make it through.

Next up was another bottle, which she went through quickly again. This time, she didn't immediately fall asleep, so I showed Knox how to burp her. While he walked around, burping her and talking to her about nonsense things like llamas, I got the playpen out of the box and set it up. When I finished, I glanced at the baby and saw her lids were closed.

"She's sleepy again. Keep that up for another five minutes and I think she'll be out fully. Then we can put her to bed."

He nodded.

"Once we get her down, I need to run home to grab some things for the night. It won't take long at all."

Knox sucked in a deep breath, then nodded again. "I should be okay," he said in a low voice.

"You will be."

After checking out the other two spare bedrooms and finding that one was an office and one had stacks of boxes and nothing else, I maneuvered the playpen into the guest room where she'd napped.

"We can put her in my office," Knox whispered from the doorway. "So she doesn't keep you awake."

"She won't keep me awake, but since we don't have a monitor, this way I'll hear her when she stirs."

"You're the boss," he said. "Do you think she'll wake up in the night and need something?"

"Most likely a bottle and a diaper change or two."

When he frowned, I reassured him, "Totally normal. Sleeping through the night at her age would be the anomaly."

"Do people really have babies on purpose?" he asked, and I laughed quietly. Juniper appeared to be passed out good. The real test would be when we laid her down.

In the darkened bedroom, Knox carefully handed her off to me, our shoulders brushing in the process. Though I could barely see him, I caught a hint of his masculine scent and felt the air he blew out when Juniper was safely in my hold. There was something about our shared mission in the dark room that created an intimacy between us.

Or maybe that was me being ridiculous and in need of a boyfriend. Preferably one my own age. Someone who wasn't paying me to spend the night.

Two minutes later, Juniper was in her playpen, still sound asleep, and Knox and I tiptoed out. We exhaled in unison and high-fived as soon as I pulled the door shut.

"Go get your stuff," he said quietly. "I'll be fine. As long as you hurry." His lips curved up in the slightest hint of a smile. I suddenly longed to see more of that smile, to see it light up his eyes. That was probably asking too much after the day he'd had.

"I'll be back in a half hour," I told him.

"Promise?" he asked, his tone lighthearted.

"Promise."

———

By the time I walked up the stairs to my apartment, I was damp clear through from the chilly October mist and wishing I'd taken my car that morning.

The lights were still on in Oopsie Daisies, even though it'd been closed for an hour. Piper was likely in the back, prepping for her busy weekend. Normally I'd go in and check on her, but I needed to hurry.

I entered the apartment and saw Jewel's bedroom light on, heard talking, either her or her TV, behind her closed door. Relieved that she was occupied, I hurried to my room to pack a bag. I wasn't sure why, but I was hesitant to talk to my roomies face-to-face about my day. It'd be easier to text them both my plans for the night once I was back at Knox's.

In my room, I grabbed a couple of changes of clothes and some leggings and a sweatshirt to sleep in, knowing I'd be up at least once or twice and that the middle of the night would be cold. I hurried to the hall bathroom Jewel and I shared and started stuffing necessities into my bag.

"What's with the sneaking around?" Jewel asked from right behind me, startling me.

"I could ask you the same," I said. "You scared me to death."

"Where are you going?"

I met her gaze in the mirror. Her face was makeup free, her dark hair pulled sloppily into a ponytail at her nape, and she had deep shadows under her eyes.

"You look like crap," I said.

"Fucking shots." She rolled her eyes and smiled sheepishly. "Whose idea was all that?"

I laughed. "Hundred percent yours, Ms. Bar Manager."

She shook her head. "Yay, me. It's lucky today was my day off. You must be exhausted after working all day." She narrowed her eyes as I threw in my toothbrush and toothpaste. "Did I miss something last night? Did you meet a guy?"

"You missed a lot of somethings last night, but no, I didn't meet a guy."

"Last time I'm going to ask nicely. Where are you heading? Watching Molly for your stepmoron?"

"No." I grinned like I always did when she called my stepmom an immature but accurate name. "I'm spending the night with Knox Breckenridge. In his guest room. Taking care of his baby."

"Wait… What?" The look she gave me said I was crazy. I laughed, because I'd done that on purpose.

Knowing the news of the dropped-off baby was already

filtering through town—Ava had said that Chloe had already heard, and not from Seth, Cash, or Holden—I told my room-mate about it.

Jewel frowned. "You're spending the night at some old dude's house you don't know?"

Throwing my cleanser and some makeup basics in my bag, I said, "I know him. I've waited on his table half a dozen times before."

My roommate's brows shot up. "Oh, well, then I'm sure everything'll be just fine," she said sarcastically.

"The Henrys know him. Technically he *is* a Henry."

"I heard about that." She leaned her back against the door-frame and crossed her arms. "That doesn't make him okay. The very fact that he hid it from them for months just means he can hide things."

"We all hide things," I said. "I don't get the serial-killer vibe from him. I'll be fine, Mom. Besides, the baby is cute as a freaking button. And he needs help with her, believe me. He'd never held a baby before today."

"Which begs the question, why would someone leave a baby with him?"

"Because he's a good-hearted man who wouldn't hurt a baby."

"And you know this how?"

"I just do."

Call it gut instinct or whatever you wanted to call it, but I knew in my bones that Knox would never hurt a baby. Not on purpose, and I doubted he'd even manage to accidentally hurt Juniper. He was too concerned to let anything happen to her.

When I had everything I needed, I turned to find Jewel still leaning there, arms crossed, looking disapproving.

"Come on," I said. "He's been in town for months. Lots of people know him."

"You don't."

"I sort of do. I've been with him all afternoon."

"What happened to work?"

I swept past her, into the living room, as I told her about Knox and Ava bringing the baby into Henry's and how he'd promised to pay me if I helped him. "He wants what's best for the baby even with the weird circumstances," I said. When Jewel was still quiet, I said, "What?"

"It's just… I worry about you." Her voice had gone from worried mom to concerned friend. "You want to be part of a family so badly. A good, loving family, I mean. One where the stepmonster doesn't run things. This is, like, a hot guy and a baby. Ready-made family."

I laughed. "I'm staying overnight, not moving in and doing the guy." I put some dry sneakers on. "And now he's a hot guy? I thought he was an old dude," I added, slinging her words back at her for fun. She wasn't upsetting me. In fact, I appreciated that she cared.

"I'm not blind. He's good-looking in an older-guy way."

She did not lie about that.

I went to Jewel and threw my arms around her. "I love you for worrying about me. I'll be fine."

She hugged me back. "Just watch yourself. And text me if he sneaks into your bedroom for any reason."

I laughed. "Maybe we'll have wild monkey sex on the nanny cam. I can send you a link." There was, of course, no nanny cam, nor would there be sex, wild monkey or any other kind.

She shuddered with exaggeration. "Don't you dare. Love you."

"Love you. Get some sleep tonight so you don't look like you got in a bar fight."

"Did I?"

Laughing, I said, "Not that I'm aware of. Tell Piper where I am if you see her. Then you two can gossip about how foolish I am."

"For sure," she said, laughing back as I walked out the door.

I went downstairs and got in my car this time. I didn't want to leave Knox alone with Juniper any longer than I had to—because I knew he was so nervous.

Not because he was a hot guy who caused butterflies in my belly at the thought of seeing him again.

CHAPTER 8

KNOX

B y two p.m. on Thursday, Juniper and I had finished at the doctor's office.

The paternity test itself, times two, was quick, but I'd opted to have Dr. Julian do a well-baby check while we were there to make sure Juniper was healthy. There'd been a wait due to a four-year-old boy who required stitches in his noggin, and I'd watched his distressed parents with a new level of empathy and held Juniper closer.

I hadn't met Dr. Julian before today, but his knowledge about paternity tests, his gentleness with the baby, and his compassion for the position I found myself in had easily won me over. He'd laughed sympathetically when I'd asked, tongue-in-cheek, whether I could get a two-for-one deal on paternity tests, then assured me he could have the lab compare my DNA to both Juniper's and Simon Henry's. His nurse would see to the details.

He might be a stereotypical near-retirement-age, small-town doctor, but he knew his stuff and had a heart of gold. I wouldn't hesitate to go back to him, for myself or Juniper. *If* I still had her in my care the next time she needed medical attention.

We wouldn't get results for a few business days—early next week would be the best-case scenario—and I'd decided to keep Juniper in my care until then. *At least* until then. If it turned out she was mine, I wasn't sure I could hand her over to anyone else, Gina included. If she wasn't mine… Well, that was an even tougher decision.

I'd parked in the lot behind the doctor's office. I liked walking, but not with a baby, not until I had a stroller. So far I hadn't given much thought to getting one, but I could suddenly see the appeal.

"You were a good baby, weren't you?" I said, catching myself using that silly voice reserved for babies as I fastened the car seat into the base and tossed our brand-new diaper bag to the floor. I touched my finger to Juniper's button nose and could admit to the gratification brought on by the smile she flashed at me before I closed her door and jumped into the driver's seat. This baby was slowly worming her way into my heart.

I'd survived nearly four hours alone with her now and figured I deserved some extra credit for leaving the house with her without an all-out panic attack. Quincy had dressed her this morning before her shift at Henry's, and Juniper had been asleep when it was time to leave for our appointment, but she'd woken up hungry during our wait to be seen. I'd had a bottle at the ready as Quincy had advised, mixed it up, and fed her like a pro, or at least not like a scared dumb ass, which was exactly what I'd been less than twenty-four hours ago. I'd remembered to burp her and changed her diaper twice—in public.

My baby-care confidence had grown since last night, but whenever she cried, my anxiety still shot through the roof.

Last night, around three o'clock, she'd had a crying jag for close to forty-five minutes, which had drawn me to Quincy's room to see if there was anything I could do. Of course, she'd had the situation under control when I'd tapped on her door. She'd explained that Juniper's diaper rash was likely bothering her and kindly told me to go back to bed, that this was what I was paying her for.

I wasn't proud that I'd done exactly that and taken my leave as quickly as I could. Fact was, I had nothing to offer except arms that weren't yet tired if Quincy's were, but she'd insisted she was fine and happy to do whatever she needed to do to calm the baby.

Since I hadn't had a chance to eat before leaving home, I drove straight to Henry's now, thankful it would again be during the after-lunch lull. Henry's was legitimately one of the best places to eat in town, but I'd be lying if I didn't admit to other reasons for choosing it.

I parked as close to the door as I could get, got the car seat out with relative ease—noting Juniper had fallen asleep during the three-block drive—grabbed the diaper bag, and went inside. I told the hostess I was there to see Seth, and she showed me back to my half-brother's office.

The room was an afterthought, maybe a former storage room behind the bar, with a desk and space for two chairs and not much else. Humble as hell, just like I'd always found him to be, at least until he'd decided I was of questionable character because I hadn't immediately told any of the Henrys about our ties. I could understand it wasn't easy news to hear, but how else did he think I could've realistically handled it?

"Hey," I said from the doorway when he didn't look up.

He set down his pen and eyed me. "Knox." He didn't bother standing. "Come on in." He noticed the car seat and leaned over the desk to look at Juniper when I set it on the other chair. "Still have your sidekick, huh?"

"Or my daughter. One of the two," I said quietly.

"That's gotta be a mind fuck," he said. If I wasn't mistaken, there was empathy in his tone.

"That's an apt description. The possibility, even if it's vague, that I could be a father… You can't imagine."

Seth sat back down, looking shaken. "Actually I can."

"You have a kid?"

He looked at the ceiling for a second, as if making a decision, then lowered his gaze, still avoiding mine. "I got a woman pregnant years ago, when I was in grad school. She swore it was mine even once I found out she was married the whole time we were together."

"Shit."

"It gets worse. The husband found out and took his own life. In the aftermath, she lost the baby."

"Jesus. That's terrible."

"Apt description."

"I'm sorry, man."

He nodded once. "I've worked through it. And that was different. I never met my baby. Never had the chance to fall in love with it."

"Remains to be seen if this one is mine. We'll know more next week sometime. I wanted to thank you for helping me research yesterday. I was in such a panic my brain locked up."

"Glad I could help." He leaned his elbows on the desk. "I talked to my dad last night— Hell. *Our* dad, I guess. He made some good points."

"About?"

"You. He pointed out you didn't have any good options once you found out the truth. He said I needed to put myself in your shoes."

I waited for more as he went silent.

Finally he looked me in the eye. "Sorry I was a suspicious asshole. I don't really think you're after anything from us. It's not like we're well-off."

I nodded, letting out my relief in an audible breath.

"Thanks. Apology accepted. Frankly you do have something I want."

He stiffened, and his eyes narrowed.

"Family," I said before he could jump to too many wrong conclusions. "That's what I want. What I don't have. You guys have a damn good one. I only hope I can someday be included."

"Give us time," he said. "It's a lot to swallow. Let us get to know you. Process things."

I nodded. I'd had months to let it sink in, plus the advantage of knowing about our ties from the first day I'd met them. "That's fair." I glanced over at Juniper, who was still asleep. "On a different topic, since test results won't be available until next week, I'll have her with me for a few days minimum."

His brows went up. "Are you going to be able to handle that?"

A nervous laugh spilled out of me. "I've made it four hours and counting so far."

"I'm impressed. Has she been asleep the whole time?"

"No, she has not," I said, grinning and crossing my arms as if I'd conquered the universe, not merely kept a baby safe for less than a quarter of a day. "Longer than a few hours though... I'm man enough to admit when I need help. How well do you know Quincy?"

"She's grown up in this town and worked for me for months. It's not easy to keep secrets around here, so I'd say pretty damn well."

"You obviously trust her, or you wouldn't employ her."

"She's honest, shows up early for every shift, and pretty much emits sunshine on the daily." He gave me a knowing look. "And she's really good with kids."

"She said she works full-time here."

He confirmed it with a nod.

"Any chance you could spare her for a while and hold her

job for her?" I asked. "I mean, *if* she's interested in helping me out?"

"Like a babysitter, you mean?"

"I'm thinking more like a nanny."

"You haven't asked her yet?"

"I wanted to make sure it was possible without her giving up her job here. I'll probably only need her for a few days, but it could end up longer."

"You need her more than I do. Lucky for you, we're over-staffed now that it's off-season. People are fighting for hours."

"No repercussions when she comes back?"

"None whatsoever. If she chooses to help you."

That remained to be seen, but I was hopeful. Quincy seemed to adore Juniper.

"Thanks, Seth." I stood up, put the diaper bag strap over my shoulder, and tucked the blanket over Juniper's feet—again. She apparently had something against her feet being wrapped up.

"Seems like the brotherly thing to do," he said.

I met his gaze, surprised at his apparent acceptance.

He nodded once and a hint of a smile tugged at his mouth as he rose too. "Are you eating?"

"Planning to."

"She's working the middle section today. I'll seat you at one of her tables."

CHAPTER 9

QUINCY

While dropping glasses and plates was something I did on the regular, fortunately I hadn't spilled on anyone for quite a while. Until today, of course.

Around three p.m., I was down to one last table of late lunchers when Seth led Knox and Juniper into my section. At the sight of the man whose house I'd slept in, my pulse sped up and a burst of energy pumped through me.

Which was completely dumb.

I barely knew the man, and even if I had, there was no reason to react to the sight of him. Yes, he was good-looking, but I was, in fact, *not* looking. Not for a relationship or a date or even a passing attraction.

Mitchell's breakup at the end of spring had shocked me, hurt me, and woken me up. It'd knocked me on my butt emotionally for a bit, but in hindsight, it was the best thing that could've happened. The more distance I got from it, from him, the more clearly I could see our relationship had run its course, probably a year or two ago. At the time, I hadn't noticed our feelings had waned, and instead I'd kept looking forward, moving toward a future with him, banking on a ring and, eventually, a family.

Without realizing it, I'd put the other areas of my life on the back burner and been content to wait tables at Henry's while I waited for my future to come to me.

I'd needed months of thinking and late-night talking with my roomies to figure out a path that spoke to me, but I finally had one, and I wasn't about to abandon it for a guy.

Even if my attention was one–hundred percent drawn to his strong, long-legged body dressed in jeans, a burgundy tee, and a flannel shirt, I wasn't interested. I refused to be.

"Hey," I said warmly, like I did to all my customers.

"Hi, Quincy." His voice was a low, whiskey-smooth timbre, quieter than usual.

When I glanced at the bundle of cuteness in the car seat, I understood why.

"Nap time for our princess, huh?" As soon as I said it, the unintentional intimacy from calling her *our* princess hit me, and I quickly jumped to a more comfortable topic. "What can I get you to drink?"

Without seeming to notice my screwup, he ordered a coffee and a bowl of lager pork chili. I poured his coffee, then went to the kitchen for his chili, which was ready fast since it just had to be served up along with some bread that Kinsey had recently taken out of the oven.

I'm not sure what happened exactly, but somehow when I went to set down his meal, I knocked over his coffee, and it spilled straight into his lap.

I gasped as he pushed his chair back to try to avoid getting hit. He wasn't quick enough, so I nearly tossed the plate and chili bowl down as I grabbed for a spare napkin at the next table. Except the chili splashed upward and nailed me in the cheek. I tossed the extra napkin at Knox's lap, somehow keeping my wits about me enough to not go for his crotch myself.

"I'm so sorry," I said. My face was burning up and not from the hot chili that'd hit it. I scrambled to the next table for more napkins. "Did it burn you?"

"It wasn't hot enough to burn." He held the cloth to his thigh to soak up the liquid. "Only a small amount hit me." He nodded toward the floor, where there was a puddle forming.

The dark liquid continued to drip from the table to the floor, and I tried to reassure myself that most of it was, indeed, on the table instead of Knox.

"I'm really sorry," I said again as I took one soaked napkin from him and held out a dry one. "I'll pay for cleaning or new jeans or whatever you want."

He reached for the napkin and trapped my hand between it and his other hand. "It's okay, Quincy." With a squeeze on the back of my hand, he looked up and met my gaze as if to show me he meant it.

I wasn't convinced. Not even close.

"Sure, sure," I said, not at all calmly. "It's fine to have a clumsy server dump hot coffee all over you and burn you and stain your pants and maybe wake up your baby."

His hands, with the napkin, were still around mine as he glanced toward the car seat, which he'd set on the floor on the other side of him—thank God because if she'd been on this side, I would've scalded sweet Juniper with coffee!

"On she sleeps. Everything's okay. I'm fine," he reassured.

He squeezed my hand one more time before releasing me, and I couldn't help noticing how much bigger his hands were than mine.

I blew out my breath and attempted a smile. "Yeah. Okay," I said, biting down on the urge to apologize again.

Dropping things always flustered me. Spilling on someone did more than fluster. I'd had a lot of practice at recovering though, and I forced myself to take three seconds now, close my eyes, and breathe in deeply. Just enough to get my brain back on the job again.

When I opened my eyes, the chili splatters on the tablecloth caught my attention, and I remembered I must still have a splotch on my face, so I grabbed one of the unused napkins and swiped at my cheek. Sure enough, it came back with a red-orange smear.

Super.

"I'm going to get you a fresh bowl of chili. I'll be right back." I picked up the original one and headed to the kitchen, relieved Zinnia was in charge today. Cash wouldn't usually say anything, but I'd know from his expression he didn't like yet another Quincy mishap.

I managed to deliver bowl number two and some extra bread to Knox without incident, cleaned the floor, and then I did my best to fade into the background and let him eat in peace.

We were low on rolled silverware, so I worked on those at the bar, making small talk with Dakota as she restocked for dinner service. My mind was split between her chatter and Knox and Juniper, who were out of my sight in the next room. There was no reason for me to feel drawn to them other than I was drawn to every cute baby. It didn't matter that I'd stayed with them last night. It was just a job. But I couldn't deny that I had to fight the urge to hover and triple-check whether the baby was awake yet and reassure myself again that Knox wasn't, in fact, hiding third-degree burns on his lap.

When I had the basket of silverware wrapped and delivered to the host stand, I allowed myself to check on Knox. He was just pushing his bowl back and sticking the last of the bread in his mouth.

"How was everything?" I asked as I sidled up next to him and craned my neck to check on Juniper. She was still asleep, looking like an angel.

"Good as always," he said, "even with wet pants."

My eyes popped wide open as my mortification flooded right back in. "I'm sor—"

"No more apologizing," he said, laughing. "I'm teasing you. Here's an insider tip for you—that's a good sign I'm absolutely fine." His laugh faded. "Really, Quincy."

I liked the gentleness in his tone when he said my name.

And that was *not* a good idea, so I inwardly shook my head at myself and took his dishes away. "Heard," I said with more confidence than I felt. I was about to ask him if he wanted dessert when Seth came around the corner.

"How was lunch?" he asked.

Knox nodded. "Damn good, thanks."

"Did you two talk yet?" Seth asked, and I tilted my head, curious.

"Haven't had a chance," Knox answered.

"I'll take those." Seth reached out for the dirty dishes. "You can take a break, Quincy. I'll cash him out."

"I haven't offered dessert yet—"

"I'm good," Knox assured me.

"Need anything else?" Seth acted as if I wasn't standing right there, ready and willing to finish up with my table. I was pretty sure he didn't know I'd tipped over Knox's coffee, so I was super confused. "More coffee?"

"I've had enough coffee," Knox said with a subtle smile at me. "I can't think of anything else I'd need."

"Okay, then. You two talk." Seth pulled out the chair in front of me, then headed toward the kitchen.

A knot formed in my gut as I tried to figure out what Knox could possibly need to talk to me about that Seth was aware of. Then it hit me that Knox had taken Juniper to the doctor today.

"Is Juniper okay?" I asked as I sat on the edge of the chair.

"Dr. Julian said she looks great. He agrees that five months old is about right. We'll hear back on the paternity test some-time next week."

I exhaled in relief and sat back farther into the chair. It took about three seconds for my curiosity to roll back in. Just as I straightened expectantly, Juniper let out a quiet snort-cry.

Knox surprised me. Instead of stiffening at the first sign of baby wakefulness, as he had last night and this morning, he glanced down at the car seat, then swiveled toward Juniper and bent over to get her out.

Maybe time alone with her had infused some confidence in him.

"Come here, little one," he said in a tender voice. "I figured my time was about up before you woke up hungry again." He straightened and cradled her in one arm as he reached to the diaper bag and unzipped it.

I'm not going to lie; I fought hard to not pop up and help him, but it wasn't my place anymore. I wasn't the hired help. Besides, I wanted to see how much progress he'd made.

He pulled out a bottle with formula premeasured, as I'd shown him, opened it with one hand, set it on the table, then dug around for a bottled water.

I literally bit down on my tongue to keep from offering to help.

Juniper's lower lip quivered, and then she let out a louder cry as her eyes popped open.

"Just a few more seconds, Juniper," he said as he unscrewed the water lid, then poured it into the bottle. Once he had the lid on, he shook it vigorously.

"You've been practicing," I said and realized a grin was spreading across my face.

"Crash course and an excellent teacher. Thanks again, by the way."

"Anytime."

He set the bottle on the table, lifted Juniper, and brushed a kiss to her forehead. She paused in her crying and studied him for a moment.

It lasted maybe two full seconds before Knox moved her

to the crook of his opposite arm and teased her lower lip with the nipple of the bottle. Juniper took it eagerly and gazed up at him with adoring eyes.

Pretty sure my ovaries stood up, did a pirouette, and spit out some eggs at the sight of him handling his baby with care and competency.

"Do you mean that?" he asked, his gaze still locked on the infant.

I had to yank myself out of my stupor to try to understand what he was talking about. "Mean what?"

"That you'll help me with her anytime."

"Oh. Of course. Whenever I can."

Knox didn't say anything else for a while. He was focused on the baby in his arms, his expression nothing like yesterday's fear and more one of determination...and possibly affection. I couldn't stop watching the two of them. There was nothing quite like a hot guy taking care of an adorable baby.

Reel it in, I told myself. I sensed there was more coming, so I waited, but I forced myself to glance around the restaurant, noting that the customers in Sarai's section had left. It was nearly time for us to close until dinner.

When I turned back toward Knox, I caught him nodding once as he watched Juniper drink, as if he was having a silent conversation in his head.

"I'm keeping her with me at least until I get the test results," he said, switching his attention from the baby to me.

"That's great," I told him. "It's definitely the best thing for her."

"I'm hoping I can convince you to help me."

The way my blood started rushing through my veins at that was all the reason I needed to say no. Because there was maybe a slight attraction on my part, and I was just starting to get my feet under me to dedicate myself to this new path I'd chosen.

I made a point of not reacting, of waiting for him to say more, because he didn't actually ask me a question.

"I might be more confident than I was yesterday, but I can't do this on my own, Quincy."

"You'll learn," I said. "Look how far you've come in just a few hours."

"And that'll continue," he said with determination. "But I'm not foolish enough to believe I can handle this princess on my own for several days."

"You know I work here full-time, right?" I asked, torn about that fact at this very moment. Part of me wanted nothing more than to go home with Knox and help him care for Juniper. Part of me recognized that wouldn't be the smartest move I could make right now.

"I took the liberty of talking to Seth. He said if you're interested in helping me out, he'd let you help me while I need it. Then you can have this job back whenever you're done."

I couldn't ignore how much I wanted to do that. "And when would I be done? What happens when you get the results?"

Knox gazed down at Juniper, who was still avidly going after her bottle. Slowly, his lips curved upward, then he sobered again. "If she's mine"—his lids lowered for moment, and his broad chest rose as he inhaled—"I'm going to keep her."

My chest inexplicably contracted at his declaration. I mean, of course I was thrilled he'd made that decision. This baby needed a responsible parent, and even though Knox was new and mostly clueless, there wasn't a doubt in my mind he could be everything Juniper needed him to be.

"And if it turns out she isn't yours?" I asked, wanting to distract myself from my weird surge of emotion.

"I'm not sure yet, but"—his Adam's apple rose with a big

swallow—"if she needs a family, I'm not sure I could let her go into the system."

That right there was proof he'd be a good father. Not that I needed it.

"So you'd want me to help for how long? What do you have in mind?"

"Let's start out saying it's a temporary nanny position with the potential for longer. If she isn't my daughter, it's a complicated decision. That's as specific as I can be right now."

I was so in. Or I wanted to be so in, but Jewel's voice rang out in my head. *You want to be part of a family so badly. A good, loving family. This is, like, a hot guy and a baby. Ready-made family.*

She was right about all of it. I knew I was predisposed to fall for the baby at least, and maybe the hot dad as well, and that would not be in my best interest. If I cared about them, it would hurt like hell when I had to go off to school in January.

I didn't want to do anything that could possibly derail me or get me off to a wobbly start.

Still, the words that came out of my mouth were, "I'll help you, Knox. I'll be your temporary nanny. If it goes beyond next week, I can give you until January, when I go back to school."

CHAPTER 10

KNOX

L ate Thursday afternoon the following week, I was finally sitting down to reread earlier chapters, trying to catch up on my writing for the first time since Juniper had crashed on the scene like a meteorite.

Ava had been understanding and accommodating, but we'd only just started this cowriting career path. I hated to be the cause of us already being behind, even if I could acknowledge I had a valid excuse.

Quincy had settled in, and we were starting to establish a semiroutine between the three of us. After living alone for years, suddenly having not one but two roommates was an adjustment. Quincy was my opposite in many ways—she was an extrovert to my introvert; she preferred Hallmark and Bravo to my Discovery and Syfy shows; I'd started college before texting was common, and she'd practically been born with a phone in her hand. Yet we got along well despite our differences. She kept me on my toes with a mix of lightheartedness and irreverence.

I didn't know what I would've done these past few days

without Quincy. She might be only twenty-eight and a late bloomer in figuring out her life plans, but with a baby, she was confident and knowledgeable, optimistic and capable. She had a knack for guiding me while letting me figure things out myself to an extent. She was going to be an excellent schoolteacher, in my opinion. If Juniper was any indication, the kids were going to love her.

Tonight Quincy had the evening off so she could stay with her younger sister later on and had left early to run errands and bring carryout from the Dragonfly Diner for me—her idea, not mine, and I sure as hell appreciated the thoughtfulness.

I was puzzling over some nuances with my main character—I was writing the male lead's point-of-view chapters, and Ava handled the female ones—when I heard stirring from the baby's room. We'd taken her out of Quincy's room and put her into the fourth bedroom after moving the boxes out and purchasing a monitor.

Pushing back from my desk, I stood, rolled my neck, then headed toward the baby. She was only stirring so far, not fussing, so I listened as I approached to see if she'd settle back down, selfishly wishing for another half hour to ponder the character issues.

It wasn't to be. Juniper let out her first coo and then a snort, drawing a smile from me. As I strode into her darkened room, I was struck by how fast life could change. Less than a week ago, those soft noises would've sent me into a panic.

"Hey, little miss."

She was lying on her back, her feet in the air, and she angled her head back to look at me. It was the simplest response, but when those baby blues spotted me, she broke out into a grin. At *me*. The dude who barely knew what he was doing.

Though I didn't pause in scooping her up, my heart stumbled in my chest at that grin.

Juniper was getting used to me, learning my voice. She was happy to see me after her nap. The wonder of that, of how it made *me* feel, was almost too much to absorb.

"Come here, Juniper." I held her above my face for a couple of seconds, then brought her nose to mine, and she let out an audible laugh. I'd never heard her do that before. "Did you just laugh?" I asked, bobbing her nose to mine again. She repeated the sound, proving it wasn't a gas bubble or an accident—she was laughing with baby joy.

For the first time, I understood what the saying *my heart is full* meant. It was a physical sensation in my chest, a light one, as if it'd been pumped full of helium.

I might be new to babydom, but one thing I'd learned already was that postnap happies didn't last all that long before postnap hungries set in.

As I snuggled her into the crook of my arm, I lowered the side of the crib, which we'd borrowed from Quincy's friend Tansy, spread out a baby blanket on the mattress, and gathered a diaper and wipes. I could tell by the weight of her diaper she needed a fresh one.

I laid Juniper back on the blanket and made quick work of the diaper change, impressed with myself even if the baby wasn't. When she lifted her feet again and grabbed one of them, I laughed, drawing her attention. Then, before I could get the fresh diaper underneath her rear, while she continued to stare at me and smile, she wet all over the blanket.

"You didn't just pee," I said, all cooing gone from my tone.

She laughed again, and damn if I couldn't help grinning despite the mess. At least she hadn't—

Damn.

She pooped next.

Right then and there, with me with a front-row seat and the blanket below her already drenched, she let out her lunch and then some.

Holy sh—

This pint-sized human could make a mess.

With a glance at the wipes to make sure we had plenty, I shook my head and couldn't help chuckling. "Quincy was right when she said baptism by fire. You like to throw me wrenches, don't you, June?"

As she stared at me with those big, curious eyes, she strained and, yep, pooped some more, as if that was her answer to my question.

What could I do besides laugh, breathe through my mouth, and clean up the mess that was Juniper?

"Such a pretty name for a baby with such a foul behind," I teased.

A few minutes later, I had her cleaned up and dressed in a clean outfit. By the time I snapped the last button on the one-piece with a woodland animal print, she was tuning up for a good fuss. I'd taken too long to get to the feeding part, no doubt.

"If you want to get to eating, you shouldn't poop all over yourself," I told her as I picked her up.

I grabbed the blanket, saw nothing had leaked through, and congratulated myself on having remembered to put it down.

I carried it and Juniper out to the kitchen, dropping off the heavily soiled blanket in the laundry room. Knowing she'd put up a royal fuss if I set her anywhere before getting that bottle made, I kept her in one arm and prepped her bottle with the other hand. It was awkward, but I was getting good at it.

And wasn't that weird as hell.

As I carried Juniper to the recliner and settled in with her and her bottle, I shook my head and realized I was smiling.

Life was bizarre.

Never would I have imagined I'd be sitting here in the living room of my new house, in small-town Tennessee, a baby snuggled up against me drinking a bottle, content. Both her and me.

I closed my eyes, listening to the soft sounds of her drinking and not at all minding the weight of her on my chest. This was peaceful. I felt a contentment I hadn't often taken the time to seek out in the past. Something about being forced to sit quietly, where the objective was to give a baby a safe place and a nourishing meal and nothing else. I didn't hate it. Not even a little.

Would I feel the same if this became my new normal? My life?

Only time would tell, and that thought reminded me I hadn't checked my email for test results since lunchtime.

Though Juniper was content with her bottle and not even halfway done yet, which meant if I carried her into my office, she likely wouldn't mind at all, I stayed put. I wasn't sure if I was ready to know the truth.

What if she was mine?

What if, from the time I opened that email on, I had a new identity as a father? Because I was certain that, if this was my biological daughter, I wouldn't be giving her up.

In fact, if Gina came back for her, I knew I'd fight to keep Juniper with me for as long as Gina refused to get mental-health help.

If the test was positive, I'd be looking at eighteen years, make that a lifetime, of being Dad as much as I was Knox, maybe more. I'd always hoped to have kids someday if I met the right woman, but as a single guy, that hadn't been foremost in my mind for some time.

On the other hand, what if she *wasn't* mine?

I imagined driving this bundle of smiles and dirty diapers to some cold, institutional office building somewhere and handing her over and…

"Shit." I said it out loud, then whipped my gaze to Juniper, as if she could understand.

I didn't know if I could hand her over even if she *wasn't* my biological child. How off-the-wall was that? In that situation, it would mean adoption, and who was I to think I could adopt this baby who'd been randomly dropped off with me and give her a good life as a single dad?

The thought was ludicrous.

And yet I couldn't shove it aside.

Before I knew it, Juniper had finished her bottle and held it out to the side, as if to say, "Get this thing away from me."

I grinned and took it, then sat up with her and breathed in deeply.

"What do you say we go check email, June?" I said it casually, as if her entire future—and mine—didn't bank on a message that, whenever it arrived in my inbox, would likely be clinical, indifferent, and irrevocable, one way or the other.

I sat down at my desk, Juniper on my lap, and opened my email platform. Somehow I knew it would be there, yet when I saw the lab name as the sender, I couldn't get a deep breath in.

After staring at it for a few seconds, I clicked. "No big deal. Just another email," I lied to myself. "Right, Juniper?"

She'd picked up a pad of sticky notes and stuck it in her mouth, completely unfazed.

I scanned the report, not breathing, then gasped.

Probability of paternity 99.9999%.

I sat back in my chair, holding the baby securely with one hand, and rubbed the other one over my mouth. Letting the message soak in. Or trying.

"Wow."

Post-it pad still sticking out of her mouth along with gobs of saliva, Juniper turned her head toward me, her wide, arresting eyes taking me in.

My daughter.

All I could do was stare back at her stupidly, reeling.

I was a father.

As many times as I'd turned over the possibility in my mind the past few days, you would think I'd be prepared for it, but no. Gazing into those trusting eyes, I couldn't quite wrap my head around the reality that I was a dad.

The sound of the front door opening and closing penetrated my attention.

I stood, pulling Juniper into my chest—Post-its, slobber, and all—and went toward the main part of the house. Quincy stood at the island with some shopping bags, including one from the Dragonfly Diner judging by the savory aroma permeating the air.

She met my gaze with her pretty, happy eyes. "Hey. The princess awoke, I see." Her gaze rested on me for a second before landing on Juniper as she lost hold of the notepad and it fell to the floor. "Does this guy have you working for him now?" Quincy asked the baby as she approached. "Taking notes? Plotting books?"

When she reached us, she bent down to retrieve the paper and continued her one-way conversation with Juniper as I tried to figure out how to tell her our news. "You bring new meaning to the phrase *sticky notes*, sweet pea."

Quincy wrinkled her nose as she held the soaked pad between thumb and finger. As she rubbed her knuckle lightly over Juniper's pudgy cheek, I said, "I got the results."

Her gaze popped back to meet mine, her eyes sparkling with curiosity. "And?"

"She's mine. Ninety-nine-point-nine-nine-percent probability. I'm Juniper's father."

Quincy grabbed on to my forearm, the one that supported Juniper. "Knox!" Her eyes had widened as she scrutinized me. "Are you… Are you okay?"

I took a slow, deep breath, considering the question. As I exhaled, I said, "Yeah." Then a smile took over my lips. "Yeah. I think I actually am."

"Oooh." Quincy bounced on her toes, and the next thing I

knew, she threw her arms around me and Juniper. My arm automatically banded around her and pulled her in. I tried not to think about the smallness of her waist or the feminine curve of her hip below my fingers.

"Congratulations, Knox," she said into my shirt.

For a moment, I breathed in her floral, sunshiny scent mixed with the baby's clean smell, and a foreign sensation stirred deep inside my chest.

Before I could think more about it, Quincy let out a sharp "Ouch!" and laughed.

I released her and peered down in question. Juniper had grabbed a chunk of Quincy's long hair, which she wore down today instead of her usual thrown-on-top-of-her-head style.

"Juniper," I said as I grasped her tiny, fisted fingers and loosened her hold. "That hurts Quincy."

Once her hair was freed from the baby's hold, Quincy stepped back, biting her lip, looking self-conscious for an instant, and then hitting me with a bright smile. Too young for me or not, she was a beautiful woman. Any man would be hard-pressed to stand this close to her, with her beaming up at him posthug, and not be affected.

"You," she said, her attention homed in on Juniper now as she took hold of her hand, "are a very lucky girl. You got a good guy for a daddy."

Quincy's gaze flitted back up to mine for a pronounced moment. I shoved my free hand into my jeans pocket to keep from touching her, pulling her close again the way I suddenly had the urge to.

A second later, she glanced at the clock on the stove. "I hate to celebrate and run, but I need to get going or I'll be late, and I'll never hear the end of it from my stepmom. Your dinner's in one bag, and I got Juniper some books in the other. If you need anything, text me. I can bring Molly here with me." She hurried toward the door.

"We'll be fine," I told her.

"Congratulations again, Knox," she said, then disappeared.

She closed the door, and the room became noticeably emptier.

I was just starting to feel more confident that I could, indeed, handle the baby by myself for the evening. What I wasn't sure I could handle was this attraction to my twenty-eight-year-old nanny.

CHAPTER 11

QUINCY

My younger siblings, Molly, Brayden, and Hannah —or half-siblings technically—were the easiest babysitting job ever. Brayden had been at a friend's house all evening, studying for a test tomorrow, until bedtime, so I'd barely seen him. Hannah's cross-country meet had run late, and she'd only gotten home an hour ago. And now that Molly was eleven, she could take care of herself, liked to help cook dinner, and preferred doing things like hair and nails instead of playing with stuffed animals or Barbies.

Tonight she'd insisted on doing my hair. As I'd learned in the recent past, having this dear tween girl do my hair was a colorful, creative event. I currently had no less than a dozen-and-a-half tiny braids on the right front side of my head, each of them with several tiny multicolored butterfly clips spaced out down the length. It looked like a cross between dread-locks and toddler gone wild, but each time I caught a glimpse of the colorful clips, my heart warmed with love for the girl with the unique way of expressing her creativity.

The younger two were asleep now, Molly since nine and Brayden for over an hour, as it was approaching midnight and they both had school tomorrow. Hannah was in her room on the lower level and quiet, probably trying to catch up on homework. I was in the living room of the split-level house I'd lived in since I was eleven, when my dad had married Cynthia. I wouldn't say it felt homey to me, because nothing had really felt like home since my mom had died, but it was familiar and comfortable.

Stretched out on the couch, I'd been bingeing a show, but for the past half hour or so, I'd been restless. Antsy. I normally didn't care how late my dad and Cynthia came home, but tonight, I wanted to get back to Knox's to make sure he was doing okay with Juniper.

He was starting to get the hang of baby care and becoming more confident. To be honest, I was still shook by my spontaneous hug earlier. Throwing my arms around him was a gut reaction, a line I never would've crossed if I'd stopped to think it through. My body's response to him had been undeniable and not at all nanny appropriate. It'd been all I could do not to either kiss him or make a hasty, obvious retreat.

I knew those inklings were ill-advised, and I wouldn't act on them, but I still felt compelled to check on him and Juniper. I'd taken my phone out numerous times tonight, about to send a message asking how he was, but I'd managed to quash the urge each time. He was my employer after all.

My restlessness wasn't only about Knox. I was getting attached to Juniper as well, for better or worse. She was such a good baby, especially considering what she'd been through in her short life. She seemed to have made the transition to Knox pretty well and a lot faster than I'd expected. It made me wonder what kind of care she'd gotten before. I hated to think Knox's ex might've been less than adequate as a parent, but I couldn't deny I had questions.

At ten till midnight, I heard the garage door open and my dad's truck pull in. I flipped the TV off, hopped up, and got my jacket on. When my dad and Cynthia came through the door, I was standing in the kitchen waiting for them.

Cynthia said a distracted, "Hi, Quincy," then breezed past me.

"Hi, honey." My dad came over and kissed the top of my head. "You in a hurry or something?"

"No," I lied. "Just tired."

"You're always welcome to sleep here, you know," he said as he set his award plaque on the counter.

"Congrats on the award, Dad. You deserve it." I hugged him and didn't respond to the part about sleeping here. I knew I was welcome as far as he was concerned, but now that I had a choice, I didn't care to wake up to Cynthia.

"Aww, thanks. It's nice to be recognized. In the end, it's just back to the grind tomorrow, I guess." He shrugged humbly. "I need to replace a lightbulb out front before I forget." He went into the pantry to get a bulb.

Cynthia poked her head around the doorway to the living room, glancing up the stairs to Molly's and Brayden's rooms. "Are they asleep?"

"Long ago," I assured her. "Hannah got home about ten thirty. She said she had biology homework to do."

Cynthia looked semi-appeased.

"You be safe going home, honey," my dad said as he went out the door to the garage, bulb in hand. "See you soon."

"Night, Dad."

"What did Molly do to your hair?" Cynthia asked, her eyes widening as she looked me over.

"She called it an experiment." I grinned, flipping the ends of the curled side and ignoring my stepmom's distaste. "Sorry to rush out, but I need to get back."

Cynthia frowned. "In a hurry to get back to that man?"

"What?" I sputtered in disbelief. I mean, there was maybe a minor attraction to Knox, but no one knew about it, and no one ever would. He was older than me, a lot older, and he was my boss, not my crush.

Mostly not my crush.

He would *not* be my crush.

The point was that Cynthia had no reason to say such a thing other than she was determined to undermine me always. She had the power to bring out my self-doubt like nobody else. Yes, my insecurities were mine, but she knew the buttons to push. She had since she and my dad had married.

"He's a handsome man. You can't tell me you haven't noticed. It's a cozy setup you have there," she continued.

I raised my brows and didn't say anything. As much as she got to me, I did my best not to take her bait. I knew the lack of affection between us bothered my dad—a lot. He rarely said anything about it, probably because Cynthia and I could be civil when others were around. She mostly saved her barbs for when we were alone, and even then, they were carefully veiled.

"I just worry about you, Quincy. You were so set on having a family with Mitchell, and then that turned into disappointment…"

I flinched. See how she did that? All concern and empathy for me…except somehow she managed to make me feel dumb for ever loving Mitchell, foolish for thinking we were going to have a future.

"I'm over Mitchell," I told her, and I hated how I became defensive. I let out a frustrated scoff. "I need to go. It's late."

"Your dad was enjoying himself with his colleagues, and I just couldn't force myself to remind him what time it was."

She rustled through her purse. We'd done this enough times, like probably into the thousands, that I knew she was getting cash out to pay me. While it was usually less than what I'd make sitting for another family, I appreciated the money, particularly since, until I'd dropped out of college and come back home, they hadn't paid me at all. Ever since Hannah, my oldest half-sibling, was born, helping with child-care had been expected of me. My contribution to the family, they called it. Mostly I was okay with that, but now that I needed to support myself, the money was much needed.

She held out some bills, and I stuck them in my pocket without counting them.

"Thank you," I said. "Good night, Cynthia." I went toward the garage, knowing my dad was still out there so it would be open.

"Night, honey," she sang out the door after me, loving as could be since my dad might be within earshot.

I couldn't say whether she even knew she did that. I suspected she bought her own bullshit.

"See you, Dad," I said as I passed him.

"Night, Quincy. Thanks for staying with the kids."

"Of course. Congrats again."

I headed to my car, forcing my stepmom out of my mind. She wasn't worth my mental energy. Instead I turned my thoughts to Knox and Juniper.

If all was well, they were probably both asleep now. The baby had likely had her last bottle around eight and usually slept a good six hours. Though I'd been a night owl for years, I was getting used to going to bed around nine so I could get some good sleep in before she woke me up for a bottle. Tonight was one of my nights off, so Knox would take the overnight shift, but I planned to peek in on her.

When I pulled into Knox's driveway a couple of minutes later though, the lights in the main part of the house were blazing. Concern bloomed in my gut. I pulled up behind Knox's SUV, killed the engine, and hurried to the front door. It was locked, and Knox had uncharacteristically not turned the porch light on. That only ratcheted up my nervousness.

Once I got the door open, I could see the kitchen and

living area were lit by the fixture over the sink. Knox's bedroom door, to the left, was open, and another dim light came from there. The hall to Juniper's room, my room, and the office was dark.

As I stepped into the kitchen and set my bag on the island as quietly possible, I listened for a hint of where Knox might be, but there wasn't any noise. The house was…peaceful. Not like something was amiss. It didn't make sense unless he was in the baby's room. Maybe she'd woken up early.

Leaving the sink light on to illuminate my way, I started toward the hallway, then startled when I noticed someone lying on the sectional. The back of one side faced the front door, so I hadn't been able to see him when I entered.

Once I walked around the end, I could see Knox, stretched out across one side. He didn't stir, so I dared to go closer because…

Oh, sweet mother of God, my heart went absolutely warm and liquid in my chest.

Knox faced the back of the sectional. The cushions were tossed on the floor, and in between him and the back was Juniper, sound asleep, her face tilted toward him.

I couldn't take my eyes from the two of them, especially not in light of the news that she was his daughter.

Several seconds ticked by with me completely entranced by the sight of this handsome man and his tiny baby girl. Without breathing, I took one more step and saw the backs of his fingers rested against her chubby, pajama-covered belly. I could swear my heart did an actual swoon.

Eventually I realized how long I'd been gawking and how awkward it would be to have Knox wake up and find me staring at him, so I backed away, tiptoed into the kitchen, shut off the light, and hurried to my room by the light of my cell phone. I closed the door soundlessly and then stood there, resting my forehead against the wood, trying to recover from the storm of emotion that had evoked.

I instinctively knew I would've been much better off to have never witnessed Knox in such an endearing situation.

Minor crush plus hot guy cuddling his adorable baby daughter? I wasn't great at math, but I could say without doubt, that added up to a big, fat danger zone.

CHAPTER 12

KNOX

"Are you sure you're ready for this?" Holden asked Sunday as he pulled up along the curb in an older Nashville residential neighborhood. My father's neighborhood.

I blew out a breath from the backseat, looking over at Juniper, whose car seat was next to me. She was sound asleep, despite the ongoing conversation for the hour-long drive between Holden, Chloe, and me. "I'm not sure about anything," I admitted.

When we'd turned off the highway, my nervousness had inched upward. Not only was I visiting my dad and his wife for the first time, but it was Simon's birthday. That apparently meant the entire extended North-Henry clan would be here in force.

"There'll be beer," Holden said, then got out of the vehicle and went around to his pregnant wife's door.

Before he got there, I asked Chloe, "You were an outsider once, right? What should I expect in there?"

Her door opened, and she pivoted until her feet were on

the ground, then looked back at me. With a sympathetic smile, she said, "In a word? Chaos." As Holden helped her out, she flipped the seat forward for me.

I held a curse in, grabbed the bouquet of flowers I'd picked up at Oopsie Daisies, and climbed out of the Mustang's small backseat. I went to the driver's-side door and leaned into the back to get the baby and her car seat.

"You going to get a family car soon?" I asked Holden.

My half-brother let out a pained groan.

"We're compromising," Chloe said. "I get the new car, but it has to be a Volvo."

As I pulled the diaper bag out, I said, "That sounds a lot better than a minivan."

"I agree completely," Chloe said as she took the diaper bag from me. Holden hefted a box with several full beer growlers from the trunk.

We walked down the block about three houses, past all the parked cars, then up Simon and Faye's driveway. They'd explained on our way here that Simon had married Faye earlier this year, and they'd chosen to live in the home where all the North brothers had grown up. It was apparently the official family hub, even when the Henrys were included, which was most of the time. Faye liked to feed as many in the family as could show up every Sunday. The Henrys, I was told, made it about once a month due to the distance and the restaurant and brewery they owned that required plenty of attention.

But birthdays? Chloe had warned me they made a big deal of them, and generally no one missed. For adults, there was a strict no-gifts policy, but there would be multiple cakes, drinks, and loads of food. All in this modest two-story house.

I might be capable of chatting people up and being friendly, but I was an introvert deep down. A group of nearly thirty people wasn't my comfort zone. Add that the people inside were my only remaining family—whether halves, steps, or any other kind of relationship, by blood or by marriage—and my inner self was huddled in a corner, sucking its thumb.

As we went up to the stoop, the inner door opened. Both my father and his wife crowded the doorway.

"Welcome," Simon said as he opened the screen door. His smile was warm and seemed genuine.

"Hey, Dad. Happy birthday," Holden said as he went in. "Hi, Faye." He kissed his stepmom on the cheek. "It's good to see you."

Chloe gave Simon a quick hug and happy birthday wishes, then hugged Faye, who directed Holden on where to put the beer.

"Knox," Simon said as I reached him. "My son." The test results had indeed confirmed our biological ties two days ago. "Still getting used to that, but we'll get there, won't we? Come inside."

"Happy birthday." I stepped over the threshold. Instantly the weight of Juniper and her car seat lightened as Simon took them from me.

"Thank you," he said. Then he turned his attention to the baby, who I'd told him about on the phone and texted photos. "My word."

A dull, incessant roar of voices came from the other side of the house. Chloe handed Juniper's diaper bag to Faye, and she and Holden headed off into the crowd.

"Heavens," Faye said, her tone dripping with sugar and love. "Look at her. She's absolutely precious." She set the bag down, pressed both her hands over her mouth, and just stared at my daughter, her eyes tearing up.

"This is Juniper," I told them, taken aback by the welcoming warmth this woman emitted.

Faye let out a happy gasp.

"We have all boys so far," my father explained. "Wonderful, brilliant little boys, but my wife has been waiting for a granddaughter."

That they already accepted Juniper as their granddaughter floored me in the best possible way and had my own eyes dampening.

"Our boys are the best grandsons ever," Faye agreed, "but this one… She's absolutely beautiful, Knox." As if remembering I'd never been to her house, she turned her attention to me and hugged me. "Come in. Welcome. We can't wait to get to know you and this gorgeous girl."

There was no way anyone could not instantly like this woman. "Thank you. Same here."

"Why don't we duck in here for a few minutes before we join the horde in the family room," Simon said, indicating a room near the front door.

"Sounds good," I said, and that was an understatement. It sounded like a lot of people, and I didn't look forward to making a grand entrance—me, the outcast, with my surprise baby.

"This used to be a formal living room," Faye said as we went in. "We don't do formal around here, so when Simon moved in, we turned it into a den."

"Otherwise known as my man cave," my father said.

"Every home needs one," I said, thinking of my office, which was as close as I came to one in my smaller place. I'd just ordered a custom carved bookshelf to make it feel like my space.

Simon's room contained a masculine leather love seat and an extra-wide chair, as well as a small desk in the corner with a computer on it. He gestured for me to take the chair, and he and Faye sat on the love seat. I set Juniper's car seat in front of me.

"How was your trip?" I asked them, preferring the spotlight to be on them instead of myself, even though I knew questions—about myself but especially about my daughter—were inevitable.

Faye let out a sigh. "It was fabulous. Perfect weather, lots of good food, and I got to meet some old friends of Simon's. But we want to hear about you. It sounds like you've had quite a bit of drama lately."

"That's one word for it." I leaned forward, my gaze going to my daughter's apple cheeks, my mind rolling over the past two weeks. "Breaking the news to you and the rest of your family about our connection was no small deal, and then the very next day, this nugget turned up."

"You said you found her in your car," Simon said. "I can't understand what whoever dropped her off was thinking."

"I thought it was a joke at first," I admitted.

"It's like something out of a movie or a novel," Faye said, shaking her head.

I'd already told them on the phone about that day and about the paternity test results, as the news had spread all over Dragonfly Lake, and I didn't want my father to hear it from someone besides me.

"Have you heard from the mother?" Simon asked.

I shook my head. "She's not answering the only number I have for her. No longer works for the employer she used to. I'm not sure what else to do to find her. And then I stop and wonder why I'd want to find her. Just to get more details about my daughter, I guess." And give Gina a piece of my mind. But mostly I'd decided that would be a waste of energy and do no one any good. I was moving forward legally to protect my daughter.

"That's something I can relate to," Simon said as he rested his elbows on his thighs, similar to my position. "I missed a lot of years. A *lot* of years." He shook his head sadly.

"You both did," Faye said.

Simon's gaze shot back to me. "That's true. I've been twisted up over missing out on your life, but you're the one who grew up without a father." He frowned. "I'm trying not to be upset with Janet, but we lost so much…"

"Yeah." I blew out my breath. "It adds a whole thick layer to the grief, believe me."

"I'm sorry, Knox. You must be going through so much," Simon said.

I managed a smile. "I've had some time to work through a lot of the stuff about my mom. She had a heart of gold. She gave up a lot for me." My throat tightened with sadness and the pain of missing her.

A young woman I hadn't met before stuck her head in the doorway. "Sorry to interrupt, but we can't find the extra plates, Faye."

"Of course you can't because we moved them," Faye said lightly. She stood and went toward the doorway. "Excuse me. You two keep talking. I need to check in on food prep and show Mackenzie where we moved everything."

Simon nodded at his wife.

Faye paused before disappearing. "I'll want to hold that baby when she's awake."

"Yes, ma'am," I said, smiling. This baby had struck it lucky with her new grandmother. There wasn't a doubt in my mind.

Simon was looking after her, the expression on his face one of a man clearly in love.

Once she'd left, he sobered, turned his attention back to me, and said, "I want you to know something, Knox. The time I spent with your mother was the blink of an eye in the overall scheme of life, but it was…special."

"I got that impression from her letter," I told him.

"It's been a lot of years. I've been lucky enough to love and be loved by two women since then. Some people would claim that the weekend your mom and I spent together was too brief for love to be involved, but I don't know. Maybe they'd be right, but maybe not. What I *can* tell you is that our connection was unique. Powerful. But always intended to be temporary. Maybe that was part of the intensity, the magic." He shook his head as if he was still puzzling it out to this day. "All I know is that meeting her when I did, spending that time together... She was exactly what I needed at that moment. Strangely enough, she helped me straighten my head out about Nita, who became my first wife, and see I was being a jackass about some things."

He met my gaze with a sheepish expression, and I grinned. "She made me see when I was being a jackass about some things too. A couple hundred times at least," I said.

Simon chuckled. Then he shifted his attention straight ahead, his focus going internal again, to memories, I guessed. "Ever since that weekend, I've felt like maybe Janet was put in my path for a reason. To give me perspective. To help me get my act together. To ultimately help me steer my life in the right direction." He let out a quiet, self-effacing laugh. "I don't know if that even makes sense, but that's what I've thought. And then I found out about you last week, and I can't help but think her life was likely just as irrevocably changed as mine was. More so. Because she came away from our time together with you."

My throat went thick with emotion again, this time not with grief but with...I didn't quite know what.

"It's as if that weekend wasn't random," my father said, then shook his head. "I probably sound like a crazy old man—"

"You don't." My voice came out rough. "My mom did her best not to let me ever feel like a mistake, but once I was old enough to understand more, it was always in the back of my mind. I knew she loved me. She loved me more than anything, so I don't want you to question that."

"I'm certain of it."

I tried to put my thoughts into words, to let him know the gift he'd just given me by telling me more about his connection with my mom. "What you just explained helps me to see it as...*more*."

"It *was* more. I mean that."

He made it sound like my conception was the result of a brief but powerful connection between two people who were never meant to be together long-term but who were absolutely destined to come together for that brief period. And that...that rearranged a part of my own story. In a good way. A very good way. I wasn't sure I could explain it to him adequately, so I just said, "Thank you. For sharing all that."

A warm smile spread across his face. "Your mom was special. Never doubt that I recognized that from the second she told me her name."

"That's something we can agree on. My mom was special."

He stood. "We have a lot more to talk about, but I'd rather do that when we don't have a zoo in the other room. What do you say? Are you ready to get to know your family?"

I glanced down at Juniper, who slumbered on, then picked her up, car seat and all, knowing she was due to wake up any minute. "Ready as I'll ever be."

CHAPTER 13

KNOX

Simon led me to the noisy part of the house. There was a big family room straight ahead, which was open to a dining room with a giant table. A breakfast bar separated the dining room from the kitchen. All three rooms were crowded with people, about a third of whom I knew at a glance.

"Want me to introduce you all at once?" Simon asked.

I shook my head. "I'll just make the rounds and do it gradually. I'll start with those familiar faces." I pointed at Ava, who stood nearby with Hayden, Everly, and another woman.

"I'll see if Faye needs more help." He pointed to the kitchen where there were several women plus Cash.

"Hey, man of the hour," Ava said as I walked up to their group. "And surprise baby of the year," she directed toward the carrier.

"Hi, half-brother." Hayden gave me a hug. "Hi, adorable niece," she whispered to Juniper.

"Hi, Knox," Everly said, slipping an arm around me to pull me into their group protectively. I didn't know if she even realized what she was doing, but I appreciated the small but welcoming gesture.

"I'm Sierra," the fourth woman, a taller brunette with her hair in a ponytail, said, holding out her hand.

I shook it. "Nice to meet you. Let's see, Cole is yours, no kids?" Holden and Chloe had gone over the couples with me on the drive in.

"Nailed it," she said. "It's good to meet you. Congratulations on fatherhood." Her gaze lowered to Juniper, and she got that what-a-cute-baby expression.

"Thank you. It's a lot to get used to." I laughed, mostly because that was the biggest understatement of my life. "How are you ladies?" I hefted the car seat up to the arm of the chair next to me to rest my arm and bring Juniper closer.

"We're basking in our auntie-ness," Hayden said. "Or at least I am."

"How can we not?" Everly said. "I've gone from zero to two, one niece and one nephew, in just a few months. Auntie-ness is awesome."

"Pretty sure we have the cutest niece and nephew ever," Ava said.

"I don't know. My nephews are super cute," Sierra said.

"Hey, your nephews are my nephews," Hayden said.

"I wonder if they're my nephews too." Ava looked puzzled, and all of them laughed.

I was clearly not in on the joke.

"Between in-laws and steps and now halves, our family likes to joke about who's actually related and how," Sierra explained. "Hayden used to be just my bestie, but now we're sisters-in-law. And stepsisters-in-law. We think."

"And they've apparently always had a rep for causing trouble together," Ava said.

They all laughed again, and this time I laughed with them even though I didn't think I'd ever keep the family ties straight, even if you drew me a family tree. I wondered if I'd ever feel a part of this instead of like an outsider and merely a half-relative.

"Where's your son?" I asked Hayden.

"In the basement with the dads," she replied.

I tried to figure out who the dads were besides her husband, Zane. Before I could puzzle through it, she said, "Mason has Calvin and Jasper. Gabe has Wyatt. Zane has Harrison. They're likely doing rowdy boy things down there."

"I haven't met any of them but your husband and son." I looked around to see who else I knew and who I didn't, now that the whole group wasn't focused on me.

"I'll introduce you to the women. They're more fun anyway," Hayden said.

Our group migrated toward the dining room, where four women were gathered at one end of the table, immersed in conversation.

"Eliza's facing us," Hayden said, gesturing. "She plays fiddle for Steele Hearts." The dark-haired woman looked up and waved.

"Married to Mason, with two kids," I recited.

"You've been thoroughly prepped," Everly said.

"The car ride in was a crash course," I admitted.

"Next to Eliza is Miranda, one of the North cousins," my half-sister continued.

"Hi," Miranda sang out, and the other two women, who had their backs to us, turned to say hello too.

"Geraldine, meet Knox Breckenridge," Hayden introduced, indicating the oldest at the table, a smiling woman with a reddish-brown bob hairstyle.

"Nice to meet you," I said. "Are you a cousin or a North?"

"Neither," the woman in her sixties said and let out a loud laugh. "I'm called the honorary auntie. I'm BFFs with Faye and her sister, Liz." She pointed at both women, who were in the midst of chaos in the kitchen and not paying attention to us.

I shook her hand. "There's a lot of aunts around here. It's tough for an only child to get used to."

"Good lord, an only child? Me too," Geraldine said. "As you can see, they don't know how to do only children around here. You and I'll have to stick together."

I winked at her. "Definitely."

Hayden threw her arms around the last woman from behind. "This is my sister-in-law Lexie."

"Married to Gabe," I said.

"Mom of Wyatt," Hayden added.

"Painter of murals," Eliza said.

"None of them lie," Lexie said in a quiet but warm voice. "Welcome to the madness, Knox. It's not too late to run away screaming."

I wanted to know more about the murals and the fiddle playing, but my questions would have to wait, as a boy around five or six years old burst into the room from the basement stairs. I was guessing he was Calvin.

"Mimi, all the boys downstairs want to know how long till eats?" he hollered.

Faye paused what she was doing, held an inviting arm out for her grandson, and looked to Cash. "Thirty minutes, Cash?"

The chef took in the different dishes in the works and nodded. "About that."

"Do you need me to sample something?" Calvin asked, eliciting laughter and comments from the family—and a mini pickle from the veggie tray.

As the boy tore off to the basement again, Juniper stirred. Just a few days ago, her waking was a stressful event for me, every single time, but today it brought a wave of relief. It gave me an excuse to step out of the pandemonium for a few minutes.

I excused myself and carried the car seat into Simon's man cave, then unbuckled the baby. "Hey, June Bug. You have no idea what I've gotten us into today. I have a feeling you're gonna get loved on like you've never been loved on before."

As I lifted her out of her cozy nest, I kissed her cheek and she cooed—so far contentedly. We were getting to a point where, if I caught her early enough upon waking, I could get her diaper changed and mix up her bottle before she tuned up into a hungry fuss. I liked to think she was learning to trust that I'd have what she needed, but more than likely, it was just that I'd figured out ways of distracting her from her basic needs for a few minutes.

I pulled out the changing pad and spread it on the floor, then did a quick diaper change. After that, I shook the premeasured bottle and settled onto the chair to feed her, needing a few minutes of quiet to process this significant day so far.

———

A few hours later, dinner was over, and we'd all moved downstairs to the finished basement where everyone could fit in one big room together for cake.

As I understood it, Faye had had the lower level finished as her family continued to expand. At one end was a play area where the boys were enthralled with a supply of toys so big it could only have been provided by doting grandparents. The other two-thirds was a family room with a giant sectional, a sofa, a love seat, a couple of chairs, and lots of floor pillows. There was a stone fireplace on one side, giving the room a warm, homey feeling despite how big it was and the fact it was underground. The egress windows helped, even though it was now dark outside.

The whole house had a welcoming feel to it. Both the Norths and the Henrys—with the exception of Cash—had been friendly and seemed interested in getting to know me and fawning over my daughter. There was nothing I could complain about, but I gravitated to one of the edges and sat next to Seth, appreciating that he was one of the quietest people here, content to watch and listen for the most part, while everyone else interacted with jokes and teasing and nonstop references to things I didn't understand. Memories, inside jokes, shared stories. None of it was meant to make me feel like an outsider, but despite their friendliness and attempts to fill me in, I did.

When my cake was devoured, Juniper needed another diaper change and was giving signs she wanted to eat. I was once again relieved to escape the nonstop clamor as I climbed the stairs with her. I was used to living alone and had only recently started adjusting to having both Juniper and Quincy in my living space. Twenty-some others was a tall order.

As I changed her in the den, I wondered what it would've been like to grow up with this, with all the people, all the love, all the connections. I'd had friends at every stage of my life, but there was a difference between those relationships and the closeness these people shared. To think the two families had only joined recently, first with the marriage of Hayden and Zane and then when Faye and Simon had tied the knot, was astounding. They all acted like they'd known each other their whole lives. Longing to be a part of it seeped through me.

After fastening the clean diaper and fixing Juniper's denim jumper dress, I grabbed her chubby feet and made bicycle circles. She laughed, as I'd hoped she would. That giggle sent a spike of joy through me more intoxicating than Rusty Anchor's Deep Waters IPA.

"You think we'll fit in here someday?" I asked her in a quiet voice.

Her eyes met mine, and I felt that connection again. It was the strangest thing, to connect with such a small human, and one I'd only met recently at that. But it was absolutely a bond that reached clear to my heart.

Next week I was meeting with a lawyer to find out what I needed to do to get full custody of my daughter. Even now though, there was a bond between us that came from knowing she was my flesh and blood, a sense of *you and me against the world.* I likened it to what my mom must have experienced, and it made me feel closer to her than ever.

The thought caused a pang of longing that robbed me of my breath. What I wouldn't give to have my mom meet my daughter. She would've been euphoric to hold her granddaughter.

Becoming subdued, I reminded myself I needed to be strong for my child. "Someday, June Bug, we'll feel like we're a part of this. We'll feel like these people are family," I said quietly, then kissed her on the tip of her nose.

I put away the changing supplies, picked up Juniper, and headed toward the kitchen to mix another bottle. Somehow thoughts of my mom had heightened the feeling of not belonging. I wasn't the large-family kind of guy who went to big, noisy gatherings. I came from a two-person clan, and I didn't know if I'd ever get used to the other end of the scale. I was starting to wish I'd driven myself so I could leave soon.

When I went around the corner toward the kitchen, Cash was there, making coffee. He turned to find out who'd joined him but didn't say anything when he saw me. I could actually feel his attitude harden.

"Hey," I said, thinking it was stupid to act like strangers when we were the only two adults on this floor of the house.

An unfriendly grunt came out of him, his back to me once again.

My eyes narrowed. Were we adults or grade-schoolers here?

Holding Juniper in one arm, I used the other to mix the

bottle. After a leveling inhalation, I tried again. "Dinner was really good."

"Tell that to Faye. She did the planning and most of the cooking," he said, his tone lacking in any sort of warmth or friendliness.

Of course I planned to tell Faye how wonderful dinner had been. That wasn't the point. The point was I was trying to find some semblance of common ground, a way for us to be civil. My efforts were obviously not well received.

Tonight had been a lot. Hell, the past week had been a fucking lot. I was weary and overwhelmed twenty-four seven. Maybe earlier in the day I could be the bigger man, but my patience was threadbare.

"Do you have something you need to say to me?" I bit out.

Several seconds ticked by, and I started to wonder if he was going to blow me off completely. I clenched my jaw, and Juniper let out a fuss. Just a prelude.

Cash scoffed, and I had to coach myself through another calming breath. I wasn't a fighter by any means, but this guy, my fucking half-brother, got under my skin.

"Okay, then," I muttered sarcastically. Nothing could be resolved through silence.

The baby's bottle was well mixed, so I turned my attention to Juniper, cradling her, then giving her the bottle. Her wide, eager gaze meeting mine took my irritation down a notch or two.

And then my shoulders stiffened again when Cash turned around and deigned to speak.

"It takes some steel cojones to do what you did."

"What did I do, exactly?" I asked in a calm voice, leaning my backside against the cabinets, keeping my eyes on my daughter, who drank earnestly.

"You came here under false pretenses and buddied up to my family without telling us your true identity."

I couldn't argue with that.

"What pisses me off the most is that I didn't trust you from the start, and I was spot on, but you managed to fool everyone and make me look like the asshole. Yet here we are."

"Here we are," I repeated.

"I went against my misgivings and extended the olive branch for Ava's sake," he continued. "Tried to be friendly with you, but how can a guy be a friend if you don't know who the fu—" He glanced at my daughter. "Who the heck he is?"

"I'm the same guy you knew. An introverted writer who fell in love with the town and the lake. Someone your fiancée trusts. You know my identity now."

"Do we?" He crossed his arms over his chest and sized me up. "How do we know what you say is true?"

I scowled and wondered why I was wasting my breath if that's how he really felt. "We did a paternity test. Was that not proof enough?"

"It doesn't make me trust you." He pushed away from the cabinets. "I resent the position I'm in. With you and Ava cowriting, I can't just write you off like I want to."

A stream of formula dribbled down Juniper's chin, so I dabbed at it with a burp cloth.

"Plus there's that family tie," I jabbed.

He picked up one of the mugs of coffee and sipped it, staring at me. I met his gaze full on.

"What would you have done differently if you were in my place?" I finally asked. "If you found out you had half-siblings and a dad you didn't know about somewhere, what would you do?"

"I wouldn't wait months before revealing who I am, all the while making friends with them."

"I never planned to. I never expected it to take so long to connect with Simon. It wasn't like I had his address or his phone number and could just ring him up and say, 'Hi, Dad.'

I also never planned to connect with Ava over writing or become friends with Holden."

He grunted.

"Look, I apologized for not being up-front about our ties," I continued, unwilling to keep hashing out the same damn points again and again. "My intent was not to hurt anyone. I did the best I could at the time."

He raised his brows. Apparently that was all the response I was going to get.

"And still, here we are," I said again.

This conversation had changed nothing. There wasn't much else I could say to argue my case. If he didn't want to see it from my perspective, there was nothing I could do.

"I'm going to the den to finish feeding my daughter. I'll be taking off soon, so you can try to enjoy the end of your night."

He grumbled something I couldn't understand, picked up the tray of coffees, then strode off toward the basement.

Trying to shrug off the whole interaction, I headed toward the den, gazing down at Juniper, whose eyes had become droopy. She'd be asleep by the time the milk was gone.

That was the excuse I needed to leave. If Holden and Chloe weren't ready yet, I'd call an Uber. I was exhausted from all the interaction and introductions.

As welcoming as everyone had been, Cash had made it all too clear I might never fit in here.

CHAPTER 14

QUINCY

Eight p.m. had come and gone when I finally got my sister Hannah and my stepmother out of Knox's house.

I leaned on the kitchen island, planting my elbows on it and wearily running my hands over my face. Trying to be a peacemaker got me in trouble every time. I hadn't volunteered for the role.

Hannah, who was sixteen, had texted saying she needed to talk and wondering if she could come over. Of course, I'd said yes. Wanting to be a nonjudgmental ear whenever she needed one, I always said yes to Hannah when she wanted to talk.

The door behind me opened, and I whipped around, on guard, thinking either Hannah or my stepmom had come back.

Instead it was Knox and Juniper, and my shoulders sagged with relief.

"Are you okay?" Knox asked as he closed the door behind them.

"Yeah," I breathed out. I sought out the adorable baby in the carrier, saw she was sound asleep, and drank in the sight of her, letting her soothe my tattered nerves. "It looks like socializing wore her out."

"Her and me both." I glanced up at Knox's face and could see fatigue in his eyes. "I'm going to see if I can get her transferred to bed without waking her. She finally fell asleep about twenty minutes ago."

"Baby babbles are the best," I said quietly, glancing down at her. "You gave me the afternoon off. I'm back on duty now. I can put her to bed."

He seemed to consider it for a moment, then shook his head. "I'd like to if you don't mind."

"Of course not. She's your daughter."

Knox tossed the diaper bag to the floor near the couch, then carried the princess down the hall toward her room as I wondered if he was okay. He seemed subdued.

Earlier he'd admitted to being nervous about the day, but knowing the Henrys pretty well and some of the Norths, I'd predicted he would be welcomed with open arms. He wasn't as upbeat now as I'd expected.

I glanced around to make sure the kitchen was clean. I'd just been finishing an early dinner when Hannah had texted.

The day was overcast and chilly, so I'd turned the gas fireplace on to an auto setting so it wouldn't heat up too much like a sauna. The house was cozy and dimly lit.

I wandered over to the sectional and flopped onto it, waiting for Knox to come out, hoping to find out how his family debut had gone. Maybe I was just the nanny, but we weren't formal around here. It felt as if we were becoming friends, maybe because he'd needed so much help with Juniper at first. He didn't treat me like he was my boss.

Maybe it would be better if he did.

Maybe then I wouldn't have naughty thoughts about him.

Ha. I'd still have naughty thoughts about him. He was too

good-looking not to. Add in that image I couldn't erase from my mind of him sleeping next to his daughter, and it wasn't just his looks. That man had taken in a baby without knowing if she was his, even though it made him fully uncomfortable. How could I not be turned inside out by a heart like that? Add in that he was intelligent, like really smart, and it was tough to ignore the thoughts…

"What's going on?" he asked, startling me. "You seem not quite yourself." He came around the end of the sectional and sat perpendicular to me, about a foot away. Close enough for me to catch a hint of his masculine scent as I lay there.

"I could say the same to you." I smiled, trying to shake off my stepmom's lingering effects. I hated letting her get to me.

"I'm fine. Good."

With a quiet laugh, I said, "You don't seem completely fine and good."

He studied me for a few seconds. "You tell me yours; I'll tell you mine," he said lightly.

My stepmom wasn't my favorite topic, but I couldn't resist the chance to find out more about his family dinner.

"My story's not that exciting," I said.

"You looked upset when I came in."

I was lying on my back, where I'd landed, and I stared up at the ceiling, thinking of how to summarize Cynthia.

"What happened while I was gone?" he persisted.

I rolled to my side and propped myself up on my elbow. "I hope you don't mind I let my sister come over. She texted me, wanting to talk."

"Is this the teenage one?"

I nodded. "Hannah. The oldest of my halves. She was pissed at my parents because they won't let her go to the big bonfire in Runner after the next football game."

"Runner's the town on the other side of the lake, right?"

"Yep. Our rivals in sports."

"So what'd you tell your sister?"

"Mostly I let her vent."

"It's good she can come to you."

"It's not easy being sixteen," I said. "Some of her friends are going, so she thinks she should be able to."

"Did you do stuff like that when you were her age? What was that, about five years ago?" he teased.

"Twelve, thank you." I laughed. It wasn't the first comment he'd made about my age. It didn't bother me. I'd had plenty of thoughts about how much older than me he was. The more I got to know him though, the less the gap felt like a big deal. We could talk as if we were the same age. "I went to the bonfire in Runner a few times," I said. "But my parents didn't know about it."

"You've got some rebel in you."

I pursed my lips to the side in thought. "Not really. Not normally. When it comes to my stepmom though..." I shook my head. "We don't get along. We haven't since day one."

"Which was when?" He propped his legs up on the ottoman and settled back into the cushions, still just as close to me.

"She married my dad when I was eleven, less than two years after my mom died in a car wreck."

"It must've have been hard to lose your mom so suddenly," he said quietly.

I closed my eyes as an unexpected wave of sadness engulfed me. The accident happened a long time ago, and I'd grieved so much, but it could still broadside me. "Yeah." I struggled to get my feelings tucked in so I could talk. "My mom was special. I mean, of course I think that, but everyone did. The whole town knew her. She was a real estate agent and good at her job. If you were selling a house, you called Reba. She was president of the PTA, in charge of all kinds of community events, and good at all of it," I said with an adult admiration I hadn't had back then.

"I see what you mean about special. Plus she raised a pretty amazing daughter."

His words spiked a warm pleasure inside me amid the sadness. "And a son. I have an older brother, Ryan. He lives in Nashville."

"How old is he?"

I did some quick math. "Thirty-seven. Actually he's business partners with Sierra's brother."

"Sierra North?"

I nodded. "Maiden name Lowell. Her brother is Jackson. Their company is Tech Horse Software."

"It's a small, small world," Knox said. "I met Sierra tonight. Liked her."

"Tell me more."

"We're not done with you yet. So your dad married in less than two years? That must've been devastating for you."

"I was not open to having a stepmom. I resented her from the first time my dad went out with her. My brother was already in college, so my dad and I were alone after my mom died. It was hard, but it became comfortable. And then it wasn't."

"It was always just me and my mom," he said. "I can't imagine how it would've felt if she met someone when I was a teenager."

I wondered what teenage Knox was like, loved getting that tiny glimpse into how he'd grown up.

"I bet you were super close to her," I said.

"Yeah," was all he said, and I could hear the emotion, the grief that was a lot newer than mine.

I checked the urge to touch the hand that clenched his jeans on his thigh. I didn't want to bring on his sadness, so I went back to my family. "I'm happy my dad is happy. He deserves to be. But it's taken me a lot of years to be able to see it that way."

"You were a kid who lost her mom. It's a blow at any age."

I nodded. "I'd like to think I've grown up, but my relationship with Cynthia hasn't changed. It's exhausting. There are times when I just wish we could be closer. I love her kids so much, and they'll always be part of my life. And my dad... He hates that we don't get along."

We were both quiet for a couple minutes. Then he asked, "Have you ever thought about sitting down with her and talking, burying the hatchet?"

"She's never asked."

"What if you approached her?"

I frowned, trying to imagine it. "I wouldn't know where to start."

"Maybe if you were the bigger person and made the first move, she'd admit she's tired of not getting along too."

"Maybe."

Before I could think more in-depth about that, he asked, "So your stepmom was here too?"

I scowled, thinking back to earlier. "She tracked Hannah down by her phone and barged in. I'm sorry. I know we didn't discuss me having people over."

"They're your family," he said. "It doesn't bother me. Seems to have bothered you though."

"There was drama." I sat up and cradled my knees to my chest. "She accused me of undermining her by letting my sister come over, even though I tried to get Hannah to understand that particular bonfire can be dangerous, especially on the night our two teams play."

"So you took your parents' side, but your stepmother was mad anyway?"

"She didn't stop to ask. All she saw was that Hannah came to me instead of her. You'd think she would just be relieved her daughter has someone to talk to besides her friends."

"Yeah, you'd think."

I reclined again and shifted onto my stomach, folding my arms under my head, tired of thinking of it, of her. "So tell me about your afternoon."

"My afternoon," he repeated. He leaned his head back into the cushion, his gaze going to the ceiling. "Mixed bag. It was weird."

"Weird how?"

"I had some good moments with my dad when I got there. Really good."

"So that wasn't the weird part?"

"That was the good part. Then I met everyone I didn't know, one by one. Tried to fit in. Failed."

I lifted my head to look at him, my brows shooting up. "That *is* a lot. Why do you say you failed?"

"I stuck out like a sore thumb. Me and my surprise baby." He laughed. "Don't get me wrong. Everyone was welcoming. Friendly. Loved on Juniper. Except for Cash, but that was expected. He's still pissed I didn't reveal who I was sooner."

"Did he say something today?"

"Sure did. After birthday cake, he and I ended up in the kitchen alone. He said some things. I said some things. Then I decided it was time to call it a night."

"I'm sorry. Cash has a good heart, but he doesn't hide when he's upset."

Knox shrugged. "He's entitled to his feelings. I'm lucky the rest of my half-siblings have made peace with me already. I hung out with Seth. It was all surface stuff, but there was no animosity."

"I like Seth. And Holden, he's so easygoing."

"Holden's been great from the start. He was welcoming before he knew who I was, and he's been accepting since I told them we're related. Hayden too."

"Cash will come around."

"Not today apparently."

"I hate that he spoiled the day for you. It was a big one," I said. "It's not every day you get to meet bunches of family for the first time."

"Bunches is right."

The fireplace turned back on automatically, filling the dimly lit room with a warm glow and the faint hum from the fan. This was cozy and comfortable like I never would've believed it could be considering I'd only been here for just over a week. My stepmom's accusation rang through my mind, about my "cozy setup." Then I shooed her out of my head, because this was just Knox and me talking, being friendly. Even if we were inches apart and my body was extra aware of every move he made.

"I always wondered what it would be like to have a big, rowdy family," he said. "Our house was always quiet, tidy. Sometimes lonely."

"And then you find out you have this huge family here," I said. "That must have been wild."

"Today I got to see what it's like to have a house filled with family, people who love each other."

"I bet it wasn't quiet."

"Not for a single second."

I rolled to my side again, propping my head on my elbow so I could see his face as he described it. He smiled faintly. Then it disappeared.

"It was fascinating to witness, but…" He shook his head.

"But what?"

He turned to his side, his body bridging from the cushion to the ottoman, which put us facing each other. "I was an outsider. It was like watching someone else's family, not mine."

"It'll take some time," I said. "You just met half those people, and the other half just found out you're one of them."

"I know. I know I can't expect to feel like I belong on the

first day. It's just...I don't know if I'll ever be more than the odd guy out with the cute baby."

"Blended families are so tough," I said with conviction. "Been there, done that, still trying to fit in. Or maybe I stopped trying, and that's part of the problem."

His hand landed on mine, just a brush of his finger next to mine but an intentional one, and I met his gaze. Dove into it and got lost for several seconds, and I could swear he was lost too, because neither one of us looked away. Neither one of us made a move. Tension arced between us, the kind that made my heart pound harder and my body respond down low, between my legs and deep in my middle.

"We have a lot in common, don't we?" he finally said, his voice lower, rough around the edges.

"We do."

Still, we didn't move. It would only take a small shift for him to join me on this side of the sectional and press his body against mine, roll me to my back, and let me feel the weight of him all over me. I stopped breathing with wanting that.

My God, I wanted that. I wanted him.

Knox rolled to his back suddenly, clearing his throat, yanking me out of that moment where time had seemed to stop.

"We should get some sleep," he said as he sat up. "The princess's schedule was wonky today, so who knows how long she'll be out."

I forced my brain to reality. "I'm covering tonight. You're meeting with Ava tomorrow morning, right?"

"Right. Monday morning planning meeting." He stood, pushing the oversized ottoman sideways to give us more room.

He turned to me and held out his hand to help me up. I did everything in my power to act like touching him was no big deal and my heart wasn't about to leap out of my chest.

But it so was.

His hand was strong, masculine, warm.

I hated to let go, but once I was upright, I did, because *no big deal*.

Forcing my mind to something besides him, I asked, "When's the last time you fed—"

My foot caught on the leg of the ottoman just as I started moving forward, and somehow I went flying forward into Knox. His hands landed on my arms to steady me, but then we were both going down. The next thing I knew, I was sprawled half on top of him, chest to chest, my foot throbbing, adrenaline racing through my veins, my heart pounding for an altogether different reason. I tried to get my brain unstunned.

"Shit," he said. "Are you okay?"

"I think so. Are you?"

A second or two passed as he seemed to assess. "I'm fine."

"I'm so sorry. I'm such a klutz. Always. God." I closed my eyes in embarrassment. "You didn't hit your head?"

"No."

As I peered into his eyes to make sure he was telling the truth, our gazes got caught up again, and my embarrassment slid away as heat and awareness rushed in.

His eyes were intense, the pupils so big that the blue was only a thin ring as he stared up at me, neither one of us moving. Without thinking, I glanced at his lips. They were slightly parted, and I instantly wondered what it would feel like to kiss a man with facial hair, as my ex had been almost obsessive about shaving.

My cheeks grew warm, and I flicked my gaze back up to his. He hadn't moved, still looked back at me, our faces only inches apart. With the smallest lean in on my part, my lips would be on his. Just a subtle shift forward to learn his taste, feel his textures, breathe his scent.

There was a tiny voice in my head saying kissing him

would be inappropriate. He was my employer. He was considerably older than me. It would be wrong.

Knox didn't move away.

Nothing *felt* wrong. Everything felt extremely right, including his solid body below mine.

Ignoring the voice, I leaned in and touched my lips to his.

CHAPTER 15

KNOX

As soon as Quincy's lips touched mine, the embers that'd been smoldering for days exploded. Lust pumped through my veins.

My arms went around her, and I drowned in the warmth of her lips, her floral scent, her sweet taste. There was no hesitancy in her kiss, as if she knew what she wanted and was going after it. Not going to lie, that was a rush in itself: that this young, gorgeous woman wanted *me*.

I roved my hands over her curves, her waist, reveling in her feminine softness even through her clothing. My fingers itched to inch her shirt up so I could touch her flesh, feel her heat directly. I wanted to peel her leggings off and strip her naked, roll her over and take her right there on the floor. As lost in her as I was though, I knew that wasn't an option.

I raised up on an elbow, palmed her cheek, and managed to break the contact of our mouths even though I never wanted the kiss to end.

"Quincy."

Her lids slowly rose halfway. "Knox."

Trailing one of my hands over her back, I shook my head. "We can't do this."

Her brows went up, her pretty, blue-green eyes seeming to focus more clearly on me, and she surprised me by smiling. "It seems like we can do this pretty well."

A lock of blond hair fell, draping over her cheek, onto me. I pushed it back and tried to summon all my willpower. "You work for me."

She tilted her head slightly, a spark of amusement lighting up her eyes. "I do, yes." Her voice was higher pitched than usual, just louder than a whisper. Magical, as if she was weaving a spell over me. "I'm the one who started this. That switches up the dynamics. Makes it okay. Unless you don't want to kiss me."

"I want to kiss you." The words poured out of me before I could think through whether they should. Fighting the effect she had on me, I managed, "It wouldn't be right though."

Her eyes narrowed, the spark dimming. "What wouldn't be right about it?"

"It's not right for a forty-two-year-old guy to boink his nanny."

Quincy laughed, surprising me like she so often did. "Did you really just say *boink*?"

I couldn't help smiling despite myself, despite my point, which was serious and valid. I needed to keep it top of mind.

Her grin faded, and she studied me. "None of that matters. The age, the job…" She made a face like the idea was preposterous. "What matters is chemistry and whether we both want it. I've fought it since I've been here. The more I get to know you, the more I like you. The more I'm crazy attracted to you. That kiss made me think you might feel the same."

I brushed another blond lock back, running my fingers through the thick silkiness, struggling to hold my line. "I do," I reassured her unwisely. "But—"

"You think this attraction is just going to go away on its own?"

"No…"

"Then there's no harm in kissing me to see where it goes. No one else has to know."

Her words made sense, and fuck if I didn't want her like crazy. She knew that though. My cock was hard as steel, and she was laid out all along me. There was no way she could miss it. I probably sounded like some old dude who worried too much, and that's the last thing I wanted. But that's not why I gave in. I gave in because Quincy Yates was irresistible in this moment, and I stopped thinking about what would happen after.

In no time, I'd switched our positions, flipping her to her back and rolling over her so I could take charge. I paused a second once I was on top to feast my eyes on her pretty face, checking her expression, assuring myself she was still on board.

"Kiss me," she whispered. "Dare you."

Laughing at the absurdity of that, I went in for her mouth, my doubts vanishing as I let sensation take over. I centered my body over hers, my throbbing dick cradled in the softness between her legs. She felt amazing, even with our clothes on. Even on the hard floor.

With half my weight supported on my forearms, I plunged my tongue into her mouth and tangled it with hers. The sexy sounds of pleasure she made were tantalizing. My blood pounded through me, and my need shot up like never before. I'd been with plenty of women, but this level of reaction was a first. I'd never felt crazed with need like this, like getting inside her was more important than breathing.

She dipped her hands under my shirt and trailed them up my back to my shoulders, back down, then dipped them into my jeans, teasing me. I slid my body to the side enough to slip her shirt up and run my palm over her flat, sexy stomach.

When I discovered the piercing at her navel, I groaned. I broke the contact of our mouths so I could lay eyes on what my fingers were feeling.

I bent closer to see it in the low light. Two tiny, thin chains with stars at the ends dangled over her navel, with a simple round stud just above it.

Fuck, that was hot.

I put my mouth to her skin, ran my tongue over the jewelry, dipped into her navel, kissed right beneath it as Quincy arched her hips upward, offering herself to me.

With a hand grasping her slender waist, I took my time showing my appreciation for her piercing with licks, nips, and kisses. I trailed my other hand up her body until I reached her delicate lacy bra. With my lips still on her middle, I raised my gaze to her breasts, taking in the hot-pink fabric covering two perfect-sized mounds of flesh that I was aching to get my hands and mouth all over.

As I kissed my way up her abdomen, I pushed the lacy material up, along with her shirt, baring her gorgeous breasts. When my fingers reached one berry-pink areola, she arched into my hand and caught her breath. I thumbed the tip of her nipple, then lightly pinched it, and she moaned. I couldn't get enough of her expressiveness. She gave me no doubt about what she liked and how it made her feel, just with sounds. The sexiest sounds I'd ever heard.

She peeled my shirt up my torso with both hands, and I rose enough for her to take it over my head and toss it to the side. I removed her shirt and bra in seconds, then relished the feel of being skin-to-skin, rubbing my chest against hers, eliciting another moan from her.

I spent the next long while tending to her beautiful breasts with my mouth, my tongue, my fingers, tasting them, loving the noises she made when I suckled her. My own need pounded through me, but it was worth it to prolong my pain just to see the pleasure in her eyes.

As soon as I felt her hands dipping under my waistband again, delving farther this time to cup my ass, I could no longer deny the need to have her writhing underneath me.

"I want you naked," I told her, needing to make sure we were on the same page.

"I'm in favor of that," she said as she trailed a circle around my nipple, then pinched it, sending a spike of desire straight to my dick.

In no time, I bent over her and peeled her leggings and underwear down her slender thighs, my eyes locked to the promised land at the apex. I pressed a quick kiss to her there, then finished removing her pants. She lifted a knee and opened herself up to me, giving me an eyeful I wouldn't forget for as long as I lived.

"You're fucking gorgeous," I said as I took in all of her, bare and eager and open.

"What are you going to do with me?" she said, all flirtation and allure.

"I'm going to carry you into my bedroom, then make you come till you forget where you are."

"What are you waiting for?" She came up on her elbows, her breasts bouncing, and I sprung into action before I died from wanting her too much.

I bent and picked her up cradle style, loving the softness of her skin everywhere. Quincy's arms went around my neck, and I thought it wouldn't suck to have her never let go of me. I pushed that ridiculous thought aside.

As I headed toward the bedroom, which was right there, thank Jesus, she kissed me, plundering her tongue in my mouth and nearly making me stumble.

Somehow I got her to my bed, got my jeans and boxer briefs off, and thought to grab the condom that'd been in my wallet for longer than I liked to admit. After flipping on the lamp on the nightstand—because I wanted to see Quincy as she came apart—I stood at the side of the mattress, then thought to make sure the condom was okay, not too old. Last thing I needed was to get this girl pregnant.

I'd just ascertained the condom wasn't too old when I felt Quincy's lips close around the head of my cock. My eyes rolled back in my head as I dropped it back, surrendering to her amazing mouth. I held on lightly to her head as she licked and sucked at me.

When I was getting too close to losing it, I pulled her upward and palmed her breasts. My heart turned over when she looked up at me with her lips moist and slightly swollen and her desire clear in her eyes. For *me*. This woman—this young, beautiful woman—wanted me. It made me feel like a fucking king.

I ripped open the condom, then held her waist, guiding her back on the bed until she was stretched out for me like an all-you-can-eat buffet that was possibly so good it could kill me. Her legs were spread for me as she supported her upper body on her elbows and arched her neck back like a seductress, silently begging me to take her whatever way I wanted her.

I made quick work of ripping open the condom and sliding it on, stroking myself a time or two as I stepped to the edge of the bed.

"I'm not going to last long," I told her as I stretched over her. I knew that had never been truer when I felt her fingers grasp me again as she impatiently tugged me forward.

In no time, I was braced over her, my dick at her opening and her hands on my ass, urging me closer. It seemed fast, but there was no denying she was wet and ready for me, so I pushed inside her, trying to go slow, the slick feel of her drawing a gasp from me. This woman was perfect.

Quincy moaned long and low. My eyes popped open to watch every flicker of wanting on her face.

"You okay?" I asked.

"Mm-hmm." She arched her hips as she said it, drawing me in as far as humanly possible.

I caught my breath and paused for a second, afraid it was really going to be over too fast. I squeezed my eyes shut and forced my mind to the creaks and sounds of the new-to-me house, anything to collect myself and slow the hell down.

Quincy was having none of it. She squirmed beneath me and palmed my ass with her small hands, squeezing and kneading as she arched her breasts into me.

I let out a gasp and met her gaze. "You're going to kill me."

"Surely you're not that old," she said with a teasing grin.

"I want to make it good, but if you keep that up, it'll be over in two seconds flat."

"Pretty sure this is going to be good."

She stilled, and I took another couple of seconds to rein myself in, trying to get my body under control. The joke was on me, though, because this girl had all the power over my control even when she wasn't trying. I peered down at her to find her biting her lower lip, her lids half-mast, watching me with those lust-filled eyes. I could no longer keep from moving, out and then in, slow for about two long strokes until I couldn't go slow.

"Yes," she said as I thrust into her faster, rocking the bed. Her ankles were crossed at the small of my back, with her arching to meet my rhythm, and holy hell, it was the most intense fucking of my life.

I got so lost in her that I stopped worrying about anything. I couldn't think straight even if I wanted to, and I sure as hell didn't want to. All I wanted to do was feel like this for the next year. Lost to ecstasy.

It didn't take long for me to feel my climax threatening. With a glance down at Quincy, I realized she was on the edge too, and then she was contracting around me, calling out my name, making the sexiest, neediest sounds. It sent me right over after her, and I came so hard I saw stars.

When I came back into awareness, I realized I was draped over Quincy, probably suffocating her. I pushed up onto my forearms. What I saw was not a suffocating woman; it was a flushed woman who looked so smugly satisfied she was practically purring.

Knowing I was the one who'd made her look like that was a rush almost as overpowering as being inside her.

Almost.

I got rid of the condom, then rolled back into her.

"It's chilly," Quincy said. "Can we get under the blankets?"

We were stretched out sideways across the queen-size mattress on top of the covers. A sheen of sweat covered my skin, Quincy's too, and she was right—there was a decided chill to the night air in my bedroom.

Still in a haze of bliss, I could think of nothing better than stretching out with her naked body against mine and drifting off to sleep, keeping each other warm.

I pulled the covers back and held them for her to crawl under, admiring every inch of her as she did. As I tumbled in next to her, I couldn't miss the approval in her eyes. That was all it took to spark my arousal again. Maybe that age gap didn't make much difference after all. We weren't getting married or spending eternity together. This was just us working out the chemistry between us.

When I switched the lamp off and turned back toward her, she ran a hand up my chest and pressed herself into my body. This had the potential to become one hell of a mind-blowing night.

CHAPTER 16

QUINCY

Juniper's cry over the monitor woke me up with a jolt.

A millisecond later, I registered that I was entangled with a naked Knox. In spite of the baby's cry, which so far was still halfhearted and quiet, I took a couple of seconds to savor the moment and the warmth and the memory of earlier.

Knox was an incredible lover. It'd been a long time since I was with anyone besides Mitchell, but I had enough guy experience to know that Knox was extraordinary at sex. I grinned at the thought, knowing he'd go all shy if I told him that, but then he'd secretly want to thrust his chest out like a champ.

Juniper's cry intensified, so I made myself roll away from Knox to go feed her.

"Where you going?" Knox's question was slurred with sleep and adorable.

"Juniper's hungry," I whispered. I rolled back toward him and pressed a kiss to his cheek. "Go back to sleep."

"I can get her." His voice was clearer, like his daughter's fusses had registered.

"I'm on tonight," I reminded him. "Nothing changed just because you *boinked* me."

He hesitated, then asked, "Are you sure?"

"Duty calls. Go back to sleep, sexy boss."

He groaned as he laid his head back down. "Yell if you need help."

"Yep." I wouldn't need help, but I would need a blanket, I realized as the chilly night air hit my naked self.

With a quick glance around the moonlit room, I remembered all my clothes were in the living room and none would make for fast dressing. I knew what would though.

I rushed out to the living room, picked up Knox's flannel shirt, and slid my arms into the sleeves. It was big on me, as I'd hoped, hanging to midthigh. I buttoned a couple of buttons and rolled up the extra-long sleeves. As Juniper leveled up another notch, I grabbed the throw blanket off the back of the sectional, then hurried in to her.

"Hey, sweet pea. I'm here. I got you."

After a quick diaper change, I carried her on my hip to the kitchen to mix up one of the premeasured bottles we always kept on hand, distracting her from her immediate needs by quietly singing a goofy song.

"We don't want to wake up your daddy," I told her as I finished prepping the bottle.

Within minutes, we were snuggled into the glider in her room, the blanket over us. As she drank, Juniper stared up at me by the light of the llama night-light with her alert, intelligent gaze, as if she worshipped me for putting an end to her hunger. Just like it usually did, my heart dipped with love for this baby. I soaked in the sacredness of the wee hours with a tiny, quiet human, as I had with my half-siblings all those years ago.

Not much time had passed before her lids drooped shut

and her drinking became lazy, sleepy. I leaned my head back and let my mind drift to her daddy. Her endearing, hot daddy, who I now knew was a generous, attentive lover. One night with him was not enough, even with the second round of mattress gymnastics earlier.

A spike of panic jabbed at me. Was giving in to our attraction the stupidest thing I could ever do? I could hear Cynthia's accusation ringing through my head, insinuating I was trying to force myself into Knox and Juniper's family.

It wasn't true, I reminded myself. I had my future lined up. Nannying for Juniper was a temporary thing, and I was fine with that. I loved that I got this time with that darling girl. I didn't hate the time with Knox either, but we weren't in a romantic relationship. I wouldn't let myself fall for him. It was only a crush, a two-sided crush that made for magical sexy times.

Breathing more easily, I studied Juniper to determine whether she was ready to return to her crib. I'd learned if I stirred too soon, she'd pop back up more wide-awake than ever and take an hour or more to go back to sleep. As much as I enjoyed this time with her, tonight she had competition. Six-foot-two-with-eyes-of-blue competition.

After giving her a couple more minutes, I gently removed the bottle from her mouth and set it aside, mostly empty. I got up and laid her in the crib without a sound, then tiptoed to the door and pulled it closed.

I paused in front of the door to my room, a moment of self-doubt trickling in. Should I go back to Knox's room? Or would that be weird? Would he misinterpret my rejoining him as me thinking this was more than it was?

I blew out an impatient scoff at myself. I was being ridiculous. There was no way we'd get confused about what we were doing. I was leaving in two and a half months.

Besides, I could absolutely give him something to think about besides the future or whether I should be back in my own bed. I could distract him from any questions running through his mind.

I ignored my door and crossed the house to his end of it. I opened his door and crept back into his room. He didn't stir. As I carefully crawled under the blankets, I held my breath, torn between wanting to let him sleep in light of his early alarm and waking him up for act three.

He decided for me when, without saying a word, he banded his arm around my waist and tugged me closer, then pulled me up against him. I watched his face, waiting for him to open his eyes, but he didn't. A faint grin curved his lips upward however.

A smiling, mostly asleep, naked Knox?

Impossible to resist.

I made my way lower in the blankets, rolled over him, and took his hardening dick in my mouth. In less than three seconds, he'd grown hard as a steel beam.

CHAPTER 17

KNOX

After three rounds with Quincy, I should've slept like the dead.

I didn't.

Tryst number three had been just as out of this world as the first two, but as soon as Quincy had dozed off and my orgasm bliss faded away, anxiety set in.

Two hours later, as the sky was starting to lighten, I was still lying in my bed, lost in worries, with Quincy a couple of inches away.

I couldn't regret what I'd done, but I needed to *not* do it again. Sleeping with the nanny wasn't okay. Yes, it was consensual. Yes, Quincy had initiated it, not me. But giving in wasn't smart.

As a caretaker of my daughter, Quincy was a godsend. I couldn't afford to screw that up in any way. I knew there was an end date of January, and I'd have to find a new caretaker by then, but right now, the less upheaval in Juniper's and my life, the better. I was a man of routines, even though I worked for myself. Juniper and I were still establishing routines, and Quincy was part of them. A big, crucial part.

I couldn't afford to have feelings screw anything up. Even if we were to agree this was just a convenient physical relationship with no future, feelings could get hurt.

I rolled away from Quincy, putting more space between us, hoping she wouldn't notice. It would've helped if she'd gone back to her own bed afterward. This sharing my bed was too intimate. It made it seem like more than just physical from the get-go.

The room was light enough now I could see pretty well. Quincy could wake up any minute. With the thoughts that had been rolling through my mind, that could only be awkward.

After ensuring she was still asleep, I rolled off the mattress as noiselessly as possible. She didn't stir, so I crept to my closet, pulled on some workout clothes, grabbed my running shoes, and exited the closet. My gaze automatically went to Quincy to make sure she was still asleep. I came to a full stop as I took in the sight of her.

Fuck, she was gorgeous.

She faced this way, and the blankets had dipped to reveal her bare breasts and slim shoulders. Her blond hair splayed over the pillow like golden silk. Her face was peaceful, her long lashes resting on her pretty cheeks. She looked so fucking young.

Not *looked*. *Was*. She *was* so fucking young.

The discomfort deep in my gut intensified.

Everything else aside, I was too old for her. Fourteen years was almost old enough for me to be her father, for fuck's sake. She might say she didn't care, but I sure as hell did. She hadn't even hit her thirties yet. The thirties were when people settled in and really started to figure themselves out. Quincy still had so much of her future ahead of her, so much to figure out. I didn't want to shut any of that down.

I made sure the monitor was on. Quincy was on Juniper duty, and I needed to get out of here.

After closing the bedroom door behind me, I went to the kitchen, put my shoes on, and took a windbreaker out of the coat closet. I walked down the hall to the nursery, cracked the door open to check on Juniper, and assured myself she was still sound asleep. I knew without a doubt that Quincy would handle her if she woke up. I closed the door again, headed back through the kitchen, and went outside.

Normally I worked out at the gym, but there had been no "normal" since Juniper had showed up, and I hadn't exercised at all. I considered hitting it today, but being penned in had about as much appeal as letting a semitruck run me over. I needed air and space.

I locked the door and inhaled deeply, hoping for relief from the shit storm in my head. Oxygen did nothing for it. After stretching, I took off at a jog down the side of Lake Road. It didn't take long for my lungs to complain, but it felt good in a punishing way. When I got to Henry's and the intersection of Main Street, I kept going straight, avoiding the heart of town, toward the Honeysuckle Inn. I wasn't going to stop by the inn that had been my home for three months, not at this hour and not when it was a safe bet Cash was there. I'd see Ava soon anyway.

At the driveway to the inn, I turned around, increasing my pace. The pain took my mind off my situation. This time when I hit Main, I turned right and ran toward the square. The time was only about six thirty a.m., but there were people out and about, most of them exercising or walking dogs.

I pushed myself to get to the far side of the square, my out-of-practice lungs screaming at me and my legs starting to shake. Worried I might embarrass myself if I didn't rest, I headed toward one of the benches in the square and sat my sweaty, panting self down. I leaned over with my elbows on my thighs, thinking I was a dumb ass not only for sleeping with my nanny but also for trying to kill myself with hard exercise after weeks off. I let my head droop between my shoulders, too exhausted to people watch and not wanting to run into anyone I knew anyway.

I was starting to breathe evenly when I felt someone sit on the other end of the bench. My head still down, I caught sight of a jogger stroller with a toddler asleep in it. He had dark hair and cheeks as chubby as Juniper's and couldn't have been much older.

I straightened and glanced next to me, marginally surprised to see a young, fit guy instead of a woman.

"Hey," he said with a friendly smile. "Want one?" He held out a full bottle of water, a half-full one in his other hand.

"Thanks, man." I gratefully took it, screwed the top off, and guzzled half of it. "It's been a few weeks since I've worked out. I managed to leave home without anything."

"The stroller makes it easy to bring multiple," the guy said.

"How old's your boy?"

There was a strange hesitation before he said, "Eight months."

"I have a five-month-old girl."

"Congrats."

"Same to you," I said. Then for some reason, I continued, "I just found out about her a couple of weeks ago when my ex dropped her off with me and ran."

"You must be Knox Breckenridge."

I whipped my head toward him, taken aback.

"There was something about it on the town app, appropriately known as the Tattler."

I nodded. "Right. That. Yeah, I'm Knox." I reminded myself this was what I'd signed up for when I'd moved to a small town. I'd been a doubly hot topic for being related to the Henry family and for having Juniper land in my life. I didn't spend much time on the app other than to see what the specials were at the restaurants.

"I'm Max Dawson." He held out a hand, and I shook it.

"Pleasure."

"This here is Daniel." Max leaned forward and straightened the blanket on the infant. "He's my cousin's son. If you spend any time on the Tattler, you might've read that my cousin and his wife died a few months ago. They'd named me as guardian, so I've been making the shift from uncle to dad."

I blew out another breath, finally feeling like my lungs were functioning again. "Damn. I'm sorry for your loss and his." I nodded toward Daniel. "That's a tough situation."

"Yeah. Thanks." He stared at the baby, seeming lost in memories. "I guess you and I have something in common. Instant parenthood."

"I guess we do. I'd say we should run together, but I normally go to the gym. I don't have a jogger for Juniper yet."

"I go to the gym sometimes, but there's no childcare this early."

"Right. I hadn't thought of that. I have a nanny."

"I've thought about trying to find one. It doesn't seem like an easy task in a town this small. How'd you find yours?"

"Sheer luck," I said. "She was a server at Henry's. Right after I found the baby, I headed to the restaurant because I was late for a meeting. I know, makes zero sense, but I wasn't thinking straight. Quincy was working and knew what to do with a baby. I had no clue."

"Quincy. That's not Quincy Yates, is it?"

"It is. You know her?"

"Everyone knows the Yateses. I teach at the high school. I had her in class my first year of teaching."

"Oh, yeah?" I did my best to act nonchalant, but my guilty conscience wouldn't let my brain forget about the naked woman likely still in my bed.

"She's a great girl. Took care of her younger siblings all the time, from what I understand, so I imagine she's a damn good nanny."

"She is. I don't know what I'd do without her."

All the more reason not to sleep with her again.

Max checked his watch. "It's about time for me to head home so I can get ready for work."

"I need to do the same," I said, and we both stood.

"Hey, a group of us single dads get together once a week to play darts or pool or watch a game. You should join us Saturday. We'll be at Chance Cordova's. Have you met him?"

"He's the marketing guy for the brewery, right?"

"That's the guy. His daughter is thirteen."

I grimaced at the thought of raising a teen girl. "I thought a baby was difficult."

"Tell me about it." Max glanced down at Daniel, who was starting to stir. "You want to give me your number, and I can send his address?"

He pulled his phone out, and I rattled off my number. We said goodbye. Then Max took off with Daniel at an impressive pace. I gave my lungs and legs a pep talk and started toward home, thinking this get-together sounded like exactly what I needed. A single dad posse.

Maybe if I made more friends and got out of the house more frequently, I'd have an easier time keeping my mind off my nanny.

CHAPTER 18

KNOX

When I let myself into my house a few minutes later, the place was full of life.

Bacon was sizzling on the stove. Quincy was whisking eggs and humming along to the kids' music that played from the speaker. Juniper was on her back on a blanket on the living room floor with her brand-new play gym arching over her.

"Hey," Quincy said, drawing my attention back to her.

This time I couldn't help but study her more carefully. Her golden hair was pulled into a neat ponytail high on her head, the strands looking silky and smooth. Her face was makeup-free and fresh-looking, her eyes bright even though I knew for a fact she hadn't slept enough. As my gaze roved downward, I realized she wore my flannel shirt. It reached to her thighs, which were bare, and I couldn't help wondering if she had anything on underneath it.

I wanted to be annoyed at the familiarity she assumed by pulling my shirt on, but I couldn't. She looked hot, with only two buttons fastened, the shoulders hanging low on her upper arms, the sleeves rolled a few times, and her tempting legs bare down to a pair of fur-lined socks. My dick went hard in no time flat.

Fuck.

"Hi." I made myself smile at her but moved through the kitchen, toward Juniper. She was content to explore her toy, her eyes focused on a plush dog that dangled from the middle. Instead of picking her up, I lay down on my back next to her, our heads side by side, me urging my hard-on to wither away. "Hey, June. Pretty cool toy you have here."

As I looked at her instead of the toy, she turned her head to me, smiled, then rolled her whole body toward me. My heart expanded in my chest, an honest-to-God physical sensation. I never understood the power of a tiny baby before. She had me wrapped around her pinky finger in no time. I kissed her nose, and she let out a giggle as her tiny hand explored my face.

My body back under control now, I rolled toward her and put my palm on her fuzzy-pajama-covered side, covering from her diaper to her armpit. It made me marvel yet again how someone so small could have such a profound effect on me.

For the next few minutes, my daughter and I lay on the floor playing—exploring the different dangly toys on the gym, doing peekaboo, kicking our legs up toward the ceiling. When I mimicked her, she stared, then smiled, then did it again.

"Breakfast is ready," Quincy eventually called out.

I sat up, tickled Juniper's tummy, and reveled in her resulting laugh. "I assume Miss Smiles has eaten?"

"Bright and early," Quincy answered.

I leaned over and blew a raspberry on Juniper's belly, then kissed her nose before pushing my exhausted body to a stand. When I headed to the island, my daughter went back to the dangling toys. Quincy had said repeatedly what a good baby she was and had told me stories about how her middle sibling, Brayden, had never been willing to entertain himself. It made me all the more thankful that Juniper was content so much of the time. The more gently I was eased into this parenthood thing, the better.

Quincy set two plates at our places, both with scrambled eggs, bacon, and toast. She'd added cheese to the eggs the way I liked. Any other day, that would make me happy. Today it felt intimate and made it hard to breathe.

"Thank you for cooking," I managed, and even I could hear how formal it sounded. I couldn't seem to help it. I was holding myself in check, refusing to succumb to her allure.

She slid onto the stool next to mine. "I knew you'd be like this."

"Like what?"

She broke off the end of a bacon slice and tossed it into her mouth, then grinned at me as she chewed. "Grave and regretful." She made her voice deeper than usual; I supposed to mimic me.

I scooped a bite of eggs in, trying to figure out how to reply. I hadn't counted on her being so awake and direct when I got back. I'd pictured her in the nursery, sleepy and peaceful and feeding Juniper, allowing me to get my thoughts better organized. I should've known by now that Quincy rarely did what I expected.

The food tasted fantastic, as it usually did when she cooked, but my appetite waned after the first two bites. She wanted to discuss this now, it seemed.

I got down from my stool, went around the island, and poured a glass of water. Stalling for time, I drank most of it, then supported my weight on the counter opposite Quincy.

"I don't regret it, but it can't happen again." When I looked up to gauge her reaction, I expected a frown. Instead her head was tilted, and she was smiling halfheartedly at me, almost as if she pitied me. "What's that look for?" I asked defensively.

"I guess it's your age."

I didn't understand what she was talking about, but I already didn't like it. *"What's* my age?"

"This Mr. Serious thing. You're overthinking last night, aren't you? Second-guessing?"

"There's no guessing. That wasn't a good idea, Quince." The shortened form of her name came out without thought, sounding more intimate than I intended.

"Did you enjoy it?" she said, picking at her bacon.

"You know I did."

"Then why can't we just go with that? You didn't propose or anything. It was...a fling."

"A one-time thing?" I asked skeptically. I was pretty sure she was campaigning for a repeat, and frankly I wasn't as dedicated as I should be to saying no.

She laughed quietly. "Three times so far, but I'm open to more. If it's casual."

"How do we guarantee it stays casual?"

"It just...does. I'm leaving for school in less than three months, Knox. Plus neither one of us is looking for a relationship, right?"

"Right," I said with emphasis.

"I just got out of a way-too-long relationship," she said. "This is my time to be free. I don't know what your reasons are for not wanting a relationship, but for me, it'd be a mistake to get involved with someone before I leave for college."

"That's fair. But what if feelings start?"

"Maybe feelings will start, but that doesn't change the rules."

She was so matter of fact about it that my resolve weakened fast. Resisting those passionate, pretty eyes was nearly impossible.

I inhaled deeply, watching her, considering my next words. "I might be open to this recurring fling idea, but I have a condition."

Her brows shot up her forehead.

"I don't want people to know. Not because I'm ashamed of you but because I can imagine what they'd say. I'm too old for you. I'm your boss."

"All the things you already threw at me," she said.

"I'm already the outsider trying to fit in. You think I'm being old and over serious, but you know as well as I do that people would go straight to *cradle robbing* and *sexual harassing* and who knows what else. If the fling isn't long-term anyway, let's keep it to ourselves."

She studied me while she chewed a bite of toast. "I'm down with that. We can do the whole secret-lover thing."

Her grin told me she was poking at me again, but I didn't care. I couldn't help grinning myself. The thought of having her again, with these conditions, was too good to pass up.

The warning voice in my head, the one that'd been squawking at me during my run, was a lot easier to shut up when I was standing a few feet away, staring at Quincy in my barely buttoned shirt.

Later, I promised myself. I had all kinds of time later to get my head straight. Right now, I needed to drag myself away to my weekly meeting with Ava.

CHAPTER 19

KNOX

As I walked from the parking lot toward the Honeysuckle Inn for my Monday meeting with Ava, I checked the cottage off to the side to see which vehicles were there. I was glad to verify Cash's blue truck was gone.

I'd suggested we meet somewhere else to avoid antagonizing my pissed-off half-brother, but Ava had said he'd likely be gone for work, and if he wasn't, he'd behave himself just fine. I had my doubts.

I was relieved we didn't have to test the theory today.

I went in the door of the place I'd called my home for four months to find the cozy lobby hopping with activity. Anna, who managed the inn, was behind the desk with Sadie, one of the newer desk clerks. They both had customers in front of them.

"Hey, Knox," Anna called as I walked by on my way to check the gathering room for my writing partner. "Ava's upstairs."

"Morning, Anna. Thanks." I backtracked to the curved staircase and headed up.

At the top of the stairs was a relatively quiet lounge area with a couch and a few chairs. The stone fireplace from the gathering room below stretched upward and bordered one side of the stairs. The room was partially open to below. There were doors to the offices and an entry to the ballroom's upper level.

Ava sat on one of the club chairs opposite the overlook.

"Morning, partner," I said, then stepped to the balcony to glance below. "I see why you're up here. Downstairs is busy."

She smiled. "Hey, you. Business is picking up even though it's off-season. Our ads seem to be working."

"That's great news."

I knew, when she'd taken the reins after her aunt's death, business had been a mere trickle. Ava had worked her tail off to start turning it around, and Anna was continuing where she'd left off.

"Anna's the best thing that could happen to this inn, believe me," she said humbly.

"She seems great at her job. How're you doing today?" I asked as I sat in the other club chair. "Did Cash give you static because I was coming here?"

"No." She shook her head. "I told you to quit worrying about that. You're welcome here anytime."

I knew I was in her eyes. I didn't know if I'd ever feel welcome in Cash's territory. They weren't married yet, and Ava was still the sole owner of the inn as far as I knew, but that was just a technicality.

Exhausted, I sat back and worked up my willpower to get my laptop out, seeing that Ava's was already powered up. I noticed she had her chapter open and had probably been working. I hadn't found the time to write for at least two days, maybe three, and had accomplished hardly anything before that, which wasn't like me at all. Yes, I'd had a baby fall into my life, but I needed to start doing better with my jobs, both for financial clients and fiction writing.

Ava frowned as she looked closer at me. "Are you okay?"

"Yeah," I said on an exhale.

"Did that sweet baby keep you awake last night?"

The question sent my mind right down the Quincy track. I took a few seconds to answer. "Quincy had her last night. I just didn't sleep much." None of which was a lie. "Ava, I'm letting you down. I was supposed to get you chapter four a week ago, and it's still not done. I'm sorry as hell—"

"Knox, shut up. You basically just had a baby."

"I mean…"

"No. No jokes about not having a uterus. You've been a daddy for two weeks, and there's going to be some adjustment."

"I know that. I just…" I expelled a breath. "You'd think I could write a couple hundred words a day."

Ava closed her laptop and set it on the table, sat forward in her chair like she meant business, and raised her brows. "Remember a couple of months ago when my aunt died?"

"Of course."

It was when I'd met her. She'd come from California to take care of this place, which I'd been living in for about two months at that point. We'd started talking and discovered we were both writers.

"Remember how much writing I got done for the next two months? Let me refresh your memory. Zero words, Knox, and I didn't have a baby depending on me around the clock."

"You did have an inn," I pointed out.

"Exactly. And that's what needed my attention."

I appreciated what she was saying, but our situations weren't the same. "I can't afford not to write for two months. Not only are you depending on me, but I've got a freelance project due on Friday."

"You need to prioritize the freelance project. I'll be here. I'm not making any speed records myself."

"Mainly because I'm holding you back with chapter four."

She exhaled heavily, blowing strands of her dark hair away from her face. "Trust me when I say I need the time to revise three and five. I'm still trying to master the differences between screenwriting and novels."

We'd discussed that before in great detail. Learning a new style of writing was no small task. Despite the challenges, what she'd written so far had been promising and usually got me pumped up when I read it because I couldn't believe my luck to be writing with such a pro. "You'll get it. I don't have a single doubt."

"Just like you'll get the hang of being a dad and fitting in work," she said, a half smile tugging at her lips.

I leaned forward, weary, the lightness and endorphins from being around Quincy earlier completely gone.

"Hello?" Ava said.

"Hi. Yeah." I debated mentioning the subject that'd been circling through my head for days, ever since my confrontation with Cash at my father's house. I decided to air it out. "I know you said Cash will adjust, but I don't want to be the cause of tension between you two. If you'd rather work on your own projects, I would understand completely."

She tilted her head and made a face like I'd spoken in Swahili. "I wouldn't."

"Seriously, Ava. At least think it over. Between my inability to be productive and your fiancé's dislike of us working together, is it worth it?"

"Hell yes, it's worth it. We're going to be amazing. It's just going to take a while to get going."

"We're not going to finish on time." With my financial clients, I never missed a deadline. You couldn't run a free-lance business and not be reliable.

"We'll have to adjust our deadlines," Ava said, "but so

what? We'll get there. We both have other income to rely on until we can launch the hell out of our cowriting career." She stared at me, raising her brows as if daring me to disagree. Then her face fell. "Unless *you'd* rather call it all off."

"No," I said quickly. "I'd be crazy to turn away the opportunity to write with famous screenwriter Ava Dean."

"Please. Screenwriter Ava quit. Novelist Ava is even newer than you."

"New novel writer, new dad. That's a lot of news. In all seriousness, fatherhood isn't going away. Even if my ex showed up tonight and wanted to take Juniper, I wouldn't let her go. I'll be preoccupied for the next eighteen years plus. I want you to rethink our deal right now. See if it's still what you want."

"It's still what I want," she said without hesitation.

"You didn't think about it."

"I don't need to, Knox. We planned out a three-book series with possibilities for another dozen, right?"

A smile tugged at me. We *had* gone overboard, but the creative synergy once we'd started had been incredible. "Right."

"I'm excited about our potential. Are you?"

I did what she hadn't done: I paused for a moment and thought about it. Fought through the sleep-deprivation fog in my head. Tried to imagine what the next year would bring, let alone the next five. Then I considered the first few chapters we'd written together. They were still rough, but the story was there, and I couldn't wait to see how it developed. Though Ava was new to novel writing and struggled with things like introspection and description, she had a way of weaving magic with her words that I could only hope to pick up.

"I am," I finally said, meaning it. "And I'm going to do better."

"All we can do is the best we can do, Knox. Juniper comes first."

"Always. But it turns out Juniper has quite the appetite, and someone needs to pay for her formula, not to mention baby food."

"She's gotta keep those darling chubby cheeks chubby," Ava said with an affectionate grin. "So let's revise our deadlines. Not a lot. We'll find a pace that works for both of us."

I growled. I hated to change our dates, but I knew she was right. We needed to adjust in order to make our goals attainable. "Let's do it."

We could give ourselves more time, but I vowed to myself I would not hold us back. I needed to spend less time pretending to have a family with Quincy and more time being productive. It was part of why I'd hired a nanny—so I could still work full-time, still do justice to both of my careers.

Yes, I'd been understandably waylaid by fatherhood, but that wasn't going away. Quincy was, and I needed to remember that. Pull back. Refocus on my priorities: my daughter and my career.

CHAPTER 20

QUINCY

The days after I'd spent the night in Knox's bed had been awkward and disappointing. By Friday night, I was sorely in need of girl time. When I'd texted Piper and Jewel about having the night off, they'd come through like only girlfriends did.

Just after nine p.m., the three of us entered the Barn Bar, which was exactly what it sounded like: a giant old barn on the outskirts of town that'd been renovated into a bar.

The lights were low. Straight ahead, in the center, was the square bar with stools on three sides—nearly all of them occupied tonight, it appeared—and a tall wall on the back with liquor-lined, rustic wooden shelves.

To the left of the bar was a dance floor. To the right were pool tables and dartboards, all of them in use. Tables were scattered throughout. A country song pumped through us over the roar of a good Friday-night crowd.

Several people called out hellos as I beelined for the bar with my friends right behind me, keeping an eye out for an available table. The smell of beer and people wafted in the air. All of it took me away from the angst of my week.

"Thank you, guys, for coming out," I said loudly enough that Piper and Jewel could hear me. "I wish Taylor would've joined us."

"I told her to text me if she changes her mind," Piper said.

"She won't," Jewel said. "We'll keep trying though."

"That house must be so lonely," I added.

Taylor was Piper and Jewel's cousin whose brother had been killed in combat a few months ago. We'd all grown up together, though I wouldn't say I'd ever been super close to Taylor. She was shy and severely introverted and had an IQ that was probably higher than all three of us put together. She'd been living in Nashville until her brother's death. When she'd inherited the family home from him, she came back to Dragonfly Lake to live. Piper and Jewel had been going out of their way to include her, spend time with her, coax her out of her shell but without much success. A night at the Barn Bar could help anyone get out of their head for a couple hours if she'd just give it a chance. That's the reason I was here tonight.

"This is exactly what I need," I said when we got to the counter.

"You and me both, sister." Jewel gave me a side hug and rested her head on my shoulder as we waited for the bartender, Piper on the other side of me. "You would think, with only three employees under me, I could have more than a third of them show up for their shifts."

"That sounds like a rough entry to management," Piper said.

"I fired one guy today, then hired a new girl." Jewel straightened and raised her arm to get the bartender Donovan's attention. "This round's on me," she said.

Once we had our drinks, we wound our way through the people and tables, stopping to talk to everyone we knew, which was, in fact, more than half the people in the place. As we wandered closer to the dance floor, we claimed a table when Shawna Jenkins and some guy left.

As we watched people dancing, mostly groups of girls, Jewel recounted tales from the week at Humble's. Highest on the gossip train was that Berwin Jepp and Dotty Jaworski, a couple of older Dragonfly Lake natives who'd both been single for close to forever, had shared a long pizza lunch together on Wednesday, sparking speculation as to the nature of their relationship. There'd been no intimate touches, according to Jewel, and notably they'd gone through multiple lemonades on the rocks *without* Berwin's usual double shot of vodka.

"I hope it's romance," Piper said. "Everyone deserves love. Berwin always seems so lonely."

"You and your romantic soul," Jewel teased. "I love you anyway."

"Can you guys keep a secret?" I asked. Knox and I had agreed to keep it private, but that didn't include these two, my most trusted confidantes. I needed their thoughts on my situation, not that it was anything close to love or romance. Sex, though…

"Of course," Piper said, then lifted her glass for a drink.

Jewel was studying me, and I dared to meet her gaze. "No judging," I said.

Her eyes narrowed slightly. "You slept with your boss."

I stopped with my mouth open, ready to tell them exactly that. "How the heck would you know that?"

Piper's head whipped toward me. "She's right?"

"One, I've seen your boss," Jewel said, tapping a finger with each count. "Two, you're living under his roof, with him twenty-four seven, and in love with his baby daughter. Three, you're overdue to find your rebound guy after Mitchell."

"There's no rule that I have to have a rebound guy," I said, choosing the one point I could legitimately argue with.

"You do," Jewel and Piper said in unison.

"I flirted with that guy from Toledo in August."

"Flirting doesn't count," Jewel said.

I looked to Piper, who shook her head. "She's right. Man-induced orgasms required."

"Did you orgasm?" Jewel asked.

I straightened and said with a drawl, "A girl doesn't *O* and tell."

"Bullshit," Jewel said with a laugh. "This is us."

Which was totally valid. I hadn't planned to be evasive anyway. That's why I'd sworn them to secrecy. I trusted these two completely.

"So?" Piper prompted. "*O* or no?"

"Ohh, there were many *O's*," I purred.

"Many!" Piper sat up straighter, and both of my friends leaned closer.

"How many times have you been together?" Jewel grasped her glass but didn't seem to remember she had a drink because she was too involved in my news.

"One night. Three times. More than three *O's*," I spilled out. Before they could ooh and ahh too hard, I delivered the downside. "But it's been almost a week, and he's avoided me since."

"Men are so stupid," Jewel said.

Not as quick to judge, Piper asked, "Have you talked about what happened?"

I recounted the morning-after conversation from Monday, before Knox had headed off to his meeting with Ava.

"Okay...secret lovers is kind of hot," Jewel said. "Except..."

"There's been nothing to keep secret," I said.

"That's so disappointing." Frowning, Piper bent down and drank from her straw.

"So he's just been locked in his room or what?" Jewel asked.

"Locked in his office. Working late into the night. During the day, he leaves to write in other places sometimes."

"He didn't do this before?" was Jewel's next question.

"He worked some during the day but nothing like this."

"Which is completely understandable," Piper said. "He'd just found out he was a dad."

"Right. I understand he needs to work," I insisted. "There's a difference between needing to work and hiding from the nanny you boinked."

"Boinked," Jewel repeated with a laugh.

Piper wasn't laughing. She was studying my face way too hard. "How into this guy are you, Quincy?"

"I'm not," I insisted quickly. "Remember, leaving for school soon?"

"Plus the age difference," Jewel said.

I bit my lower lip, then said, "I don't know how that'd work long-term, but in bed… Let's just say he knows what he's doing."

"Ohh?" Piper said.

I leaned farther into our huddle, even though no one around us could hear over the music. "Of course, it's been forever since I was with someone other than Mitchell, and sex with him was fine, but Knox?" I lifted my brows way up my forehead for emphasis. "Seriously suggest you test out the older-guy theory. Not with Knox," I added quickly, then laughed as if it was a joke, but I couldn't stand to think about Knox even going on a date with someone else. Even though we were a temporary thing, if a thing at all, that would hurt.

"So he's magical in bed," Jewel said. "And now he's running scared. But you obviously want a repeat."

"I wouldn't argue with a repeat." I couldn't wipe the smile off my face as I thought about the look in his eyes as he'd climbed over me that first time. "That's what I thought we'd agreed on."

"I'm sure he's freaking out about sleeping with the nanny," Piper said.

"The much younger, hot, sexy nanny," Jewel said.

"The whole keep-it-secret bit proves it," Piper added.

"My opinion?" Jewel leaned her elbows on the table and sat up straighter. "This is too much worry over a temporary thing."

"It is," I easily agreed. "But I can't help being a little upset and medium offended."

"Justified." Piper patted the back of my hand. "Sorry, hon."

"I'm sorry too. The best remedy is to have fun tonight," Jewel said. She scanned the room. "Plenty of age-appropriate guys here. I'm thinking we should dance with a few of them."

"If you feel like it," Piper said empathetically. "Let's be real. We don't need guys to have fun."

That was something I wanted with all my heart to get behind. I raised my glass. "Here's to girls' night with the bestest friends ever."

"Love you, girls," Piper said as we all clinked.

"Yeah, screw that boss of yours," Jewel said with a grin.

"Screw him," I said with absolutely no conviction. Because I knew, if Knox made any opening at all to me, I'd take it and screw him for real. There was no reason whatsoever to turn down a repeat of level-ten sex.

But when a good-looking, age-appropriate guy in a cowboy hat asked me to dance five minutes later, I made myself say yes. Knox was a short-term good time that was apparently over, and I didn't need to waste any more time pining.

CHAPTER 21

KNOX

As I walked from the far back of the parking lot to the main entrance of the Barn Bar, I wondered what the hell I was doing. I had no business—and very little interest in—wasting an evening at an overcrowded bar among people half my age.

Holden had convinced me to join him for a drink. I'd never been here before but had driven past it a few times in broad daylight. I'd had no idea what I was getting into.

As I neared the back of the building, I spotted a couple against the outside wall, kissing, grinding against each other, oblivious to everything but each other, not noticing—or caring—they were illuminated by the security light and the nearby shrub did nothing to hide them. Nor did they seem bothered that the temperature was dipping down toward the forties. Even when I was in my twenties, I didn't remember ever losing my mind so much over a girl that I couldn't make it to privacy with her.

Ahead of me, a group of five young women, barely of legal drinking age, decked out as only females on the hunt for mates could be decked out, made their chattery way to the door. There were so many threads of conversation among the five I didn't know how anyone could make sense of any of it, but I did gather that the redhead hoped Shane, whoever that was, would show up as he'd promised, and the blond was sure he would.

They turned the corner to the front of the barn, and I gave serious thought to hightailing it back home. I'd told Holden I'd be here though.

After an evening with him and Chloe, Hayden and Zane, my father and Faye, plus Harrison and Juniper, I felt like I'd made some progress with half of my family. On the way home from Nashville, Holden had suggested we have a drink sometime. Chloe, who was six months pregnant and said it was past her bedtime, encouraged us to do it tonight. I'd agreed as long as I picked up my SUV from home first, and here I was.

When I opened the main door, the roar of a crammed bar on its busiest night smacked into me. All I saw at first glance was a crowd of about two hundred more people than I usually spent time with. And didn't I sound just like the old man Quincy teased me about being?

The lights were low and drinks were flowing as I walked through the clusters of people toward the bar. Holden had texted me he was saving a seat at the counter, on the right side, so I headed that way.

Once I neared the bar, I spotted him easily. As I made my way to him, he called out to someone at a pool table, then joked with the bartender, then made a comment to the guy sitting next to him, all in the thirty seconds it took me to reach the empty stool on the other side of him.

"Hey, bro," he said, his voice inviting and jolly like only Holden could be. He gestured to the bartender. "This is Donovan. This is my half-brother, Knox."

Donovan and I exchanged greetings.

"What can Donovan get you?" Holden asked. "This one's on me."

I sat down and ordered a Rusty Anchor beer, impressed they carried Holden's brand. "Thanks."

Holden nodded at someone seated on the opposite side of the bar, facing us, then said to me, "I was starting to think you'd changed your mind."

"I considered it," I told him. "Not going to lie, I'm feeling old. This is about ten times crazier than the Fly gets."

"That's the truth. This place packs 'em in, particularly when they advertise their drink specials on the Tattler. You're not old though. Take a look around."

I did, and I saw more twentysomethings than at a college graduation. I shot my half-brother a raised brow of disbelief. Donovan set a mug of cold beer in front of me.

Holden nodded toward the pool tables. "Over there we have Lyle and Jerry. They're both close to seventy, as are half the people watching their game." He turned partway around and indicated a table near the outside wall. "That group is in their fifties and then some. There's Davis Morten over there with Tony Wall and Jeannette Ditmer."

They were clearly closer to retirement than middle age, but the clusters of older patrons didn't make me feel any more at ease.

"It's more of a lifestyle thing than an age thing, I guess," I told him. "There was a time when a scene like this was important to me. During college. In my twenties. Maybe even in my early thirties. But there came a point when I figured out I prefer a peaceful night at home or at a movie to this chaos."

"I get it. I've been out a lot less since connecting with Chloe. Why didn't you say something? We could've gone somewhere more low-key."

"We're here now," I said, glancing around again, smiling to soften my complaints. "I'll get over my old self in about five minutes. Things like this are useful for filling the creative well. Besides, I've hoped for months to one day be able to grab a drink with one of my brothers."

"It's cool as shit," he said, grinning.

"Glad you think so."

"Cash will come around eventually. Tonight was a good time, right?"

"Tonight was good." In part because Cash wasn't there.

Hayden and Zane had invited us all for an impromptu dinner. Seth and Everly couldn't make it because they had plans with Everly's producer, Gin, and her husband, Tucker. Cash was working the dinner shift at Henry's, and Ava had plans with Magnolia, so it was just the nine of us including the kids. I chuckled at that. "Our partial gathering of nine was a huge family get-together in my world."

"Better get used to it fast," Holden said. "But then you've already had a sample of full-on Henry-North chaos."

"Overwhelming. Mostly in a good way." I sobered. "You think Faye and Simon are okay with Juniper overnight? I'm not sure I should've taken them up on the offer."

"Oh, hell." Holden laughed. "Those two are in grandbaby heaven. As soon as ours is born, there's no one I'll trust more than Faye."

I relaxed a degree. "Not only am I not used to having a child, but I'm not used to having family to rely on," I said, keeping my tone light.

"Both will take some getting used to, huh?"

"Understatement. Good beer can only help." I took another drink.

I'd been warned, plus witnessed it myself, that Holden knew everyone in town. As if to further prove it, two guys stopped to say hello on their way to the dartboards.

"Levi Dawson, Nick Carlisle, have you met Knox?"

"Hey," Nick said. I'd met him through Seth.

"Good to see you," I said, then held out a hand to Levi. "Dawson. Is Max your brother?"

"Afraid so," the other tall, built guy said. He didn't have the look of an office guy, more like he did physical labor of some kind. Both of them actually.

"And his younger sister, Dakota, tends bar at Henry's," Holden said.

"Ah, yes. I know Dakota. She's a sweet girl."

Levi's brows shot up. "She's something," he said with a laugh. "I don't usually use the word *sweet*."

"I met Max a couple of days ago," I said. "He invited me to a single dad group."

"That sounds like Max. He's got his hands full with that baby." Levi's expression—as well as Nick's and Holden's—washed into sorrow as he shook his head, and I remembered Max had said Daniel was his cousin's baby. Levi had clearly suffered a loss too.

"I'm sorry to hear about the baby's parents. That's a terrible thing," I said.

"I'll say. Max seems determined to do right by the little guy. I help when I can, but it's a drop in the bucket, you know?"

I said, "I'm sure everything is appreciated by your brother."

"You're the guy with the surprise baby, aren't you?" Levi said, as if just realizing it.

"That's me."

"I admire you for stepping up," Levi said.

"Yeah, that takes some steel balls," Nick added.

I tried to laugh that off, but my laugh felt hollow. "We do what we have to do, I guess, right? I never expected to be in this position."

"And now he's head over heels for that cutie," Holden said, lightening the tone, to my relief, and making everyone laugh.

"She's irresistible, in my biased-as-hell opinion," I said.

After more small talk, Levi and Nick wandered off. I was

just starting to relax when a blond head on the crowded dance floor on the other side of the bar caught my eye, and my heart skipped a beat.

I could swear that was Quincy, but she was on the other side of a tall guy with a cowboy hat, so I couldn't verify. Taking another swallow of beer, I kept my gaze locked on the back of the guy, hoping for another glimpse of his dance partner.

I nearly dropped my mug a second later when the couple shifted and I got a full view of Quincy.

She was stunning, the prettiest girl in the place, with tall boots, a short skirt, a barely there top that revealed her navel piercing, and an open sweater over it. Her long, blond hair was down, falling everywhere as her body moved to the beat.

One look at her and I was suddenly burning up.

"You watching Quincy?" Holden said, apparently following my gaze, jolting me back to the awareness that I'd been staring for too long.

"Wasn't sure if that was her," I fibbed. "Who's the guy?"

Holden sized him up and shrugged. "Probably some out-of-towner."

Whoever he was, I didn't like that he was dancing with my nanny.

My nanny, I repeated in my head to my dumb-ass self. *Not my girlfriend.*

"How's it going with her?" Holden asked, eyeing me. I couldn't tell if it was a loaded question or innocent conversation about my daughter's caretaker.

"Going well," I said, endeavoring to keep any expression off my face. I went for a drink to cover.

"Is she not supposed to be here tonight?"

"She has the night off, so she can be wherever she wants to be." I realized once the words were out that they were more of a snap than I'd intended. "She deserves a night off," I said to smooth it out.

"It looks like she's put herself back on the market after her breakup."

I was taking another drink and coughed as it went down wrong. Holden eyed me again, so I attempted to make conversation like a normal person who hadn't slept with Quincy and then avoided her all week.

"Is her ex from Dragonfly Lake?" I managed.

"Born and bred. He moved to Memphis after the breakup," Holden said.

Good riddance.

"She hasn't said much about him," I continued, digging for more intel despite myself. "I get the impression they were serious?"

"They were together for a few years. She was pretty upset when it happened—for a couple of weeks. She seemed to bounce back quickly."

I wanted to ask what kind of a guy he was, whether he was a dirtbag, why they'd ended it, but I didn't want to wonder about these things, let alone make it obvious to Holden I wondered about these things.

Apparently holding back didn't work, because Holden asked, "You interested in her as more than a nanny?"

My beer was almost gone, so I resisted repeating that stall. I scanned the dance floor again. I scanned the dance floor and didn't take long to spot Quincy's golden hair. The cowboy was nowhere to be seen, but now there was a tall, skinny guy dancing with her, all grins. The punk.

"Don't you think that age gap would be a bit much?" I finally asked my half-brother.

He shrugged. "I think attraction is attraction. Love is love. She's legal and then some."

It sounded good in theory, but this was real life, not theory.

"She's going to college," I pointed out. "It's been so long since I was in college that I barely remember the name of the dorm I lived in and only recall a handful of my professors' names."

"Should I buy you a cane for Christmas this year, old man?"

"I trust we're close enough now I can tell you to fuck off?" I said, laughing.

"Sounds like typical brotherly love to me."

Our conversation moved away from Quincy on to more comfortable topics like beer and business and fatherhood. Holden's excitement about pending fatherhood was tangible. It made me wonder how I would've felt to be in that position, with a woman I loved and eight or nine months to get used to the idea before the baby arrived.

During the next two hours, I met more people than I'd ever remember and counted no less than six male dance partners for my nanny. I was doing my damnedest not to let it bother me, but...

Fuck. It bothered me. It bothered me a lot.

It particularly bothered me a lot when the original cowboy took a seat at Quincy's table, where she'd been sitting alone for about two minutes. It was as if he'd been watching her, waiting for an opportunity, after dancing with her at least two more times after that first one.

I'd switched to soda after one beer, recognizing fast I needed every ounce of good judgment and willpower intact if I was going to sit here and watch my daughter's nanny flirt and touch guys who didn't deserve her.

Not that I did.

Holden returned from the restroom as I settled my stare on the guy in the fake Stetson across the way. The smile Quincy gave him was strained, not genuine at all, as if she didn't care to have his company. I straightened so I could see them better.

"It's getting late for this married guy," Holden said as he

flagged down Donovan to clear his tab. "I'm going to head home to Chlo. Are you ready yet?"

"I'll stay a few minutes and finish this drink," I told him, my gaze barely leaving the big, ugly cowboy hat. "I won't be far behind you."

Donovan slid him a bill. Holden set some cash on it and handed it back.

"Need anything?" Donovan asked me.

I shook my head.

"You're good?" Holden asked.

"I'm good. Go home to your wife. Thanks for convincing me to come out tonight," I said. "It was great to talk more."

"Agree. Take care. Don't do anything too crazy." He glanced toward Quincy, then raised his brows at me suggestively before heading out.

"See you," I said, ignoring the look. I wasn't going to do anything crazy, joke or not.

As he walked off, I leaned on the bar and cradled my drink between my palms. My gaze went back to Quincy just as she said something to the cowboy. It looked clear as day to me that she said, "No, thanks," and her smile was nowhere in sight, so I went on alert.

When Quincy very clearly said no again and shook her head at the guy, I stood, trying to decipher what he was asking her for. I waited for the tension in her expression to lighten up and her to flash that smile I couldn't get enough of.

Quincy cast a look at the dance floor, leaning one way, then the other, and I wondered if she was searching for her friends.

Maybe I was misinterpreting things, but I didn't like the vibe she was putting off. I made my way around the bar. My view of her disappeared temporarily as I got closer, thanks to the crowd, but when I was fifteen feet away, I saw her shake her head at the guy and scoot a couple of inches farther from him.

I walked up behind Quincy, put a gentle hand on her shoulder, and said into her ear, "Let me know when you're ready to go. I'll drive you home." I kept my words innocuous because I didn't know how she'd react. As far as I knew, she hadn't seen me yet tonight and had no idea I was here. I hadn't been overly friendly to her all week, so she had good reason not to welcome my presence.

The way the cowboy's eyes narrowed as he watched me squeeze her shoulder told me I hadn't been wrong to be concerned.

"Knox," she said, smiling up at me. "There you are." She grabbed my hand and tugged me toward the stool next to her, opposite the cowboy.

"Here I am," I repeated.

With narrowed eyes and all friendliness gone from the asshole's face, he said, "You two together?" to Quincy.

"We live together," I said.

"You didn't tell me you had a boyfriend," he said, assuming exactly what I'd hoped he would assume.

"Knox doesn't like to dance," Quincy said.

"Fucking dick tease," he said, his words just slightly slurred.

I stood up and leaned toward him, ready to advance on him if he pushed any more. "I suggest you leave, Cowboy."

Quincy grabbed my hand as if to hold me back. I was generally pretty coolheaded and not one to fight, but if he said one more thing about Quincy…

"Please," she said emphatically to the guy. "It's never pretty when my boyfriend breaks out the black belt."

Wisely, without another word, only a scowl, the asshole got up from the table and stalked off toward the pool tables. I took a breath and looked at Quincy.

"Thank you," she said, the sugary-sweet "boyfriend" warmth of thirty seconds ago gone, replaced by obvious relief and a tinge of disgust I was pretty sure was aimed at the cowboy.

"Are you okay?"

"Yeah. I'm fine. Just annoyed. He was all charm at first, but he sure didn't know how to take a *no, thank-you.*"

I took her at her word that she was okay. "I meant what I said about the ride home."

She searched the dance floor again and smiled when she found Piper, who was dancing and singing—at the top of her lungs, it appeared—with three other females.

"They'll be closing the place down if I know them," Quincy said.

"You going to join them?" I made my voice matter of fact, not hinting at the disappointment I'd be hit with if she said yes.

After another glance at her friends, she met my gaze with her pretty, green-blue eyes. I'd missed looking into those eyes this week.

She picked up her phone and started typing. "That douchebag was exhausting. If you don't mind, I'd love a ride home. Let me finish telling Piper and Jewel I'm leaving with you."

I nodded briefly, acting nonchalant, but I felt anything but nonchalant at the thought of being alone with her.

As she smiled at me and preceded me toward the door, I put my hand on her lower back. I knew it still wouldn't be smart to give in to this attraction, but I was desperate to touch more than just the small of her back—and I sure as hell didn't want any fabric between us.

CHAPTER 22

QUINCY

Knox on a regular day was good-looking and tough to resist.

Knox when he was being all gallant and protective of me… He was hot as hell and totally bangworthy.

Even though he'd rescued me from the idiot cowboy, however, and there was a throbbing of desire deep between my legs, I was not going to climb him like a monkey in heat. He'd have to make the first move.

As we walked out of the bar, his hand was on my lower back. I loved feeling the heat of him on my skin below my cami. Even better was the veiled claim on me, whether that was his intention or not. When I said goodbye to the people we passed, I could tell some of them noticed Knox's hand. I spotted more than a couple of looks of speculation. I just smiled and waved like everything was normal, in spite of the way my body was lighting up.

We stepped outside, the door closing behind us, blocking the nonstop racket of all those people—and the warmth of them. The chilly, late-fall air hit my thighs above where my boots ended.

Knox slid his hand to the side of my waist, his warm flesh touching even more of my skin.

"You're being unboss-like tonight," I said lightly, flirtatiously, as I moved closer into his side.

"Want me to stop?" he asked, all seriousness, his voice lower than normal.

"Nope," I said easily. To prove it, I slid my arm around him, then stretched up and laid a kiss on his cheek. "The way you rescued me from that jerk-off was hot...*boyfriend*."

His hand crept up from my waist toward the edge of my bra.

Keep going, I silently urged.

"Guys like that deserve to be castrated," he said in a low growl that did nothing to cool my jets.

"He didn't seem so bad at first. The more he drank though..." I shook my head in disgust.

Knox didn't say more, which was fine with me. Jed the loser wasn't worth the oxygen it took to discuss him.

"Where's June Bug tonight?" I asked.

"Faye and my father volunteered to keep her overnight. I'd like to say it was to give me an evening of respite, but I suspect they were more motivated by baby snuggles and toothless grins."

"I can't blame them. Those are pretty irresistible. So you decided to go out to the biggest bar in the county and get your drink on alone or what?"

A quiet laugh rumbled out of his chest. "Holden convinced me to get a drink. For some reason, he thought the Barn Bar was a good place."

"It wasn't?" I'd seen Holden sitting at the bar at one point but not Knox.

"Well, we had a drink, had a decent conversation despite the four-dozen interruptions by people he knows, and I was able to save a young damsel in distress from an ugly creep with my storied black belt skills, so I'd say it worked out okay."

"Always a good night when the knight can save the damsel in distress."

He laughed again, and that sexy rumble... Oh, God, it resonated with something deep inside me, as if the frequency of it unlocked all my female hormones to storm through my body.

I sucked in the night air, trying to rebalance myself from what this man did to me. Maybe keeping it light would help. "Confession," I said as we stepped from the blacktop lot to the gravel section even farther from the building. "I'm not really a damsel in distress. I could've saved myself."

We moved as one through the packed lot, our steps the same, our bodies flush, our arms around one another.

"Confession," he said as he walked us up between his SUV and a car, falling behind me so we could fit. At the passenger door, I turned to him, anxious to hear what he was going to confess. He moved close, our bodies nearly touching again, and peered down at me. "I'm not really a knight. I just...want you."

The lightness of our banter dissipated as his stare pulled me under. Next thing I knew, he stepped even closer, pressing me into the side of the vehicle. The hardness of his body told me his words were true. The question was whether he was willing to do something about it.

Then his palms cradled my cheeks, and his lips were on mine, his tongue demanding entrance to my mouth. In less than a heartbeat, I let him in happily, wholeheartedly. I'd been dying for this for days.

Knox plundered my mouth insistently, making me believe he'd been wanting it just as much. I put my hand on his denim-covered ass and squeezed it, making sure he got my message loud and clear. With my body throbbing for him, I wrapped a leg around his thighs, angling our bodies so his erection hit me at my center.

His fingers reached the bare skin on the back of my thigh, then trailed upward to my butt, also bare since I was wearing a thong. The contrast of his hot skin and the cold air hitting me where it didn't normally hit me spiked my need even higher.

"Knox," I managed between urgent, frenzied kisses.

He kept kissing me, one finger straying between my legs, to my core, dipping inside me. My body clutched at him, needing to be filled. Dropping my head back, I clung to his flannel shirt, a needful moan coming out of me. I didn't know if anyone was close by. Didn't care. I just…needed.

Knox abruptly ended the kiss and said, "I need to get you home. Get in."

He gave my ass a little tap and a squeeze, lowered my leg, then opened my door. I stood there for a couple of seconds, trying to get blood to my brain so I could function, make sense of his words. He nuzzled up next to my ear, his breath hot on my lobe, and said, "Quince. Climb in. I'm not going to fuck you against the car."

He took my hand and guided me. My legs shook as I managed to put one on the running board and step up, then slid onto the cold seat.

The door closed and I let out a breath, trying to think whether a guy had ever made me lose my mind so fast before. The answer was an easy no. I would've let Knox bang me against the car in a heartbeat.

CHAPTER 23

KNOX

Once I shut Quincy in the passenger seat, I headed around to the driver's side and sucked in a deep breath of cold air, hoping it would cool my blood.

It didn't.

I'd never reacted to a woman the way I did to Quincy. Never gotten so lost in someone I forgot where we were.

I'd tried my best to stay away from her all week, but look where that had gotten me. Desperate to get inside her. In a fucking parking lot, for God's sake.

Fighting my desire for her wasn't working, so I was damn well going to surrender to it, assuming she was still on board by the time I got her home.

After one more greedy gulp of brisk air, I opened the driver's door and climbed in.

Immediately I caught Quincy's feminine scent. I started the engine, cranked up the heat, then pointed the vents upward while the engine warmed. Just long enough to get home.

I took Quincy's hand, noting it was cold, rubbing it

between both of mine. When she looked over at me and smiled, I couldn't help myself. I leaned toward her and kissed her, just a taste before I took her home.

She met me eagerly, her lids lowering. Her mouth was like some kind of drug I couldn't live without now that I'd tried it —the softness, the warm heat, the sweetness with a trace of liquor.

My dick throbbed against my jeans to the point of pain that only Quincy could soothe. I tugged her toward me at the same time I pushed the seat all the way back, letting my body override anything my brain might've said.

"Come here," I growled out.

As she straddled me with no hesitation, I grasped the backs of her bare thighs underneath that sexy, fluttery miniskirt. My hands slid up to her perfect ass, and I reveled in the feel of her cheeks, squeezing and kneading them, eliciting a moan from her as she kissed me.

Our tongues met, swirled, danced together as I arched up to press my aching cock into her softness. The friction between our bodies made the pain better and worse at once. Attempting to sidetrack my dick from being too selfish, I pushed her sweater and her bra up to unleash her luscious breasts. I palmed them, molded them, feasted my eyes on the milky orbs in the near darkness.

When I could no longer resist the berry-pink tip, I brought her nipple to my mouth and fastened my lips over it, suckling and swirling my tongue around it, toying with it, learning what she loved most based on the telling sounds she made.

Her hands on my shoulders, breast in my mouth, she ground her pelvis into me, circling and rubbing herself over my dick until I was ready to explode out of my jeans.

"Fuck, Quincy," I managed.

Abruptly she lifted away from me. My eyes popped open in confusion. She stretched over the console and grabbed her purse, unzipped a compartment, and took out a condom.

When she'd lowered herself back onto me, sitting on my thighs, she ripped the packet open, gazed at me with a hungry look, and went to work on my belt buckle. While she undid my pants, I helped myself to her gorgeous breasts again, pinching her nipples, kneading all that smooth flesh in my palms, trying to sidetrack myself from the blood still pounding to my dick.

Once she had my pants unzipped, her fingers closed around me. Sweet Jesus, she was an angel with a magic touch. I raised my hips so she could get my jeans down far enough to free me. She stroked me, fondled my balls, swiped a finger over my tip, all of it making my eyes cross and my breath catch. I'd nearly stopped breathing altogether by the time she rolled the condom down my length.

Somehow enough blood got to my brain for me to figure out to recline the seat, giving us more room. Still wearing her hot-as-fuck, knee-high boots, Quincy rose above me, pulled her barely there panties to the side, and lowered her gorgeous body until she impaled herself on me, her slick heat making my eyes roll back in my head.

"Mmm," she said as she circled her pelvis against me, taking me deeper inside. "You're perfect, Knox."

Her words revved me as much as her tight body did. She rose and lowered herself slowly, as if she were savoring every inch of friction. In ecstasy, I wove my fingers through her silky hair, palmed her cheek. Our gazes met and locked, and though there was barely enough light to see, her eyes sparkled with intensity. It was somehow the most intimate, soul-baring moment of my life.

As she slid down again, her lids fluttered closed and she moaned, the sound sensual and primitive and so fucking erotic. In the confines of the SUV, I was at her mercy, without enough room to move. I'd never been more content to give over my control.

When Quincy moved faster, my hands landed on her ass

cheeks beneath her skirt, grasping her, feeling the contraction of her muscles, pulling her into me with every thrust of her hips. She clung to me as a sheen of sweat covered both of us, the SUV turning into a steamy sauna now that the heat was blowing out of the vents. I couldn't be bothered with doing something about it as she took me higher, became more frantic, our bodies moving as one in perfect concert, like this was meant to be. Like we were meant to be.

"Knox," she said in a shallow exhale. "I'm coming. Oh, God, oh, God, oh, God." She let out the sexiest sound as her body contracted around mine.

I couldn't have held on if I wanted to.

Grasping her ass, I arched up into her and came so hard I nearly ended up inside out.

With her arms around my neck, Quincy collapsed on top of me, breathing hard, her face nuzzled beside mine. Weakly I wrapped my arms around her, thinking I'd be fine if we never, ever moved.

Quincy burrowed in closer, a satisfied purr rumbling out of her. I laced one of my hands with hers, my eyes closed. I could feel someone's heart pounding, and I didn't know if it was mine or hers…or both.

A couple of minutes passed, or maybe more, with us lying there without words, just…breathing. Being.

After a while, I felt Quincy's body shaking. With laughter?

"Are you okay?" I asked.

She nodded against me and laughed again. "Just…you surprised me is all. I wouldn't have thought the serious, proper, boss-like Knox would get down and dirty in the parking lot of a busy bar."

Her words served to jolt me out of my post-orgasm bliss and slammed me back to reality. "Oh, hell, Quincy. I'm sorry."

She laughed again, seemingly unconcerned. "From where

I'm sitting, there's not a thing to be sorry about." She hoisted herself up to look at me, pressed a kiss to my lips. "That was…" She inhaled, then blew out a breath, as if there weren't words.

"That was incredible," I said, my worries easing slightly as I took in her flushed cheeks, her unquestionably satisfied expression.

"Mm-hmm," she purred. Then she kissed me again, this time lingering, probing me with her tongue, burrowing her fingers into my hair.

I kissed her back, but when a loud engine revved close by, I stiffened, and not in the good way. I propped up on my elbows, one arm banded around her, so I could figure out what was going on. That's when I realized the windows were steamed up good, the outside world invisible, which meant, hopefully, no one could see us either.

I relaxed further. "You…" I kissed her forehead, pushed her tousled hair behind her shoulder only to have it fall forward onto my chest again. "You turn me inside out and make me lose my godforsaken mind, Quincy."

"Yeah?" she said, her grin making her cheeks look like a pair of apples. "Good."

I laughed. Somehow she took me from worried and repentant back to pure joy in mere seconds. Her irreverence and her unpredictability were some of my favorite parts of her in addition to her irresistible body.

"I've never done anything like this," I told her. "Never *not* been able to make it to privacy. Never understood how people could get so lost in someone that they dropped inhibitions."

"Now you do?" she asked smugly.

I shook my head, unable to stop grinning but refusing to admit it out loud, just because she wanted me to.

"I need to get you home and into my bed so I can do things properly."

Staring down into my eyes, she said, "I don't know. I liked improper. A lot. It might be hard to top."

"Is that a challenge?"

"Yes, it is, sexy boss of mine."

"Challenge accepted. And maybe I'll have to fire you beforehand just to get you to hush about the boss thing."

"You don't scare me at all," she said as she started righting her clothes.

As she went back to the passenger seat and my thinking became clearer, I had a wisp of a thought that *she* scared *me* —a lot.

I pushed it aside, redid my pants, and raised the seat back so I could take her home and make good on my threat.

CHAPTER 24

KNOX

Saturday evening, I pulled up in front of the address Max had sent me for Chance Cordova and parked. As I got out of my SUV, nerves fired up in my gut as they always did before social events, particularly ones where I barely knew anyone.

Who was I kidding? I didn't normally go to events where I barely knew anyone. Home was my happy place.

Back in Texas, most of my socializing had been with business associates: other writers, financial bigwigs, clients. I hadn't had a close group of friends since my twenties, when I was still in touch with my college buddies.

Though it was out of my comfort zone, I was ready to make connections here in Dragonfly Lake. More than ready. I'd hit a point in my life when I longed to settle in every way, like I hadn't before. Previously I'd been focused on my career. Now that I was branching out, the freelancing was still important, but it was only half my career, and my career was only a sliver of my life.

I was working on connecting with my new family, making

progress, but that came with expectations and pressure. I found myself, for the first time in a lot of years, longing for a group of guys I could call friends.

But damn did it suck walking into someplace I'd never been into a situation I had very little info about. The geeky researcher in me would've been content to have biographies and backgrounds of everyone who'd be present.

After checking one more time to be sure I had the right house number, I knocked.

A lot of seconds passed before I heard anything from inside, and I started to doubt myself yet again. Finally there were heavy footsteps and then the door opened.

"Hey, Knox." Chance opened the screen door and extended a hand, friendly as could be.

"Chance. It's good to see you. I was told to bring snack food." I held out a donut box from Sugar.

"You brought the good stuff. Come on in. Welcome."

"Thanks for including me," I said. "Nice place you have."

His house was in a neighborhood on the other side of downtown, away from the lake. The houses appeared to be twenty or thirty years old, family-oriented, like a slice of small-town America. Chance's was two stories with a connected garage and a well-kept yard.

"Thanks," he said, his tone suddenly less jovial. "I bought it with my late wife a couple of years after we got married."

Though I'd met him at Henry's and chatted with him a couple of times at Rusty Anchor, where he was the marketing manager, I didn't really know him. Hadn't realized he had any kids until Max had brought up this gathering tonight. Since their group was single dads, it followed that he wasn't married, but I hadn't known his wife had died.

"It suits my daughter and me well," he continued.

"Max said she's thirteen?"

"That's right."

"Teenagers scare the shit out of me," I said.

"You and me both. She thinks she knows everything."

"I suppose I did too at that age. Parents are stupid, right?"

"I always thought so until I became one," he said with a laugh.

The basement was a walkout and had one big L-shaped room with some doorways off it. On the bigger side of the L was a bar, a pool table, a dart board, and a poker table. On the other, a big-screen played a football game, and a couch and a couple of recliners were situated in front of it.

Max and another guy sat on the couch, a coffee table in front of them laden with bowls of chips, peanuts in the shell, dips, and two Humble's pizza boxes that were wafting out an aroma that made my stomach growl.

"There's beer in the fridge," Chance said, pointing behind the bar. "Water and soft drinks too. Help yourself."

I went over and shouldn't have been the least bit surprised to find a full stock of Rusty Anchor. I picked up an IPA. "Nice setup down here."

"Thanks," he said. "It started as a place for my daughter to hang out with her friends, but she couldn't care less about it. She'd rather hole up in her bedroom with them and giggle." He shook his head, and there was an air of concern in it. I didn't know much about parenting, but I could guess that having a teenager was cause for concern in itself.

Beers in hand, we went to the TV area.

"Hey, Knox," Max said, standing. "Glad you could make it."

I shook his offered hand, then nodded at the other guy, who also stood.

"This is Luke Durham. The others couldn't make it tonight. You'll meet them later."

"Knox Breckenridge," I said as Luke and I shook.

With a reserved smile, Luke said, "I read about your situation. Life is crazy, huh?"

"Batshit," I verified. "Nice to meet you."

"Imagine running into a fellow insta-dad in the square," Max said. "I gotta think we're few and far between."

"I hope so," I said. "Particularly in a situation like what happened to your cousin."

"No shit," Luke said. "It's hard enough to just be a dad on a regular day. Throw in a tragedy or some other odd situation…" He shook his head. "I'm thankful nothing bad has happened to Addie's mom."

"Are you divorced then?" I asked.

Luke nodded. "Jess's career Army. We split up when my daughter was nine months old. I have full-time custody, but when Jess's stateside, I give her all the access to Addie she wants. We weren't a good couple, but we're pretty good at co-parenting."

"How old's your daughter?" I asked.

"She's four."

"Is that age easier than a baby or harder?" I dared to ask, hoping for an encouraging answer.

All three men replied with a roar of laughter.

"We have a saying here," Chance said. "We borrowed it straight from the Navy SEALs."

"'The only easy day was yesterday,'" Luke said.

I laughed with them even though, after only two weeks, I sensed it was a thousand percent true, and that worried the ever-loving shit out of me.

We settled in front of the TV with pizza. We watched the game, but the volume was low, no one too engrossed. There was a thirty-point difference in score that explained it.

"What's the story with your daughter's mother, if you don't mind me asking?" Chance said to me. "Is she still in the picture? Coming back?"

I picked up my beer. "I don't mind you asking, but I'll need a long drink first." I took a long swig while the others raised their bottles in support and drank too. Maybe it was corny, but I appreciated that.

"My ex has some mental health issues," I said frankly. "I mean, who doesn't, but she's bipolar."

"Shit," Max said. "That's not an easy situation."

"No." I filled my hand with peanuts, leaned back again without cracking any. "Finding the right balance of meds is a challenge, but she'd gotten to a pretty good place with hers. We had a good couple of months where she was stablizing." I shook my head. "It was becoming clear that we weren't a good match on a good day. Then she decided she didn't want to mess with her meds anymore. Insisted she didn't need them."

"Oh, hell no," Chance said.

"Yep." I nodded. I set the peanuts on my plate and picked my pizza back up, took another bite, chewed. "I tried to stick it out to be supportive, see if I could help her get help again. I didn't want to desert her when she wasn't okay."

Luke made a face like he didn't figure it ended well. Max growled and shook his head.

"I'll take a stab in the dark and guess that didn't work out?" Chance asked.

I shook my head. "She did everything she could to push me away. I finally let her have her way. If she'd wanted help, it would've been different."

"Hell yes," Chance said, then shoved the last of a slice into his mouth.

"We broke up in October last year. I don't think she knew she was pregnant then. If she did, she didn't tell me." I took one of the peanuts, crushed the shell with my fingers, and tossed the bits into a bowl. With a look at each of the other three, I said something out loud that I'd thought multiple times to myself but never dared to utter. "This sounds awful, but part of me's relieved Gina wasn't on a bunch of psychotropic drugs while she was pregnant. I have no doubt she needed them, but I don't like thinking about what that might've done to the baby."

"Your daughter's health is your top concern now," Max said.

I nodded, letting out a breath, relieved he seemed to understand. "Right. I tried repeatedly to help Gina get the help she needed. If she'd gone back on the right meds during the pregnancy out of necessity, with a doctor's supervision, I would've supported that too, had I known. But hindsight... I'm glad Juniper doesn't have a history with those."

"Absolutely," Chance said.

"We get it," Luke added.

"So does your ex want to share custody?" Max asked.

"My ex 'never signed up for this,' which makes me pretty sure she's still not on the right medications. I'm meeting with a lawyer to make sure she can't pop up whenever she wants."

"You need to go for full-time custody," Luke said.

"Agreed," Max said.

"That's the plan," I told them. "If I could track Gina down, I'd see if she'd sign away her rights. I think she would."

"You can't find her?"

With a head shake, I said, "I haven't heard from her since the note she left with Juniper."

I'd looked up the mentions on the Tattler and knew the drop-off had been detailed for everyone, so I didn't need to explain.

"That baby girl is where she's meant to be now," Max said. "I just hate what she's been through so young."

"Lucky thing is she won't remember any of it," Chance said.

"Damn straight." Max stood and tossed back the rest of his beer. "It's great you have Quincy's help for a couple of months."

"I don't know what I would've done without her. She has a magic way with June." I did my best not to think about her magic ways with *me*.

"With kids of every age," Chance said. "She babysat Sam a

few times back in the day. She's gonna make a fantastic early ed teacher."

"Agreed," Max said. "The world needs more people like her to go into teaching."

"I don't know Quincy well," Luke said, "but her dad does my insurance. I was in a couple of weeks ago to see him. He's happy as hell she's finally figured out what to do with her life. He said the same thing as you: she was born to be a teacher. He just wishes it hadn't taken her so long to figure it out."

"Better late than never. Waiting tables was never her strong point," Chance said. "She's a great girl, but…"

"Clumsy as hell," Max said, which was no exaggeration. "Who's up for some darts?"

"This game isn't keeping my attention," Chance said, gesturing toward the TV. "Let's do it."

Relieved to not be the center of attention anymore, I stood eagerly, taking an extra pizza slice toward the dartboard.

"I'm in," Luke said.

As we played 501, we made a hell of a dent in the food. Over the next couple of hours, I learned that Luke and Addie lived with his dad on his family's farm outside of town, where they grew strawberries and apples. Max was the high-school football coach as well as a math teacher. He'd had an active social life until the day his cousin had died in a car accident. Chance's wife had died when their daughter was four. He hadn't dated anyone since. Had some flings apparently, but he was dead set against getting involved with anyone else, at least until his daughter was grown and out of the house.

I also learned that Max was as good at darts as anyone I'd seen. I razzed him for being a typical jock, good at all things physical. He beat us all, multiple times, but it didn't matter.

When the football game ended, SportsCenter continued to

play in the background while we went for round two of food and switched to pool.

Somehow, deep into the third game of pool, we got onto the topic of college funds for our kids.

"Shit," Max said. "Something else I haven't had a chance to think about."

"I've thought about it," Luke said. "Jess has a small fund started but I'm trying to figure out how to contribute to one regularly. It's been a tight year at the farm."

"I've got nothing," Chance said. "Raising a kid isn't cheap. I've been meaning to look into it, but I don't even know who to go to for advice."

It was my turn, and I took aim at the cue ball, shaking my head as I nicked the ten ball at not quite the right angle and it rolled and bounced off the side. "I could give you some tips," I said, straightening. "I'm not a financial advisor, but I've written dozens of articles on that topic alone. I'd be happy to help you sort things out."

"Hell yes. Please. Do you have a financial planner?" Chance asked.

"I do, and I can get you his contact info. Any of you."

All three of them shot questions at me, questions I was able to answer. Eventually conversation turned to other topics, beer changed to water, the food was nearly gone, and it was going on midnight. Luke needed to get home to relieve his father of childcare duty. Max had told his babysitter he'd be home by twelve too. While I had Quincy working tonight, I was ready to get home and check on my daughter and—I only admitted it to myself—I wouldn't be upset if Quincy found her way into my bed.

Just the thought got my blood pumping.

As the three of us helped Chance with the mess, mostly empty food bowls and boxes, I said, "This was a good night. Thanks for including me."

"Hey, we're glad to have you," Chance said. "We meet just about every Saturday night. I hope you'll come next time."

"I will," I said without hesitation as we headed upstairs.

I might not be an avid football fan, I might suck at pool and be not much better at darts, but none of that mattered. Single fatherhood formed a bond between us the second I'd come in the door.

While my relationships with the Henry family were tentative, on the stressful side, and works in progress, and Quincy tied my thoughts up in goddamn knots, these guys were chill. This was good.

For possibly the first time since I'd come to Dragonfly Lake, these guys made me feel like I might belong here.

CHAPTER 25

R eality checks were a good thing even when they were painful.

I'd been hesitant when Quincy had suggested we ride to Nashville together and combine her campus orientation with my trip to the baby superstore. Quincy could be persuasive though, especially when we were in bed together sans clothes. I'd given in to her request embarrassingly easy.

The first Thursday in November was a beautiful late-fall day, and the trees along the highway and across the urban campus had slipped on their seasonal coats of amber, scarlet, and lava, with hunter-green and silver-green conifers sprinkled in. The sun shone brightly outside the window of a common area in the student union, where Juniper and I were waiting for Quincy to finish her morning sessions.

Next up was the last thing on her list—the dorm tour—which I'd agreed to accompany her on. Then we were meeting her older brother, Ryan, for lunch. I hadn't let myself think too hard about that. I'd met her stepmother when I'd taken Juniper to Dr. Julian's office, but that was because she was the reception-ist, not because of my ties to Quincy. I hadn't been introduced to anyone else in her family. That she'd spent every night in my room lately made the thought of meeting them uncomfortable.

I sat in a low-slung easy chair in a quiet corner. I'd spread a blanket on the carpeted floor for Juniper, who'd been content to sit and play with her toys after her snack. My attention was divided between people watching and watching my daughter at my feet.

One of June's favorite toys was a plastic cube with shapes cut out from the top and matching blocks that fit through the openings. She'd started to figure out how to fit the pieces in, but half of her time was spent exploring them with her mouth. She had the yellow star, her favorite, in hand now, or rather in mouth. When she lost hold of the star, it rolled a few feet away.

I'd started to reach out and get it for her when she leaned forward and ended up on hands and knees, rocking like she sometimes did, her eyes on the star. I sat back, waiting to see what she would do.

Juniper, eyes still locked on that beloved star, put one hand forward, rocked for a second, then moved her leg, then her other hand, her other leg… Within seconds, my daughter was crawling, closing the three feet to the star. Her squeal of joy when she reached it, sat back on her behind, and picked it up matched the elation and pride in my heart at her milestone.

"Look at you, June Bug," I said, leaning forward, making eye contact with my gleeful baby. I held my hands out to see if she'd crawl back my way.

She let out a happy shriek, the star tumbling from her hands and mouth again, but this time she didn't care. Her avid eyes were locked on me as she crept toward me on shaky hands and knees. When she reached my feet, I scooped her up, cuddled her to my chest, and congratulated her with words and kisses, my heart overflowing.

I picked up the star and handed it to her, perched in the crook of my arm. She took it and happily obsessed over it some more.

Two minutes later, the auditorium door opened and several people filtered out, all of them in their twenties or younger. Quincy emerged, seeking us out, and I stood, still psyched about Juniper's milestone. I held it in, though, looking forward to hearing how her advising and introduction sessions had gone.

"There's Quincy," I told Juniper, who broke out into a big smile as soon as she spotted her nanny. "Hey," I said as Quincy reached us. "How was it?"

Quincy was all grins. "Good. The people seemed to legitimately like their jobs, which says a lot, and I got tons of information. Plus classes. I'm all enrolled." She dragged in a deep breath. "It's starting to get real." Grabbing on to Juniper's arm, Quincy said, "Hey, sweet pea." She kissed June's nose, eliciting a giggle.

"You're on countdown." I forced cheer into my voice even though I was dreading when Quincy left—for multiple reasons.

She wrinkled her nose. "Not quite yet. Are you trying to get rid of me?"

"You know better," I said in a private voice.

Her eyes met mine, then flitted down to my lips as if she wanted to kiss me. She didn't though, which only made me ache more for a taste of her. I stifled that as Quincy's attention went back to my daughter.

"How's my favorite June Bug?" she asked. "Were you a good girl for your daddy?"

"More than," I said, grateful for the distraction. "Should we tell her the news?" I asked Juniper, who answered with a babble.

"What?" Quincy said, looking from Juniper to me.

"Juniper crawled."

"What?" Quincy's mouth fell open as she reached out for the baby. "You crawled? And I missed it?" She took Juniper into her arms and peppered her with kisses, making my daughter laugh some more. "That's a big deal, sweet pea. We're in trouble now. You'll be into everything."

"She will, won't she?" I'd thought we might have a couple more months to prepare, but obviously my precocious daughter thought differently. "What time is your tour?"

Quincy pulled out her phone to look at the time. "Eleven. We need to go now, or we'll be late."

"It's close by, right?" We'd located it on a map earlier, and it was no more than two blocks away.

"It is, but I want to get there early."

"Of course."

Quincy's penchant for being fifteen to twenty minutes early for everything was a surprising quirk, seeing as how she wasn't particularly organized in any other way, but she was militant about it, and I respected that. We had more than twenty minutes to make a three-minute walk now, but I quickly packed up June's toys and blanket and readied her carrier.

"I can't believe I missed her first time," Quincy said, hugging my daughter to her.

"I'm sorry you missed it, Quince." I hooked the diaper bag over my shoulder, took Juniper back, settled her in the carrier, and picked it up. "I didn't think to try to get it on video. It happened so fast." I recounted the play-by-play.

"Cutie patootie, next time wait for me," Quincy told June. "I guess I'll miss a lot once I come here full-time."

"You can visit her when you're home for breaks," I said, not letting myself think too hard about what it would be like once she was gone.

I was keeping my ears open for leads on a possible nanny,

but the truth was I wasn't sure I wanted a full-time, live-in nanny again. Not unless it was Quincy. I was working on balancing my time better, and Juniper was sleeping longer at night. It was a luxury to have Quincy's help when she did wake up, but I was considering looking for more of a daytime sitter just for when I was working. I had time to figure it out. Time for the right person for the job to show up in our lives.

We hurried down the main boulevard to the dorm Quincy had been assigned to.

"Wow," I said as we walked up to it. "Back in my day, living in the dorms meant roughing it. This doesn't look too shabby."

"It just opened last year," Quincy said. "I think I only got into it because I requested a single room in a suite. It's harder if you have people you request to live with. I'm a leftover they could stick anywhere, which is awesome for me."

The door opened as we neared, and a tall, college-age guy wearing his ball cap backward came out. When he saw Quincy, he held the door open, his eyes locked on her in obvious interest.

"Heyyy," he said to her, stopping to give her his full attention. "You live here?"

Quincy smiled and shook her head. "Not until January."

The kid glanced at me and Juniper, then turned his attention back to Quincy as if we weren't standing there. "I'll definitely see you in January."

He didn't look at me again as I took the door, my heart pounding with annoyance, adrenaline spiking in a protective rush, as if Quincy needed me to fend off this dude.

Two steps into the building and I realized she didn't, of course. Come January, if she wanted to talk to backward-cap guy, she could. If she wanted to flirt with him, she could. If she wanted to date him, fall in love with him…

Fuck.

She could, and I'd have to be okay with it.

I was going to need time to come to terms with that.

As Quincy walked to the desk, I waited out of the way, closer to the door than the desk, not wanting to interfere. Trying to get my head in check—or was it my heart?

I shook my head, as that was the dumbest thought yet today, then made faces at a wide-eyed Juniper until she laughed.

A few minutes later, Quincy and a smiley, petite girl who couldn't be more than eighteen came over to us.

"Hello. My name is Sumi, and I'll be showing you around today. Let's go this way." She led us to one of the wings, held her ID card in front of a scanner, and let us in.

I allowed the two of them to walk side by side in front of me, listening but not participating as they chatted.

As we turned a corner, Sumi glanced back at me with a smile and said to Quincy, "Is this your dad with you today?"

Somehow I managed to keep my smile pasted on my face, but her assumption hit me like a physical blow.

"Oh, no," Quincy said with a surprised laugh. "Knox is my...boss. I nanny for this cutie patootie." She touched Juniper's nose affectionately as we all stopped at one of the doors.

"She's adorable," our guide said. Then she used a key to unlock the room and let us in.

In the meantime, I tried to act like everything was A-okay when what I really wanted to do was duck out and get the hell back to my real life, the one where I wasn't sleeping with a girl young enough for people to mistake her for my daughter. One who I employed.

At the same time, I knew damn well I'd sleep with her again tonight and savor every damn second of it.

As the guide showed us the common area in the four-bedroom apartment—a living room and full kitchen plus laundry closet—I tried to pay attention. While we were en route to one of the bedrooms—with its own private bathroom —a thought struck me so hard I stopped for a second.

That smart-ass, backward-cap punk at the entrance hadn't been threatened by me because he too assumed I was Quincy's father.

I shoved the thought down deep. This was Quincy's day, a big deal for her, and I needed to not let my hurt feelings show.

The bedroom was empty of staging but contained a twin bed, nightstand, dresser, and desk. Everything she'd need— plus the attached bathroom. They didn't make dorm rooms like they used to…and that thought made me sound like the old fucker I was.

At some point during the apartment tour, Quincy had become subdued. I couldn't help but wonder what was going through her head. On the drive into Nashville this morning, she'd chattered nonstop about the college, her possible first-semester classes, the campus, and everything else under the sun. As she glanced around at the bedroom and checked out the bathroom, I realized she'd gone quiet. She still answered Sumi's questions, asked a few of her own, but her enthusiasm had dimmed for some reason. Looking around at what her new home away from home would be like, I couldn't fathom why. Maybe she was just tired.

Once the room tour was done, we made our way back out to the hall to see the common areas of the building—study areas, recreation areas with Ping-Pong and pool tables, a kitchen, for God's sake, in case the one in your apartment wasn't good enough?

Sumi, it turned out, was also in the elementary education program, a sophomore, so Quincy peppered her with questions about classes and requirements.

I already knew the program had a top-notch reputation because I'd researched it. This was a stellar opportunity for Quincy. I remembered what the guys at Chance's had said about how cut out for being a teacher she was, and I couldn't argue. It hit me how it was more than possible Juniper could have Quincy as a teacher someday. If so, my daughter would be lucky.

I myself would have some shit to work out in my mind.

At the end of the dorm tour, we thanked Sumi and said our goodbyes. As we walked toward the parking lot, I reminded myself again to get out of my thoughts.

Today wasn't about me. It was about Quincy and her future.

She'd be in a good place with all kinds of opportunities, and I needed to be happy for her.

I'd be back in Dragonfly Lake with my daughter, and we'd be lonely but just fine. Better than just fine.

Coming with Quincy today, it turned out, had been the right decision. God knew I needed all the help I could get to prepare for her moving on.

CHAPTER 26

QUINCY

The campus was picture-perfect. It was a slice of green space—and gold, orange, and red if you wanted to get technical—and majestic, old buildings in the middle of the city, like an escape from the chaos. I knew college would be its own kind of stress and chaos, but it was hard not to fall in love with the setting.

Knox drove us toward Clayborne's, the restaurant where we were meeting Ryan, my older brother. It was situated on Hale Street, the cornerstone of the redeveloped neighborhood close to both downtown and the college, and owned by Sierra North's brother-in-law, Hunter Clayborne. I hadn't been there before but had heard buzz about it, particularly since Hayden's home decor store was down the street. I hoped to explore before we headed off to the baby superstore.

First, though…Ryan.

I adored my older brother. Even though we didn't see each other all that often, we were close. He worked too much, thanks to the success of Tech Horse Software. He and his partners, Jackson Lowell and Keaton Hayes, were launching a new product I couldn't pretend to understand, and Ryan had been traveling more than he'd been home for the past couple of months.

I was excited to see him and dreading it at the same time. Knox and I were short-term and secret. We were alone so often that it was an adjustment to be with others and to act like *just* boss and employee sometimes. I was worried we might accidentally reveal too much. I'd have to be on guard.

Knox parked in a garage by the gorgeous and stately Wentworth Hotel at the opposite end of the short street, which gave us the chance to check out all the shops as we walked by.

"That's where Everly records," Knox said, pointing to the Hale Street Recording Studio, an unassuming building on the opposite side.

"I've heard a lot of big names are in and out of there."

"From Hayden, right?" Knox said with a laugh. "She would know since her shop is right next door. Do you mind if we stop in there after lunch?"

"Do you mind if we stop in half these stores?" I asked, noting a boot store and a boutique and a bakery. "I've heard about that place." I pointed at Sugar Babies Sweet Shop at the same time the aroma of baked goods mixed with a delicious fried-food diner scent—Frank's Diner—reached my nose.

"I'm up for it. The baby store won't take long. I'd like to be home by dinnertime so I can get a few hours of work done this evening."

"Deal. Ohh, maybe we can find some books for this girl at Angry Cat Books," I said, squeezing one of Juniper's soft-bootied feet.

"Because my poor, deprived child only has about three dozen board books. I could never say no to a bookstore."

We reached the door of Clayborne's on the Corner and went inside. From the street, the bar and grill looked unassuming, clearly a building with historical roots. On the inside, it was lively, full of chatter and energy thanks to a near-capacity lunch crowd. A long bar ran the length of the place on the left side, with a small stage at the front end by the windows. In the back half was a loft area with more tables.

I scanned for my brother, but we were twenty minutes early. Ryan tended to be the right-on-time type. We grabbed one of the last open tables by a window on the Hale Street side and settled Juniper into a high chair.

Once we'd ordered drinks, Knox asked, "So what'd you think of the college? I didn't expect the campus to be so scenic in the middle of the city." He took out Juniper's favorite cereal, swiped over the table with a wipe, then set several pieces on a napkin in front of her.

"It's beautiful. I was there a few times growing up, but I never did an official visit before I applied. I went based on the reputation of the education program and because it's close to home."

"That dorm is downright posh. It's a few steps up from my guest room." He grinned and then set Juniper's sippy cup in front of her.

She picked up her cup with the happiest laugh and then hit it on the table. She startled at the sound of it hitting, her eyes going wide and adorable. I leaned in with a smile, kissed her forehead, and said, "It's okay, sweet pea. That's what happens when you bang things on the table."

The baby studied my face, then broke out into a grin and babbled back to me.

"The dorm is nice but has nothing on your place," I told Knox. I raised my brows suggestively. "And it's been a while since I've slept in your guest room."

"If I get my way, you won't," he said in a private voice.

"That twin bed in the dorm will be lonely."

"You'll be so busy with school and a social life that you won't even notice. And if you do, the backward-ball-cap guy would love to keep you company." He said it like a joke, but I wasn't sure how to take it.

"Is that what you want?" I asked without thinking. "For me to hook up with some nineteen year-old guy?"

He leaned his elbows on the table and brushed my hand briefly. "Quince, it doesn't matter what I want. This is your future, and not to sound like some old dude, but it's a bright one."

I made myself smile at his humor attempt, but I wasn't feeling it. I was feeling uneasy. Everything would be changing. It was a lot to wrap my head around now that I'd been on campus, enrolled in my classes.

"Hey, Quincy." My brother broke me out of my thoughts as he approached and extended his arms for a hug.

I hopped down and threw my arms around him. He had more of a beard than before, but it looked good on him. His blue eyes sparkled with energy even though I saw fatigue underneath. No surprise with his workload.

"Ryan, this is Knox Breckenridge and his daughter, Juniper. Ryan Yates," I said.

They shook hands and greeted each other, and my brother fawned over the baby.

"You're going to be a heartbreaker," he said in an indulgent voice as she stared up at him. "I can tell already."

"Don't go there," Knox said with a laugh. "I'm still getting my head around bottles and diapers."

"I heard you've had quite a whirlwind," Ryan said as he sat next to me.

Our server showed up and took our orders, then hurried off.

"How's my favorite older brother?" I asked.

"Still your only older brother, smarty. I'm doing well. Work is keeping me out of trouble."

"Quincy said you're one of the founders of Tech Horse,"

Knox said. "You guys are having quite a year from what I've read."

"We are. It's been a crazy ride, mostly in a good way. We're planning to go public in March."

"I read a rumor about that in one of the financial blogs I follow," Knox said.

And just like that, they were off, talking about a subject I didn't understand in depth, but I was fine with that. Business wasn't my thing, especially not the financial aspects of it. Hello, eye glaze, but I loved that my brother and Knox connected—and then I had to remind myself it didn't matter. I wasn't bringing a boyfriend home to meet the family after all.

"So how's the fam, Quincy? Any Cynthia drama of late?" Ryan asked once their business talk had been interrupted by our food arriving.

"Isn't there always Cynthia drama?" I asked after I finished chewing the first bite of my burger.

"When it comes to the two of you, always," my brother confirmed.

Looking between Ryan and me, Knox asked, "Is this mainly a Quincy-Cynthia thing?"

I nodded, and my brother said, "They're like water and oil. Always have been. To be fair, I was out of the house by the time my dad remarried. I've never had to live with Cynthia. But I think there's also some kind of unspoken female dynamic going on."

"There is," I acknowledged. "Knox suggested I try to make peace with her."

I looked up in time to catch Ryan's appraising look at Knox.

"And?" Ryan popped a fried mushroom into his mouth.

"I'm thinking about it. I want peace," I said. "I'm just not sure how to go about it, what to say. I don't know if it's even possible."

"I can tell you for sure it's not possible if you don't make the first move," Ryan said.

I narrowed my eyes and looked between him and Knox. "Are you sure you two have never met before and discussed this?" I accused, joking.

"It might just be easier to see with some distance," Knox said.

"So let's say I take her to lunch." I dipped a pretzel bite into the cheese sauce and let it drip. "What do I say to her?"

By the time we'd finished eating and hashed out my Cynthia problem, I'd decided to give it a try and ask her to brunch. I knew the guys were right when they said my stepmom would never make the first move. She seemed to have issues with being the bigger person even though she was the mom.

Once the server had cleared our plates, Knox excused himself to change Juniper's diaper, picked her and the diaper bag up, and headed to the restroom, leaving me alone with my brother.

"I like him," Ryan said as soon as Knox was out of earshot.

That shot a spike of relief and happiness through me, but I quickly tamped it down, reminding myself my brother didn't have to like my employer. Particularly my very short-term employer.

Instead I said, "He's easy to work for. I was lucky to be working when he first brought Juniper into Henry's." I laughed. "You should've seen him and Cash and Ava. None of them had any experience with babies." Though my brother had never lived in the same house with Cynthia and our half-siblings, he'd been around plenty and had helped with diapers and feedings and baths many times.

"He was lucky you were there." He pushed his empty plate back. "You two seem close."

I went on alert. "I guess we've become friends," I allowed.

It wasn't a lie, just wasn't the whole truth. "I've known him for less than a month though."

"You live in his house."

"That's what a live-in nanny does," I said with a laugh.

I racked my brain for whether Knox or I had slipped up and said something to get my brother on this topic of our "closeness."

"Has Dad met him?"

"Not that I know of. He could've gone in for insurance from Dad or something."

My brother nodded once, looking thoughtful.

"What?" I said grumpily, my heart pounding harder. "Whatever you're thinking, just say it."

"I would say"—he began as he swished the ice around in his water glass—"unless you want Dad and Cynthia figuring out what's going on between you, you should avoid being with all of them in the same room."

"What's that supposed to mean?"

We hadn't slipped up. Hadn't accidentally said anything about…*us.*

"When I got here, I saw him touch your hand. It wasn't a boss-employee touch."

"We didn't—"

"I'm not here to judge you, Quincy. You know me better than that. But I'd have to be in a coma not to sense the feelings between you two."

"There aren't feelings," I said automatically.

He chuckled quietly. "Oh, there are. Maybe you're denying them to yourself, but they're plain to see. On both sides."

I stopped my denial before I could start it, curious. "Like what?" I challenged.

"The way Knox looks at you, for one. When you're talking, he studies you, hangs on your words."

"No, he doesn't."

"And the way he knows you. You said you haven't even known him a month, but he seems as if he's known you for years. He gets you, lil sis."

His words caused a warm rush and a surge of panic at the same time.

Knox didn't have feelings for me.

I mean, of course he had the kind of feelings that made him want to sleep with me. And he trusted me with his baby. We got along well, but that didn't mean love or those kinds of feelings. To him, I was a secret lover he didn't want anyone to know about.

Before I could argue any of this out loud, my brother continued. "Are you going to tell me you don't have feelings for him?"

I should. But this was my brother, and I trusted him. And though I didn't know what my feelings were exactly, I couldn't deny there was *something*.

I expelled a breath. "I have feelings. But that's irrelevant. I'm going to school in two months."

"An hour away. You could make it work if you wanted to."

"That's not what I want," I said. I'd been over this in my head. I'd been over it with Piper. "I wasted years of my life with Mitchell, ignoring what was best for me. Ignoring my future other than Mitchell, and you see where that got me."

"Okay." Ryan straightened, his expression saying he surrendered. "I'm not trying to tell you what's right for you. Only you can figure that out. If that's focusing on school and waiting till afterward to get involved with someone, then that's what you should do. Probably."

I frowned at the *probably*.

"That's what's right for me," I said with a touch of defiance, toward what, I wasn't sure, because I wasn't upset with Ryan. "Why do you say probably? Of course it's what I should do."

"It's a good plan...unless you find the right person along the way but don't pursue it. Because who knows if that right person will still be there by the time you finish school and finally have *relationship* inked into your plan?"

I tilted my head and sized up my brother because I could swear it sounded like he had personal experience with exactly that. But I didn't know of any right person or even remotely possibly right person he'd had in his life.

"I'll keep that in mind," I said to appease him, because I finally had my plan, and I wasn't going to veer from it because of really good sex or even because of possible feelings that I couldn't define. "He's coming back, so drop it please."

"Happy to. But me dropping it doesn't mean you should too."

As Knox came back to the table, I pasted my nanny grin on my face, cooed to Juniper, and ignored her father.

CHAPTER 27

QUINCY

Piper and Jewel and several of our friends were hitting the Fly tonight and had invited me since I had the night off. I'd shocked them and myself by saying no. A month ago, I would've joined them in an instant, but tonight getting prettied up and being social for hours on end didn't appeal.

I'd just finished feeding Juniper her early dinner when Knox came out to the kitchen grinning.

"Well?" I asked as I wiped baby carrots from Juniper's face and hands. "How does it look?"

"It's perfect. Even better than I was hoping for."

"Will you show me?"

"I'd love to. It's incredible, Quince." His voice was chock-full of the most endearing little-boy enthusiasm.

I finished cleaning the messy princess, then lifted her out of the high chair.

"You're about done with June Bug duty," Knox said. "I can take her."

"As if this is any hardship," I said, kissing the baby's rosy cheek. "You're much more than just a 'duty' to me, aren't you, sweet pea?"

Juniper patted my shoulder and voiced her opinion in baby babble as I followed Knox to his office.

The bookshelf he'd waited weeks for had finally been delivered an hour ago. It'd been crated up tight, so I hadn't even caught a glimpse as he and the delivery guy had moved it in.

As I followed him into his work haven, I gasped. "It's a work of art, Knox."

On the wall opposite his desk stood a tall bookcase made of a dark wood with a gorgeous grain to it. The showpiece part of it though, and the reason it'd taken more than a month to arrive, was a hand-carved dragon out of the same wood that crouched along the top, his head dipping down on the right side as if to guard his books, and his long, glorious tail trailing down the left outer side of the bookcase almost to the floor. Built-in, blue-green lighting under the shelves added to the fantasy-novel aura of it.

I walked over to it, my mouth gaping. When I glanced at Knox, he was smiling hard, his eyes lit up.

"Wow," I said.

"I know. It's incredible. Better than I ever imagined. So much more so than the photos on the website could convey." He shook his head. "It's perfect. I can't wait to get my special books unpacked in their new home."

"Want some help?"

"Really? You want to pull dusty books out of boxes with me?"

"I'd love to." I wasn't much of a book person, but I was totally becoming a Knox person, and I loved seeing him so happy.

"Don't you have plans with the girls?"

"I told them no, so"—I shrugged—"I'm all yours." I kept

my tone light and held my empty hand out to the side, offering myself up.

His brows shot up. "That's a heck of an offer."

"I know," I said, grinning. "I don't make it to just anyone."

"I was planning to wait till after June Bug went to bed so I could focus on the task."

"We can bring the playpen in and start right away. I know you're dying to."

"I might be dying to. The boxes are here in the closet. I'll treat you to pizza delivery afterward."

While he pulled multiple book boxes from the closet, I brought the playpen from the living room to the office.

Knox relieved me of the playpen and set it up out of the way, though with so many boxes of books, we were running out of space. I set Juniper inside, then went to gather some board books and toys for her. When I returned, she was on her knees, peering out at Knox as he cut the tape on the first box.

"She wants to get her hands on Daddy's books," I said.

"Someday I'll introduce you to them, June Bug, but not today." He pulled the flaps of the box open and removed the top books. I heard him sigh in contentment.

"These are your *first* babies, huh?" I asked.

Knox frowned. "Two months ago, I would've said yes, but now…" He looked at Juniper, love in his eyes. "There's no comparison. These are just books. Special books. Damn good books. But just books."

"With a bad-ass custom bookcase to call home," I said.

"And a dragon to watch over them," Knox said, glancing at the carving with a sparkle in his eyes.

"Just like Juniper has you. Speaking of, any luck tracking down Juniper's mom?"

He scoffed. "She doesn't want to be found. Once I have paperwork drawn up, I'll hire a PI to get her to sign away her rights."

"Do you think she will?"

"Her disappearing act says it all."

Nodding, I sat next to him on the floor, peering down at his prized possessions. "So these are the good ones, huh?"

He took out a hardcover. "This is the first epic fantasy I ever read. My seventh grade English teacher, Mr. Cranden-berry, recommended it. I'd never read anything like it. He started feeding me fantasy recommendations, and later some hard-core sci fi, and I never looked back. I'd stay after class to talk books with Mr. C."

I could so totally imagine thirteen-year-old Knox falling in love with these books with the moody, beautifully illustrated covers. The dust jackets were nearly pristine even though the books were clearly old and well loved. "I bet you were teacher's pet."

Knox took three more of the thick hardcovers and shelved them on the bottom row. "He was a mentor to me, almost like a father figure. Would you believe I still went to see him when I was in high school?"

"Yes," I said, laughing. "Easily. I'm glad you had someone like that in your life. My favorite teacher ever was Mrs. Tolbert. Third grade. She picked the best books to read out loud."

"Mr. Dawson wasn't your favorite, huh?" Knox asked, his tone teasing.

"Mr. Dawson," I said with a sigh. "A lot of girls had a crush on him."

"Should I be jealous?"

I tilted my head, shooting him a flirty look. "Nah. Math is a total turn-off. I hated trig with the heat of a thousand suns."

"He had nice things to say about you at one of our dad nights."

I went on alert. "You guys were talking about me? At this super-exclusive single dad party?"

"Only in terms of nannying and teaching. They all agreed you'll be a hell of a teacher."

"Oh. That's nice of them." I wasn't quite used to people praising my plans, mainly because I hadn't had any for so long.

"They were sincere. Both Max and Chance seem to know you pretty well."

"I'm sure they think they do. That's life in a small town when you've lived here your whole life."

"Or had your personal business posted all over the town app," he said good-naturedly. "It still pulls me up short when I meet someone and they know all about me and my daughter and half my life story."

"You'll get used to it fast. How about I take the books out and hand them to you and you can put them where you want them."

I handed him another four books after looking at the titles. All four of these had different authors, but each one had at least one dragon on the cover. "I'm starting to see where the dragon thing came from."

As Knox took the stack from me, his phone sounded with a message. He took it out of his pocket, read the screen, and frowned.

"Everything okay?" I asked, digging another three heavy books out.

"I'm not sure." He typed something in and waited, staring at his phone. "It's Cash."

"Texting you?"

He nodded, his forehead creased with concern. When another message came through, Knox stood. "Ava's upset. Something to do with writing, and Cash has to run to Henry's because Zinnia cut her finger badly enough she's going in for stitches."

"Right at dinnertime," I said.

"He wants to know if I can come talk to Ava, see if I can calm her down."

"Okay," I said, also standing. "He reached out to you, Knox. Progress?"

"Maybe." He typed again, then stuck his phone back in his pocket, then stopped short. "You have tonight off. I can take June Bug with me."

"I told you I'm staying in. I'm happy to take care of her while you're gone. Take your time."

He studied me for a second, then nodded. Flashed a hint of a smile, closed the space between us, and kissed my forehead. "Thank you, Quincy."

"Of course. We can tackle the rest of the books when you get back."

"There's no rush. If you get too hungry, order pizza without me. I don't know how long I'll be."

He kissed me again, this time on the lips, and then hurried out. It was only a short kiss, but it warmed me to my toes. *He* warmed me to my toes.

I went over to pick up Juniper and heard the front door shut.

"It's just you and me, sweet pea." I lifted her over my head, her eyes going big and that smile I loved popping up on her face. I perched her on my hip, went over to the half-full bookcase, and ran my fingers up a few of the thick spines. Now that several of the boxes were unpacked, the room somehow smelled even more like Knox. I breathed it in.

"You are one lucky baby girl," I told June. "Your daddy is a special one."

Juniper stared at me as if she was puzzling out what I said, and then she giggled and grasped on to my shirt with her fist. She rested her darling head on my shoulder.

I breathed in and closed my eyes, taking a moment to appreciate where I was, how I was feeling. Content. Comfortable in a way I hadn't felt for…years? Ever? Maybe not since before my mom died.

My heart felt at home here, with this man and his daughter. Knox was so quietly caring and compassionate. He'd been counting down the days until his custom-made shelf showed up and been like a kid opening birthday presents with every book we unpacked, but when Cash texted him, when Ava needed help, he'd never once hesitated.

Just like he hadn't truly hesitated when Juniper came into his life. He might not have admitted it to himself in the first couple of hours, but he'd accepted responsibility for this child almost immediately, long before knowing she was his. His heart was big, soft…irresistible.

Then it hit me like a rock crashing through a window—I'd fallen for Knox.

I was in love with him.

How could I not be, between that loving heart of his, the kind, intelligent, unselfish person he was, and the way he worshipped my body at night?

I. Loved. Knox.

My heart raced out of control with the realization and, grasping to Juniper, I caught my breath, leaned against the wall next to the shelf.

Because loving him wasn't okay. It was never part of the plan. And that was a giant problem.

CHAPTER 28

KNOX

I pulled up to Ava and Cash's cottage next to the inn. The place looked cozy, lived in, like a home, the way my house didn't yet look from the curb.

Love lived here. It was plain to see in the pots of mums along the walkway and the two chairs with pillows and the low, warm light in the windows.

I got out and hurried to the front door. It took a while for it to open after I knocked, and when it finally did, Ava stood there, blinking at me in confusion, her eyes bloodshot and swollen.

"Knox, what are you doing here?"

"Are you okay?" I asked.

"Of course I'm okay." She blinked again, glanced at the driveway, then tilted her head back up at me. "What... Did Cash contact you?"

"He said you were upset."

Her eyes fluttered closed. "I love that man to pieces, but he's ridiculous. I told him I'd be fine."

"He's worried about you," I said, wondering when I'd started defending my unfriendly brother.

"Come in out of the cold." She stood back so I could enter. A lamp shone on a low setting from the living room on the left, the only illumination on the main floor. "I can't believe… Did he really call you?"

"He texted. Said you were upset about writing, threatening to quit—"

"I'm not going to quit." She frowned. "I don't think I could if I wanted to. I was just ranting. You know how it is."

"Sure." I narrowed my eyes at her. "So you're not upset anymore?"

"I didn't say that. But I don't need an intervention. Would you like a drink?" She gestured to the kitchen on the right, open to the dining and living areas. I followed her over.

"What do you have?"

"Beer, soda, tea, water."

"Got any Rusty Anchor?"

She walked around the island, opened the fridge, and took out an IPA. I was touched she knew my preference without asking. I'd never had that kind of closeness with people in Texas.

Grabbing a tea for herself, she leaned on the island. I took a seat on the opposite side.

"What's going on?" I asked her as I opened the bottle. When she didn't say anything, I said, "Talk to me, Ava."

She spun her tea around in circles, her eyes locked on it, avoiding me.

"This is me," I said in a coaxing voice.

Still not looking at me, she let out a breath. "I sent some of my chapters to a writing coach," she finally spit out. "It's someone I knew from school."

"You don't need a writing coach."

She scoffed. "I definitely need a writing coach."

"Ava, the screen play you wrote is a TV series."

"I can write a screen play, but I'm so used to being brief and paring down details that I can't write a novel."

"Untrue. You're writing one."

"Not well."

"Says who? The writing coach?"

"And me. You know I've been working hard to get the right amount of description in, to add introspection."

"You have. You've gotten a lot better at it in just a month."

"Yeah, well, the writing coach thinks I overdid it."

I clenched my jaw, frustrated that she'd been unsure enough of herself that she'd even gone to this writing coach. "Ava, you've been working your ass off to expand your writing. You expanded your writing. You overdid it? That's fantastic. That's what we wanted."

"I wanted good writing."

"You're a damn good writer. Stop it."

"I'm holding you back, Knox," she said quietly. "We're spending so much time on me trying to figure out the right balance that we can't move forward."

"We're almost to the midpoint of the rough draft. That's progress."

"But my last three chapters are overwritten."

I couldn't help a grin. "Ava, come on. Listen to what you're saying. You overwrote. Your problem before was underwriting. This is a win."

She looked at me finally, her expression saying I was crazy. "Overwriting is not good writing."

"But you can edit it down. We can edit it down. Three chapters of overwriting? We'll go through it together and fine-tune it. Piece of cake. Compared to vomiting out extra words and details, polishing is nothing."

"I can't figure out the balance. I don't know if I ever will."

"Whatever, Ms. Professional Writer. You're smart. Give yourself half a minute to adjust."

Her shoulders lifted with an inhalation, then relaxed

slightly with the breath out, her gaze averted to the counter again.

"Don't you dare even think about making me go solo," I said.

"I'm not going to make you go solo."

"Promise?" I leaned down to try to get her to meet my gaze.

"I promise," she finally said begrudgingly when she glanced at me.

"Thank God." I injected lightness into my tone. "We've got two characters halfway to falling in love, and I can't get them there by myself. I don't know a thing about romance."

Now she raised her head and looked me directly in the eye, her brows climbing her forehead. "Really though?" Her tone was deliberate. Stronger. None of the unsure writer of two minutes ago.

I became wary, narrowing my eyes at her. "Really. Remember me? Fantasy and sci-fi guy?"

"Are you sure you're not romancing your nanny?"

My eyes went wide, and I reared my head back before I could control the reaction. "Where did that come from?" I asked, trying to play it cool while I gathered my thoughts.

In a one eighty from the distraught woman I'd found when I showed up, she tilted her head and studied me. "I notice you didn't deny it."

Hell. She wasn't going to let this go. It wasn't a random attempt to divert the focus from her to me. I suspected she'd been dying to ask me about Quincy for some time. I was surprised she hadn't before now based on a couple of veiled comments she'd made.

I picked up my bottle, swigged half of it down, and decided to be honest.

"You'll keep this between us?" I asked, still holding my bottle.

"Of course." She said nothing else, just eyed me. Waited.

"Quincy and I are...involved."

I couldn't bring myself to use the word *romancing*. I wasn't sure what that entailed, though I didn't think it meant just shagging for shagging's sake.

My lids closed with that thought because...I was lying to myself if I said it was just sex between us.

It'd become more.

"I knew it," Ava said with glee. "Awesome." She apparently got a good look at my face, and her smile disappeared. "Not awesome?"

I leaned my forehead into my hand and rubbed it, trying to find words. Despite being a guy who made a living off them, I was sure as hell struggling now.

"She's too attached?" Ava guessed when I didn't say anything.

I shook my head. A half grin popped out. "Quincy's pretty carefree." More carefree than I'd ever be. "We set boundaries, and she respects them."

"Are *you* having a hard time with boundaries?"

"Nope," I said quickly. "We agreed it ends when she goes to school."

Ava studied me. "Did you grow feelings?"

Shit, this conversation had gotten uncomfortable fast.

"I care about her," I said. "It's impossible not to care about Quincy."

"Yeah, I can see that. She seems like an awesome girl. Caring, dedicated, funny. Cute." She emphasized the last word.

I couldn't argue with any of that.

"You don't seem like you're happy," Ava said.

"I'm not unhappy. Just...worried, I guess."

"What are you worried about?"

"It's...probably a mistake. The longer it goes on, the more we could start to care. The more we start to care, the more someone gets hurt."

"What if you took away the end date?"

I shook my head. "That's the only thing making it okay. Keeping it temporary." I folded my hands together and leaned my forehead on them. "I'm forty-two, Ava. She's in her twenties and about to go to college. She has her whole life ahead of her, her whole future. She's going to be a teacher." I cracked a grin, thinking about how good she'd be. "It wouldn't be right for me to plan a future with her. She needs to go into the education program with no ties, nothing holding her back. Her *twenties*, Ava. When I was in my twenties, bars and friends were just as important as books and tests. If she drove home to Dragonfly every weekend to see me and Juniper, she'd miss out on college life. That stuff is important."

Ava looked thoughtful as she nodded. "It is. I get it. You're in homeowner and fatherhood mode. She's in English 101 and frat-party mode."

"Exactly."

"Are you thinking you should put an end to the fling sooner rather than later?"

The thought of having Quincy under my roof but not in my bed... I didn't like that thought. At all. "Do you think I should?"

"I think that's entirely up to you. Would it make anything better?"

It'd make everything downright shitty and awkward. I shook my head.

"There's your answer then, Mr. Romance. Keep on romancing until your deadline. Respect the boundaries. You'll miss her when she's gone, but you knew what you were getting into from the beginning."

And that was the bitch of it. I'd known, at least on some level, and I'd done it anyway.

I had a feeling I'd pay for it later in the form of missing Quincy like crazy, but I'd get through it.

CHAPTER 29

QUINCY

The Sunday before Thanksgiving, I dashed through a light rain into Henry's as soon as they opened for brunch. I glanced around for Cynthia, but she wasn't here yet. Not surprising since we weren't supposed to meet for another few minutes.

"Quincy," Arielle sang out as I walked inside.

"Hey, Ari. How are you?"

The hostess, who was twenty years old, curvy, and gorgeous, came around the host stand to hug me. "I'm good. We miss you."

"I miss you too." I did miss the people but not so much the job itself. It had never been a good fit for me, the queen of clumsy. I'd been planning to hold on to the server job for school breaks and summertime, but the longer I was away, the harder it was to think about coming back. I'd much rather help Knox with Juniper, but he'd have a new nanny by then and wouldn't need me.

That thought caused a sharp pang in my chest that stole my breath.

"Are you here for brunch?" Ari's question distracted me from those unpleasant thoughts.

"I am. There'll be two of us. Is table ten available?"

"Of course," Ari said over her shoulder as she led me through the bar and to the left.

When we turned into the middle dining area, the fire was already glowing, emanating warmth throughout the room. The fireplace was on the back side, opposite the wall of windows that looked out over the lake. Ari took me to the table in the corner, the most out of the way.

Strategizing wasn't my strong point, but Knox had helped me plot out the details of this meeting with my stepmom to help me be as comfortable and confident as possible. We'd chosen Henry's because it was as close to my territory as you could get. The out-of-the-way table would afford us more privacy than others. I'd been banking on the fireplace being on, hoping the cozy atmosphere would put both of us at ease.

Ari let me know Jack would be our server, then returned to the host stand. I'd been hoping for Jack. He could charm anyone and might help put Cynthia at ease. While I waited for her to arrive, I sipped on a mimosa and joked with Jack that I hoped he'd convince my stepmom to have one too.

When Cynthia appeared, my insides tensed, but I inhaled deeply as she approached, doing my best to put a genuine smile on my face. The mimosa helped.

"Quincy," she said as she sat across from me. Her smile was thin, but it was better than a scowl.

Jack assured himself of a large tip when he did, in fact, convince her to join me in Mimosaville. While we waited for her beverage, she told me about Brayden's basketball tournament and reminded me of Molly's upcoming dance recital.

When Jack set her mimosa down, she practically leaped on it, which told me she too was on edge. She took several sips, then set the glass down, fidgeted with the silverware roll, and said, "What's on your mind, Quincy?"

Here goes nothing, I thought.

"I…" My voice wavered. I remedied it with a drink, then blew out a breath. "I hate that there's so much friction between us."

Her forehead furrowed, and she cradled her glass with both hands. Maybe fragile champagne flutes were a bad idea. We should've gone with straight whiskey in an old-fashioned glass. If we got through this without me dropping any glasses or her crushing one with her tight grip, it'd be a feat.

"It's always been that way," I continued, "and I think… I *know* a lot of that's my fault. So I wanted to start by saying I'm sorry I was so…against you when you married my dad."

Cynthia let out a shaky "Ohh, Quincy." She turned her lips upward in a flash of a sympathetic smile, and then it disappeared, giving way to a nervous fluttering of her features. "We did get off to a bad start all those years ago, didn't we?"

"I was closed off and took my feelings out on you."

Cynthia stared at her glass, nodding. Eventually she met my gaze. "Thank you. For apologizing." She opened her mouth to say more. Closed it. I waited. "I imagine it was really hard for you to see your dad remarry."

I nodded. "Yeah. It didn't matter who it was. He could've married Beyoncé and I would've hated it."

We shared a big grin imagining my dad with Beyoncé.

"I understand that now. Back then it was harder for me to grasp." Cynthia studied her drink again. "As much as I loved your dad, it wasn't an easy time for me either. There were all these…expectations." With a frown, she continued, "I was as much to blame as you were, I'm afraid. I don't care what anyone says; it's tough to step into the role of a stepmother. Add to that a grieving girl who I didn't know how to help, and the pressure I put on myself to be what your dad needed…"

"You were what he needed. I wish I'd been mature enough to see that."

"You were eleven, Quincy. You'd just lost your mom, and it wasn't just any mom but the incomparable Reba Yates."

She *was* incomparable, but I'd never expected that compliment to come from Cynthia. I peered more closely at her, trying for once to see *Cynthia*. Not my "evil" stepmom.

"Did you know her?"

With an uneasy laugh, she said, "Everyone knew Reba. Everyone loved her," Cynthia said, not noticing how closely I was watching her, probably with a weird look on my face, as understanding struck me.

"She's a lot to try to live up to, huh?"

"Lord, yes." Cynthia sipped her drink thoughtfully, set it back down. "Every single person in town knew her and loved her. She was a successful career woman, involved in every cause known to mankind, and Super Mom as well. And I was scared that if I didn't measure up, your dad wouldn't be happy."

"Oh," I said, sitting back in my chair as I let that sink in.

"I'm pretty secure in my career," she continued. "I've been with Dr. Julian since my early twenties. I run that office for the dear man. I've tried to stay involved in town events, causes, fundraisers, all those things over the years. But motherhood…" She expelled a breath that sent her long, auburn-brown bangs flying away from her face. "Some people have a knack. A strong maternal instinct. Like Reba. She had it in spades. You do too, Quincy. Me?" She scoffed and shook her head. "I don't have that instinct. A squirming newborn can still send me right over the edge. I have to talk myself down, remember I've had three babies. But it doesn't come naturally. No surprise to you, I know."

"Kind of like waiting tables, or really, walking in general doesn't come naturally to me." I grinned self-consciously.

Her sympathetic expression said she couldn't debate that.

"Hannah, Brayden, and Molly know you love them," I went on. "That's most important."

"After Hannah was born, I suffered from postpartum depression for months. I was so afraid I was a disappointment to your dad."

It was my turn to frown. My dad was one of the most devoted people I knew. "He loves you, Cynthia. I've never doubted that."

"I know that. God bless the man." Her face slipped into a deep frown, and I thought I saw her lower lip quiver. "It's my own insecurity. I know that too. I let Reba get in my head from the grave. Trying to measure up." She let out a self-effacing laugh. "No one can measure up to Reba, and I say that with full respect. I don't care what year it is or how far we've come; there's still a lot of pressure on us women to be good at everything, isn't there? To have the successful career and make a living. To run the household and keep a beautiful, clean house. And to be Super Mom."

It was the first time she'd ever spoken to me as an equal, woman to woman, as if we were in the same boat. And we were.

We absolutely were, I realized.

Her words dug down deep and rustled something awake in me.

"I need to knock that right off," Cynthia said. "All of us women do. As long as we let ourselves feel inadequate for not being as amazing as Reba, God rest her soul, we'll all be going in circles trying to find some unattainable happiness."

"Yes." I nodded, my thoughts suddenly spinning out of control.

"I've not set a good example for you, Quincy. It's never been my intent to replace your mom, but I should've been a better role model. A better stepmother. I'm sorry."

"Isn't that falling into the same trap?" I asked. "Saying

you weren't good enough, when you were doing the best you could?"

She looked pensive for a few seconds, then met my gaze. Slowly her mouth curved into a slight grin. "You might be right," she said sheepishly. Her grin faded. "I'm glad you initiated this conversation. It's long overdue."

I breathed out and nodded. I was glad too.

"I hope we can find a way to start fresh. Not really start over, because we're different than we were back then."

"Older and supposedly wiser," I said.

"Supposedly."

We both laughed quietly.

"I'd like it if we could get along better. Treat each other better," I said.

"Yes." Cynthia reached across the table and put her hand on mine, squeezed it. "Yes, let's."

I wasn't naive enough to think we'd be best friends or even close. That would take time. But today we'd connected on a level other than insecure stepmom and difficult step-daughter. We'd connected as two women trying to do their best. Failing sometimes but trying.

She raised her mimosa glass, nearly empty, and said, "To being happy with ourselves and better to each other."

"Cheers." I clinked my glass to hers, sipped the rest of it down, and dug into my quiche again.

Silence settled in around us as we caught up on the eating we'd half neglected while we talked. My thoughts rained down on me, only slightly clearer than five minutes ago.

I'd realized I felt that pressure Cynthia described. The driving belief I should try to live up to my mom. How did that even make sense?

She'd been an amazing person. She'd loved what she did —the job and the involvement and the family, everything— and had been good at all of them. That was Reba Yates, but it didn't have to be Cynthia, and it didn't have to be me.

While my dad hadn't intended it, he'd wanted nothing more than for me to find my career path, my life's calling, even when I was still with Mitchell. I'd chosen teaching because it seemed the best fit for me with my maternal instinct, as Cynthia called it.

But did I really want to spend the next however many years going to college just so I could have a career, as opposed to a job I loved that paid the bills?

I'd been so determined to forge ahead and make something of myself, I'd forgotten to think about what would make me happy.

While I could fully admit waiting tables wasn't my life calling, what about nannying? I adored what I was doing for Knox and Juniper. I knew I was good at it.

My eyes had been opened, and ideas were filling my head, ideas that made me smile. I'd spent a lot of time figuring out what career path might suit me. I wasn't going to change plans on a whim. But I definitely had some soul searching to do, and fast.

CHAPTER 30

QUINCY

Despite having slept no more than an hour or two last night thanks to racing, life-altering thoughts that stemmed from yesterday's brunch, I was feeling light and optimistic, humming quietly to Juniper as the sun rose in a dramatic splash of violets morphing into soft pinks and corals over the lake. It might be three days before Thanksgiving, but Monday had dawned a breathtaking—if brisk—morning.

June Bug and I were sitting on the shore with a doubled-up blanket beneath me and the baby in a sling on my chest. I'd put her fuzzy white polar bear hat on her head and wrapped a heavier blanket around the two of us to keep us toasty as we listened to several birds serenade us and watched a pair of hearty ducks paddling across the water.

Though Knox's shoreline was currently empty of any benches, seats, or docks, it had the potential to be the heart of his outdoor space. I could easily imagine Juniper learning to fish off a dock as a toddler and sunbathe on the shore as a teenager. I could picture Knox helping her onto a family boat

—and then holding my hand as I climbed on, maybe with another baby in my arms.

The image in my mind was so vivid, so easy to see all of a sudden, that it took my breath away with longing.

That was what I wanted. I wanted Knox and Juniper. I wanted a family, but not just any family. I wanted Knox's family. His babies and him.

As if I summoned him with my thoughts, I heard the door to the house close behind me. I took in a shaky breath, straightening, preparing.

Juniper's gaze locked on something behind me.

"Is that your daddy?" I asked her, then brushed a dark lock of hair off her forehead. I knew without looking Knox was getting close. I could feel him in my blood.

He came to the end of the path and sat on the blanket next to us.

"Morning," he said, his voice still with a hint of sleepy gravel.

"Hey," I said, smiling at him, trying to hold in all the feelings that were on the verge of bursting out of me.

"It's early. Are you warm enough?"

"We're toasty in here, aren't we, June Bug?"

Juniper reached for Knox with a toothless grin and big eyes.

"You want your daddy." I raised my brows at him to see if he was ready for his daughter.

Knox's face brightened as he gave the baby an exaggerated smile. "Come here, princess. I need morning kisses."

I watched father and daughter laugh and kiss and play, my heart threatening to explode with affection and hope. And nervous energy.

"Do you have time to talk, or do you need to get to work soon?" I asked as Knox rubbed noses with his daughter.

His smile slipped away as he supported Juniper in a standing position between his legs. She couldn't stand on her own yet, but she loved to try, loved to bounce with someone holding her. She was building her muscles, getting ready, and would master it before we knew it.

"Sure. We can talk. Want to go inside for it? Get this girl warmed up?"

"Good idea." I'd bundled her in a thick one-piece footie outfit so that her feet would stay covered, but now that she was out of the sling and my blanket, it was too cold to have her out for long.

We stood, and Knox walked next to me, carrying Juniper inside, still playful with his daughter but subdued. Was that my imagination or was he concerned about our upcoming discussion? Maybe he thought I was going to quit early. I allowed the faintest private smile to creep onto my lips, anticipating his reaction when I said basically the opposite.

A few minutes later, we had June settled on the living room floor with some toys. I sat on one side of the sectional, the blanket pulled around me even when Knox started the fireplace. He came over and sat on the other side, a few inches away.

"What's going on, Quincy?"

I inhaled deeply as I met his concerned gaze, gathering my courage. "I've decided not to go to school after all."

His expression went…not at all the way I expected it to. His features dipped in a frown, brows wrinkled in confusion. Not happiness.

I moved to his side, letting the blanket fall away, kneeling on the cushion next to him so I could make him understand. With my hand on his strong forearm, I sought out eye contact. "Knox, I love you and Juniper. I want to be here with the two of you, not an hour away—"

He shook his head, frowning, and I tensed, my chest locking up with fear. "No, Quincy."

"What?"

"You can't do that." He shook his head in a tight, insistent movement. "I can't let you do that."

"You can't let me do what? Love you?" An incredulous, half-crazed laugh came out of me. "Too late, Knox. You don't get a say in that. My feelings are already there."

He surprised me again by bolting off the couch and putting space between us, his gaze locked on the floor.

A sick feeling washed over me as I watched him, my hope crashing that he'd maybe misunderstood me at first and would realize this was happy news.

As the situation sank in, my mouth gaped. I was too stunned to find words to convince him or argue.

"You're on the verge of...everything, Quincy," he said. "Your life is getting ready to take off in a good way. Your future, your goals—"

"Changed," I said decisively, but he was shaking his head again. I perched on the edge of the cushion, my whole body tense as I struggled to find the right words to make him understand.

"You're twenty-eight years old. You're about to embark on the career path you were put on this earth to follow. Everyone agrees you're going to be a stellar teacher. I'm not going to let you give that up. Not for us. This was always supposed to be temporary."

"You can't tell me you don't have feelings for me."

He didn't look at me. "Of course I have feelings for you. I care deeply about you. That's why I can't let you give up everything you want."

"I told you; I want you and Juniper." Anger was burning through my disbelief. I shot up off the sectional, no longer able to fight this battle sitting down. I shouldn't have to *fight* this battle at all. This was crazy. "Why can't you understand I changed my mind, Knox? As you pointed out, I'm twenty-eight. Old enough to decide what I want. Old enough to figure out that the whole women-can-do-everything schtick isn't for me. I don't want to do everything. My mom was the queen of doing everything and doing it better than every-body." I shook my head, tears dampening my eyes. Angry tears. Frustrated tears. "I'm not my mom. Believe it or not, Cynthia helped me see it's okay if I don't want to be."

"You can't just throw away all your plans because of us. You've said it yourself—you made that mistake with your ex."

I reared back because that stung. More than stung. It crushed me, got it through my head that Knox didn't want what I wanted. I sat back down on the edge of the sectional, all my optimism draining.

As I fought to get my brain to work, to figure out what to do next, Knox lowered himself to the ottoman in front of me, facing me. He leaned his elbows on his thighs, not meeting my eyes, not touching me.

"We're in two different life stages, Quincy. You're about to get started. I can't wait to see what you become, because you're going to be amazing. I refuse to stand in your way."

I opened my mouth to argue, but he held out a hand and said, "You have to try it. Juniper and I will miss you, but you can visit whenever you're in town."

I couldn't imagine how awkward that would be. It was irrelevant though because I wasn't going to school. I'd decided that deliberately, separately from loving Knox and June. I loved being a nanny. I didn't know why it'd taken me twenty-eight years to figure that out, but it had.

But clearly, Knox didn't care what I wanted. He wasn't open to listening to me, didn't think I could make up my mind about my own future. I stood and stepped past him, needing space.

I walked over to the kitchen island, leaned my elbows on it, and covered my face with my hands. Putting physical distance between us didn't help a thing. I couldn't begin to figure out what my next move was. I was still trying to wrap my head around how everything had gone sideways in a matter of minutes.

"Why don't you go to your apartment for a few days," he said, startling me because he was so close, right behind me. "Give yourself some space from me and June so you can think straight."

I stood upright. Just when I'd thought it couldn't get worse… "You want me to leave?"

"I think it'd be best. You need a clear head, away from us."

Don't tell me what I need. I bit down on the words, keeping them in, acknowledging that nothing I could say would change his stance. If I had to convince him, beg him, then it wasn't the right thing anyway. I shouldn't have to convince him to spend the future with me, or even the next month and a half.

Feeling like the rug had been ripped out from under me, I couldn't utter an answer. I looked him in the eye, trying to reach the man I'd fallen for, checking to see if he would back down.

He didn't.

I glanced at Juniper. Adorable, chubby Junie Bee. A tear spilled over the rim of my eye, splashing down my face.

"June Bug and I'll be okay," Knox said, as if that would make everything fine. "You've prepared us to go it alone. We've got this."

I fought to swallow. Nodded once. Battled hard not to let any more tears fall. Not in front of him. "Fine," I managed, doubting I'd be okay.

I took less than two minutes to gather my toiletries and some other belongings I might need in the next few days. I left most of my clothes, figuring I'd be back soon, when Knox came to his senses.

Even though I was completely unsure he would come to his senses.

When I came back into the living room, I went to Juniper,

picked her up, and squeezed her to me, burying my head in her fresh baby scent. "I love you, little girl. I'll see you very soon," I whispered.

At that, tears drowned my eyes and streamed down my face. I fought to keep silent, struggled hard against the sobs that needed to escape.

Junie grabbed my hair and tugged affectionately, babbling like she did. Telling me she loved me too, I imagined. The thought had a pained smile forming on my lips, still pressed against her shoulder.

Not that Knox was looking.

He stood in front of the door to the deck, peering out, as if the lake was the most interesting thing ever. Not the heart he was breaking behind him.

I couldn't bring myself to let go of Juniper for a good minute or two. Once I got my tears to stop falling, I took in the shakiest of breaths, gave her the most heartfelt kiss, and set her back down amid her toys, handing her the stuffed monkey she loved.

Straightening, I said to Knox's back, "Goodbye, Knox. Let me know if you need help with June."

His only reply was a nod, still not facing me, and that told me all I needed to know.

I'd misjudged everything. Mistaken what he felt for me as more than it was. Gotten sucked in by the "coziness" of our setup.

Once again I'd let myself want a future with a man. Once again I'd let myself get my heart broken. Except this time, it hurt so badly I could barely get a breath in. Because this time, I'd truly fallen in love.

KNOX

I stared out at the lake, not seeing a damn thing but knowing, if I turned around and watched Quincy walk out the door, I'd probably stop her.

I needed to let her go.

I'd always known I had to let her go, but fuck. This was harder than I'd ever imagined.

The door clicked shut, and still, I didn't move, listening to be sure she was gone. The only sound was Juniper's favorite rattle she used as a teething toy.

When I heard Quincy's car drive away, I closed my eyes. My jaw was locked tight, giving me a headache I hadn't noticed until now. My arms were crossed, fists clenched tight, as if I was fighting myself.

Probably accurate.

In my head, I knew what I'd done was right. There was no way in hell it was okay for Quincy to throw away her college opportunity and the teaching career it would lead to. Even though she said she was okay with it, I would never be.

"Ah-gah!"

Juniper's baby babble jolted me out of my thoughts, reminded me I had a six-month-old to care for. Breakfast to make. A day to figure out now that I'd ensured we were on our own, for better or worse.

"Come here, June Bug." I turned, found her on her tummy with the rattle flung to the side as she reached for her stuffed monkey. "I didn't even ask Quincy if you had your breakfast yet."

Scooping her up, I inhaled her baby scent and let my love for her wash over me, like a blanket of calmness, of protection from...the hard stuff.

I stood behind my suggestion of spending time apart. Quincy needed to see things objectively. She needed time to go out with her twentysomething friends and be carefree before she had to buckle down at school and study. She needed a reminder that she wasn't forty and married and the mother of an infant. She had all the time in the world to get to that place in life—later. Much later.

I shook my head. I couldn't think about Quincy now. I was going to be the dad Juniper needed.

After blowing a raspberry on Juniper's belly, I sniffed her to be sure she didn't need a diaper change, then lowered her into her high chair while I found myself some breakfast.

Quincy didn't cook every day, but she made breakfast often enough that I'd gotten spoiled.

"I can make breakfast," I muttered, determined. I was fine with cooking. I'd done it all the time before Juniper. Before Quincy.

As I opened the refrigerator, my daughter started banging her hands on her tray and vocalizing. I let the fridge close and turned to her.

"Are you hungry, or are you playing me?"

Of course, my daughter only hollered louder and continued her rhythm on the tray. It was a happy holler, I noted. Maybe she was just feeling musical.

Quincy would know exactly what she wanted.

It was high time I learned to figure out the same.

"Cereal?" I asked her as I went for the box. I spread a few oat rings in front of her, earning a wide grin. "That's what you wanted."

I had enough time to pull the eggs and a pan out before I noticed Juniper was systematically picking up each piece of cereal, dropping it over the side of the tray, and watching it land on the floor.

"Maybe we'll get a dog." As if I needed another living creature depending on my caretaking. "June." I went over, bent down and picked up the cereal, and tossed it in the trash. So that wasn't the answer after all.

As soon as I had the stove warming for an omelet, my

good-natured daughter started to crank. I knew there was some ham and diced onions and jalapeños in the refrigerator, but I decided scrambled would be easier and good enough.

"June Bug, what's wrong?"

Before I committed and poured my eggs into the pan, I lifted her and did a more thorough check of her diaper. It was dry, light, and unstinky. She quieted, her grumping turning more chatter-like.

She waited until the eggs were cooking to start fussing again, and I closed my eyes, searching my mind for what she could possibly need right now. I could hear Quincy's voice in my head saying, *Babies don't cry for no reason. The trick is figuring out if it's a legit reason and what it is.*

As I went back toward her high chair, a stench that wasn't there two minutes ago hit me. "Okay then," I said, flipping off the burner on my half-cooked eggs. "Maybe your tummy hurts."

I had her diaper changed in no time, then brought her back out to the kitchen. As I walked up to the stove, still holding her, I eyed the runny, half-cooked eggs. My hunger had vanished. Eating seemed like too much.

Cleaning the kitchen seemed like too much.

The day itself seemed like too much.

Leaving the mess, I did a one eighty to the living room, stretched out along the sectional, settled Juniper between me and the back, and closed my eyes.

I'd done the right thing. Quincy would be better off this way.

Juniper and I would be okay too. We'd get used to being on our own. We'd master all of it.

But right now, I couldn't deny...nothing felt like it would ever be okay.

CHAPTER 31

QUINCY

I might still be a mess, but I was maybe a little less of one today than the past two days.

Maybe.

I pulled my car into the back of the lot behind the flower shop, cut the engine, and climbed out later than planned.

The sky was heavy with winter clouds, and it was close to dusk even though it wasn't five p.m. yet. Ignoring the back door of the shop, knowing it was locked during business hours, I went down the narrow alley beside our building, passed the stairs to our apartment, and went inside Oopsie Daisies.

"There she is," Piper called out from the sales counter in the back of the room.

"It's about time," Jewel said.

Their cousin Taylor was there too, smiling quietly, standing stiffly in front of the counter. She waved briefly. We'd all made plans for a quiet movie night at home tonight.

"I'm here, impatient wenches. Hi, Taylor," I added since we weren't close enough for me to lovingly refer to her as a wench. I pushed the door closed to shut out the cold. "This place looks fantastic as always."

Though most of the stores on the square were closed or closing soon for Thanksgiving Eve, Oopsie Daisies was lit with a warm, welcoming glow. The showroom was stuffed with its usual assortment of pretty things, plus an abundance of stunning Thanksgiving centerpieces. They were Piper's newest brainchild, and she'd outdone herself.

There were all sizes, from simple candles in wide hurricane vases with acorns, mini pinecones, and twig accents, to three-piece sets that would span a long table, overflowing with pumpkins, squash, greenery, candles, and hand-painted signs saying "Grateful," "Give Thanks," and "Family."

"You still have stock," I said as I made my way to the sales counter. Jewel was sitting on top of the work counter behind it, and Piper was futzing with an arrangement next to her.

"She's still churning them out," Jewel said. "Not because she needs them but because—"

"She can't be idle," I said along with Jewel. We shared an amused look.

Taylor laughed. "Some things never change."

"We've had a lot of walk-ins for the centerpieces," Piper said, ignoring our teasing. "And we still have eleven orders to be picked up."

"They're incredible, Pipes." I stopped at a display to look more closely at a piece with gnomes peeking out from among pumpkins and vines, making a point of not touching it. I didn't want to break it.

"We've been worried about you," Jewel said.

My eyes teared up out of nowhere, and I swore as I wiped them. "I'm fine," I said, smiling to show it. "I mean, still messy, but I'm doing a little better."

"We filled Taylor in on what happened…" Piper said.

"Because you're afraid I'm a walking disaster and might lose it at any second?" I asked, grinning.

"Something like that," Jewel answered dryly.

As I reached for a pumpkin decoration, I bumped a basket of decorative apples and they spilled all over the floor. "Something else that never changes," I said to Taylor, rolling my eyes at myself.

"I'm sorry about Knox," Taylor said as she pushed back a strand of her dark red hair that had escaped her ponytail.

"Thanks," was all I could say, pausing from picking up the fake apples that had rolled everywhere to grasp her wrist for a second.

I'd left Knox's house Monday, made a beeline to my apartment, and been relieved to find it empty. After sinking into my own bed, which wasn't nearly as comforting and familiar as it'd been just a month before, I'd cried myself into a long, fitful sleep, feeling the heavy weight of sadness smothering me every time I turned over.

My roomies hadn't realized I was there until evening, after both of them had finished work for the day and heard me sneak to the bathroom. With the three of us piled onto my bed, I'd poured out the story, cried another ocean's worth of tears, then agreed to a movie-sized box of Milk Duds for my dinner.

Yesterday hadn't been much different as I slept and grieved and made a point of responding to texts from Piper and Jewel so they wouldn't come home from work just to check on me. I wasn't proud of losing two full days to tears, but let's be real; it wasn't like I had anything else I needed to do now that Knox had cut me off from my job. Both my jobs if you counted Henry's.

Jewel hopped down, came around the counter, and hugged me. Then Piper joined us.

"I was medium okay until these wenches had to hug me," I said to Taylor over Jewel's shoulder, trying to laugh as my eyes leaked anew. "Love you weirdos."

"We love you," Piper said.

"Now tell us about your day." Jewel squeezed my hand.

"It was...okay," I said as I blew out my breath, making the wisps of my hair fly outward. "I wouldn't say good but...helpful."

The bells on the door jingled behind me, and Rosy McNamara glided in. "Hello, beautiful girls." We all greeted her. "I've heard about these centerpieces from everyone," Rosy said. "Stars above, these are gorgeous, Piper. I need one."

Piper laughed. "We've got you covered. What are you looking for as far as size and style?"

Rosy glanced around, her eyes sparkling as they darted from one arrangement to the next. "All the boys will be here for dinner tomorrow, so nothing small. For style, they won't give a hoot, so I'll go with what *I* like." She sized up some of the options. "That one. You've outdone yourself, darling girl."

Piper rang up the centerpiece with sunflowers, dahlias, eucalyptus, apples, and more, then packed it in a box.

"The apples are genius," Rosy said. "Everyone else will have pumpkins." She affected a smug expression. "We'll have apples."

"Local ones from Appleberry Farm," Piper told her.

"I don't imagine it's a hardship to do business with Luke Durham," Rosy said as she took out her wallet from her oversized purse. "Still a hottie."

"He's great but not my type," Piper said. "Even if I was attracted to him, the instant parenthood thing is a turn-off for me, you know?"

Jewel's gaze swung to me, and she frowned sympathetically.

"That's just me though," Piper added quickly, as if remembering I was the exact opposite.

"Are you doing all the cooking tomorrow?" I asked Rosy, hoping she didn't catch on to my friends' meaning.

"You bet I am. Thanksgiving is my favorite meal to cook," Rosy said with her usual hippie-tinged sparkle.

Minutes later, the door closed after her, leaving the four of us alone again.

"You were telling us about your day," Jewel said impatiently, leaning against Piper's work counter, watching me. I still stood near Taylor on the customer side, nervous energy pumping through me at the same time I was bone-tired.

Piper came around the counter to rearrange merchandise, filling the space from Rosy's centerpiece. "Yeah, how was your trip to campus?"

I glanced out the windows, checking that no one was heading toward the store.

"We're alone for now." Piper came up beside me, leaned against the main counter, and wove her arm through mine. "Tell us about it." To Taylor, she said, "She insisted on going to Nashville alone."

"To think," I explained.

"I get that," Taylor said with a sympathetic smile. "Believe me. Although lately I've maybe overdosed on alone time."

"Which is why we wouldn't have taken no for an answer tonight," Piper said.

Taylor expelled a breath. "Yeah. Thank you for including me. Most of the time I'm okay, but holidays…and being in that house…"

"You're welcome to join us anytime," Jewel said. "We've told you that."

"Maybe we should set her up with someone too." Piper was eyeing her as if she was getting ideas.

"No," Taylor said emphatically. She smiled though, as if this wasn't the first time Piper had brought it up. "I mean, I wouldn't mind having a boyfriend, but a setup sounds terrifying."

"If you start coming out with us, we'll introduce you to single guys," Jewel said. "If that's what you want."

"You know a lot of the guys around here anyway." Piper wiped some dust off the counter. "Or you could take a page from Quincy and try the older set. She says they know how to please a lady."

"I'm good," Taylor said. "It's getting a little easier. Quincy was going to tell us about her day."

"Pour me a drink, and I'll talk," I said.

"Sold!" Jewel headed into the back room.

"Brilliant idea," Piper said.

"Red or white?" Jewel called out.

Piper looked to me.

"Red." No question.

It went without saying that red wine was for butt-hard emotional times.

A soft, sympathetic sound came from Piper, and she put an arm around me and squeezed. Yet again, my burning eyes filled.

A cork popped from the back room, Jewel swore, and Piper, Taylor, and I laughed, me through tears. Even though Jewel was a bar manager, she hated opening anything with a cork.

"Scares her every time," Piper said quietly.

"Even though she's expecting it," I added, grinning.

"Suck it," Jewel said as she rejoined us, carrying the bottle and three wineglasses.

Once we'd split the bottle into our glasses—hand-painted by Piper in a fall motif—I took a healthy swallow or five, appreciating the warmth as it went down.

As Jewel retook her place on the work counter, I leaned against the checkout area next to Taylor, facing Jewel. Piper tidied the top surface, straightening the hand-painted gift cards, the daisy keychains, the flower-shaped votives.

"Let's hear it," Piper said.

"So I walked around the campus," I started. "A lot of it was closed for the holiday, and most of the buildings were locked, so I spent most of my time by this quiet pond behind the dorms. It was peaceful. Mostly deserted. I found a bench and just sat there, trying to shut down all my thoughts and listen to my heart. To figure out whether school's the right thing."

"What did your heart say?" Piper asked.

I pressed my lips together, waited for any misgivings to arise. None did. "I'm not going."

There was silence for two full seconds. Then Piper said, "Okay then. Decision made."

"Decision made," I repeated, nodding. "Again. It still feels right. I've been turning it over in my head since brunch with Cynthia. I think I was mostly going to school because that's what's expected of me. I picked teaching because it fits better than other degrees." I shrugged tiredly. "Could I be a teacher? I think so."

"You could be a hell of a teacher," Jewel said. "But you shouldn't unless you burn to."

"School's a lot if you're not totally into it," Taylor said.

"How would you know?" Jewel asked. "There was never a second you weren't into it."

"That's a valid point," Taylor said sheepishly. She'd skipped two grades in grade school and graduated before any of us even though she was younger than Jewel and the same age as Piper and me.

"I think I'd like teaching for a couple of years." I traced the edges of a daisy key chain. "That's not what I really want to do though."

I glanced up at my friends. Jewel's head was tilted as she listened to me. Piper raised her brows as if waiting to hear more.

Taylor asked, "What do you really want to do?"

"I want my own family, first and foremost."

"We know," Jewel said with an affectionate smile. "Not shocking."

"Don't judge," I said. "I know it's out of the nineteen fifties but—"

"Hush," Piper broke in. "You want what you want."

"Screw societal expectations," Jewel added.

I let out a quiet laugh, grateful for their understanding, then sobered. "The family I want... Yeah. That didn't work out." I swallowed. Fought to maintain my composure. I was wrung out and so tired of crying.

"I know, hon." Piper stopped her tidying to rub my arm. "He's blind."

"Men are stupid," Jewel added with emphasis.

"You'd think Knox would be wiser since he's older and all..." Piper said.

"Nope," I said, emphasizing the *p* sound.

"He's still a male." Jewel sounded bored with her own pronouncement.

"You like men just fine as long as they're short-term," Piper told her.

"I don't like men when they crush my bestie's heart."

My attempt at a laugh came out shaky. "Me neither."

"So...what are you going to do? You can't keep working for Knox, can you?" Piper asked.

Closing my eyes tight against the physical pain the question caused in my chest, I tried to imagine living at Knox's again, caring for Juniper but not sleeping in his bed. *Just* being the nanny. Loving on his daughter. Avoiding him on my days off.

There was no way I could go back to how it had been, to the sex, the sleeping together, the waking up together.

We'd fallen into it before, and stupid me, even after he'd said we were a secret, even with all the ways he made it clear I was just convenient, a part of me had dared to believe it could go somewhere. Dared to believe my heart could get it right for once.

That was *my* problem though. He hadn't led me on, had never made promises he couldn't keep. He'd been honest from the get-go. I'd just been wearing blinders.

They were off now.

"If he needs help, I can take care of June until he finds someone else. He has to find someone else fast though."

Jewel hopped down from the counter and wrapped her arms around me, pulled me into her. "I'm so sorry, sweetie."

With a watery laugh that sounded more like despair, I said, "You warned me. I should've listened."

As Piper closed in and joined the hug, Jewel said, "You can't help what you feel. I was just afraid you were *going* to feel."

"And you were right." I swallowed around the gob of emotion in my throat.

"Dammit," she said with a caring smile.

Piper gestured to Taylor to join us, and she did.

"Will you go back to Henry's?" Taylor asked.

"My job there's supposed to be waiting for me," I said. "But no." We stood there with our four foreheads pressed together, arms around each other, as I worked up my courage to say the next bit out loud for the first time. "I'm going to look for another nanny position."

"I love it," Piper said.

"That's a solid plan," Taylor said.

"It feels right." I sniffled. "Righter than teaching or Henry's or anything else."

Jewel was noticeably quiet. I straightened and eyed her.

"What?" I asked.

"You'll be a rad nanny." She looked me in the eye as a partial smile tugged at her lips.

"I hear a but."

"Same thing as before. You care too much. You'll want to make your nanny family your own. I worry you'll get hurt again."

"You're sweet," I said with another sniff.

"I'm not sweet," she huffed. "I'm practical. Another

couple of heartbreaks like this and we'll need a lot of red wine."

Grinning, I said, "I'll start a wine fund with my earnings." I grabbed my almost-empty glass from the counter and held it in front of me. "You girls are the best. Love you bunches."

They clinked their glasses to mine and Jewel replied, "Love you bunches too."

"You're going to be fine," Piper added. "Better than fine."

I took a swallow, then lowered my glass, nodding.

Becoming a nanny for a different family meant opening my heart to more precious babies. I knew I'd fall in love with whatever kids I was lucky enough to care for. Knew it would hurt when I had to say goodbye to those kids and their families. I was reasonably sure, though, that I wouldn't ever get hurt as badly as Knox had hurt me. I knew that because I was pretty damn certain I wouldn't get over this heartbreak any time soon. My heart, where romance was concerned, was out of commission for the foreseeable future. You couldn't break what was already destroyed.

"Yeah," I said on an exhale. "I'm going to be okay."

It was just going to take some time. Maybe a couple of decades.

CHAPTER 32

KNOX

Thanksgiving with my new, extended double family was unlike any Thanksgiving I'd ever experienced. It was how I imagined a Hallmark holiday would be but louder.

The Henrys and Norths—all twenty-two of them, or twenty-four when you counted Juniper and me, plus Drake and Mackenzie's two dogs, Tank and Gunner, and Gabe and Lexie's dog, Saint—had gathered at Seth and Everly's home. It was situated on the lakeshore a few houses up from mine and had been in the family for nearly fifty years. This was where my half-siblings had started their childhood. When they'd moved to Nashville, their grandmother—*my* grandmother, Guinevere Henry—had stayed. This house had served as her full-time home, a summer retreat for the family, and a second home for Holden, who'd preferred high school here in Dragonfly Lake to the large, overcrowded one in Nashville.

Admittedly, with the Henrys and Norths, even this generous four-bedroom home felt cozy and small. The main dining table in the kitchen and the one in the formal dining room had all their leaves in, and chairs and high chairs crowded around them. Both rooms, and the living room in between, had been rowdy, chaotic, and filled with laughter all afternoon.

June and I were still sitting in the dining room with our half of the group after the meal was cleared away and dessert had been devoured. My daughter was out of the high chair, sitting on my lap, spellbound by a clean spoon. Hayden, Chloe, and Eliza were sharing some of the worst parts of being pregnant, eliciting cringes from those of us who hadn't lived through it with them and shudders from those who had.

Unlike last month at Simon's birthday celebration, I was becoming comfortable with everyone, relaxing more with them as well as with my daughter, and starting to feel like I fit in. As the only single guy present, I'd taken some teasing for that. I preferred being teased over the stiffness of my debut any day. If these folks were kidding around with me, their guard was down, which relaxed mine as well. Even though I was the new guy, I no longer felt so conspicuously like the new guy.

I had a bunch to be thankful for, the warmth and welcome from this family second on the list, right below June Bug.

I'd probably clung to Juniper harder than usual for the past three days as I tried to adjust to Quincy being gone. Truth be told, my daughter had been fussy and out of sorts, likely because of Quincy's departure. Maybe also because I was fussy and out of sorts.

We'd get over it eventually, Juniper probably faster than me.

Despite being able to relax with these people who were beginning to feel like family, there was a heaviness in my chest I couldn't shake. The cause of it was no mystery. I ached for Quincy like I'd never thought possible. Like I'd never ached for anyone before. I wanted her flipping me shit as we shared a meal. I wanted her loving on my daughter as much as I did. I wanted her lounging on the sectional near me as we watched a movie or talked. I wanted her in my bed, and it wasn't just because sex with her turned my world upside down. I couldn't sleep well without her, couldn't seem to fall into a deep rest.

"When I was pregnant with Calvin," Eliza said, pointing over her shoulder toward the kitchen where her older son was sitting on Faye's lap and playing with a tow truck, "all I wanted to eat was bologna."

"I'll eat almost anything, but bologna is nasty," Drake said, laughing. "Why bologna?"

Eliza shook her head and made a face. "No idea. I can't eat it at all anymore, but I begged my roommate, Grace, to go on a bologna run in the middle of the night once."

"Knowing Grace, she did it too," Hayden said.

"She sure did. She deserves a medal."

As talk continued, Juniper's body stiffened, and I could tell she was about to dirty her diaper. I picked her up and headed upstairs to Seth's office, where Everly had suggested we store our baby gear and change diapers.

"Definitely time for a change, huh, June Bug?" I said to her as we walked into the quiet room and I got the first hint of baby stench.

I spread her changing pad out on the floor, laid her on top, and bent over her, talking to her, giving her some time to finish going before I stripped her down. As I dug out her plush monkey and gave it to her to keep her hands out of the "work area," someone entered the room behind me. I turned to see who it was and tensed.

"Hey," Cash said, looking down at us, a beer in his hand.

"Did you take a wrong turn?" I asked, trying to figure out why he was here.

He'd said hello earlier, but that was the extent of our inter-action. He'd been in charge of cooking since Everly was a self-professed newbie in the kitchen, and I'd given him a wide berth. I wasn't up for a repeat of the scene at Simon and Faye's house. I'd made a point of finding a spot at the table he wasn't sitting at.

He shook his head, grinned down at Juniper, then reared back as the odor must have hit him.

"Delicate operation. You might want to exit quickly," I said, giving him an out.

"I've smelled worse," he said lightly, which made me look at him a second time. Cash hadn't been light toward me since before he found out we were half-brothers. "Sorry to follow you up here like a stalker. It's not easy to have a private discussion."

"I'm not up for another round," I told him as I undid and folded Juniper's nasty diaper, then cleaned her up.

Cash sat on the edge of the leather love seat. "I wanted to thank you for helping Ava the other day when I texted you."

"It was no problem," I said, caught off guard. "She talked me down a week or two before that. In case you haven't figured it out yet, a writer's brain can be a scary place."

With a chuckle, he said, "I love that woman's brain. It's fascinating, but she was so full of despair, and then I got called away…" The antagonism from the past was missing from his tone.

I relaxed slightly, not yet convinced we were at peace but willing to take any concessions. "I'm betting she let you have it later for contacting me."

"She did." He grinned, and I could see his love for her in his eyes even now. It felt like a knife in my chest, and that made exactly no sense. "We worked it out."

"I don't need details," I said.

"Wouldn't give you any if you asked," he shot back, but there was no bite to our words. He stood, paced toward the desk, and gazed out the window. Just looking at his back, I could tell he'd gone more serious. Tense. He pivoted toward me. "So…I'm sorry I've been an asshole. Ava and I talked a lot about you and your mom, our dad… It's a fucked-up situation that she never told you before, but I can see now that's not your fault. It just took me a bit to get there. So." He cleared his throat. "Anyway. I'm sorry."

With Juniper's fresh diaper in place, I was able to give him my full attention. "Apology accepted." I nodded, a little overcome, a lot relieved. "My mom meant well. I don't want to say anything bad about her, but I would've liked to know you all from the beginning."

"And there were days I begged to be raised as an only child." Cash chuckled. "I imagine it was pretty damn quiet."

"Compared to your life? Like a morgue."

We both smiled, like maybe there was a new chance for us to get along.

"You got that cute little turkey cleaned up yet?" He nodded toward Juniper.

"About as clean as she gets, but now I have to wrestle with this outfit Faye got her."

It was two pieces—a white onesie that said *Little Turkey* and a tutu-type skirt in oranges, golds, and browns—plus the socks June Bug pulled off multiple times a day. I much preferred a one-piece outfit with feet, but when Mimi bought her granddaughter a special outfit for the holiday, I knew enough to dress her in it.

"I don't know if I'd let them put me in something that said *Little Turkey*, Juniper," Cash said. "That might be one of those photos that ends up surfacing at your wedding rehearsal."

Juniper vocalized back to him. Once I had her socks on again, I stood and picked her up. She held out her stuffed monkey to Cash. My brows shot up.

"She doesn't offer the monkey to many people," I told him. "It's her most prized possession."

"Enjoy it while it lasts. One of these days she'll prefer sparkly, expensive things." Cash took the monkey and pressed a kiss to its furry head, eliciting a laugh from my daughter.

"You're probably right." I said to my daughter, "Let's stick with stuffed monkeys for a good long while, okay, June Bug?"

She lifted her toy with a flourish and babbled as if she was proclaiming the stuffed toy her prince, making Cash and me laugh.

"She's gonna be a heartbreaker in no time flat." Going serious again, Cash shrugged and said, "I thought it was a good day to make peace." He held out his hand. "Glad to have you in the family, brother."

A surge of emotions washed over me, good ones—relief being the primary one. Gratitude. For the first time since I'd arrived in town last summer to search out my family, my misgivings and worries about revealing the truth faded away.

"Thanks, Cash," I said, my voice strange as I shifted June to my left side and shook his hand. "June and I look forward to getting to know your peaceful side."

"Hey, you two." Ava appeared in the doorway. "Just making sure my fiancé's behaving. Everything okay? Hi, Junie." She stepped in and squeezed my daughter's hand. Ava held out her arms to see if Juniper wanted to go to her, and June leaned toward her, smiling. I handed her off.

"Everything's good," I said, bending down to pick up the changing pad, the toxic diaper, and the wipes.

Cash palmed Ava's waist and planted a kiss on her lips, then made funny faces at the baby and kissed her nose.

"I need to talk to Knox," Ava said to her fiancé as I packed away all but the dirty diaper.

"Want me to take this cutie downstairs so you can have a few minutes?" Cash asked me.

"Sure," I said, wondering what Ava was so determined to talk to me about that we'd need privacy. There'd be no shortage of people downstairs willing to look after my daughter though. "Be good, Bug," I told Junie.

Ava transferred June to Cash, kissed both of them again, sent them on their way, then turned to me.

"What's going on?" I asked her. "Did you hate the last chapter I sent you?" I'd sent it late last night, managed to string some words together over the past few days while Juniper napped, not ready to confess to Ava I was on my own with childcare. It was admittedly not my best work.

"I haven't had a chance to read it yet, but I won't hate it. Dork. I came up first and foremost to do exactly what I said— make sure Cash was playing nice."

"Did you put him up to apologizing?"

"He saw the light mostly on his own," Ava said, making me laugh. She perched on the love seat, so I pulled the desk chair out and sat.

"Thanks for any part you had in it. That's a weight off my shoulders," I said.

"He's a stubborn one, but I love him. What's this I hear about Quincy not nannying for you anymore?"

There it was. The real reason she wanted to talk. I frowned. I'd mentioned Quincy's leaving in passing at the table, but Ava had been in the other room. I'd made sure of it. She was the only one I'd ever fessed up to about my involvement with my Quincy, the only one who would read more into it than just my nanny moving on. "You have good ears."

"Hayden told me. But I knew something was wrong even before she said anything. You're not yourself today."

"I'm doing okay," I lied. I'd gone to great lengths to be upbeat and holiday-cheerish all afternoon.

She narrowed her eyes at me and crossed her arms. "I don't buy it, but if you don't want to talk about your *feelings*, I get it." She said it like a challenge.

"No feelings to talk about." Another lie. Ava knew it, and I knew it.

"What happened, Knox? I thought she was staying until mid-January."

I looked away, debating whether to open up.

"She decided not to go back to school. She's staying in Dragonfly Lake."

"Because of you?"

I winced. "She used the L word."

"And how did you respond?"

"I told her I couldn't let her throw away her future."

Ava cringed visibly. "I was afraid of that."

"Afraid of what?"

"That you'd push her away." She leaned her head back into the cushion, her eyes closed, as if there was no hope for me.

"You and I talked about it," I reminded her. "The age difference?"

Her eyes popped open. "She changed everything up when she told you her feelings."

"We're still in different life stages, feelings or not."

"You were worried about her missing out on college life. She decided against college life altogether. It sounds like she's not so much in frat-party mode after all."

"I can't let her throw that away for me."

"That's not your decision to make."

"Maybe not, but I don't have to support it or make it easier for her to make that mistake."

"Who's to say it's a mistake, Knox? She might be younger than you, but she's the boss of her life."

I clenched my jaw, unable to argue with that, but still…

"This might be presumptive," Ava said, "but it seems like you're trying to do the same thing your mom did."

I reared my head back. "My mom? What does this have to do with her?"

She leaned forward, her forehead furrowed. "With all due respect, because I suspect she meant well, she made a giant decision when she was pregnant that affected Simon's future and yours."

"Sure. The way she saw it, she sacrificed for my father's sake. Because she knew he'd be happy with Nita, and she didn't want to intrude on their life."

"What if she had let Simon make that decision?" Ava asked quietly.

"He never would've agreed not to have his child in his life," I said without hesitation.

"I think so too." She stared at me as her meaning sank in.

"You think I'm doing the same thing," I said.

"You are."

"You think I should let Quincy quit school before she even starts and work for me full-time."

"I think the school part is Quincy's decision. Whether you employ her is yours."

I sat forward and leaned my elbows on my thighs, trying to argue in my head that my situation was different from my mom's. I couldn't. Not if I was honest.

I growled, burning to argue. "What if she eventually regrets dropping out? Giving up a teaching career? For me?"

Ava put her hand on my forearm, and I met her gaze as she asked, "What if she doesn't? What if Quincy's your one, Knox?"

I swallowed, trying to keep my face blank as I flinched inwardly.

Her expression softened. "Tell me something. Do you love her?"

Running my hands over my face, I let my mind churn over what I already suspected. What I didn't want to face.

"If you didn't, you probably wouldn't be in a knot over her leaving," Ava said.

A knot. That was an understatement. My appetite was off. My sleep was nonexistent. My mood was shit.

I took in a deep, lung-expanding breath and let the admission sink in.

I did.

I loved Quincy.

I let out a halfhearted laugh that sounded more like a scoff.

I loved her spirit and her spunkiness and her take on the world. I loved her with my daughter. I loved her naked and writhing underneath me. I loved her when she fell asleep during a movie. I loved her courage to tell me how she felt and her braveness to be different, make different choices. I loved when she gave me a hard time for being old and stuffy. I just…loved her.

"Yeah," I finally said, my voice wobbling with the weight of the realization. "I do love her."

"I knew it! Knox, this is so great."

"This…" My gut tightened and started churning. "It's not so great."

"What?" she said, her voice pitching high.

"I don't know what to do about it. I think…" The look on Quincy's face before she'd left my house was burned into my mind. "Pretty sure I screwed everything up."

She studied me. "You might have to do some groveling to get her back."

"Groveling how?" I asked, my shoulders sagging more.

"Pay close attention," she said, pulling her legs up on the love seat and getting comfortable. "You'll need to know this for the romance arc in our book anyway, so take notes. You're about to put your heart on the line."

CHAPTER 33

QUINCY

I was more than ready for Thanksgiving to be over.

Unfortunately the annual Dragonfly Lake holiday tree-lighting ceremony was starting in a few minutes, and our family never missed it, so I was stuck.

"You hangin' in?" my brother Ryan asked me privately, our winter coats rustling against each other as he sat next to me on the stone landscaping border. This had been our regular spot for this event since I was in single digits, first with my mom and now with Cynthia and our younger siblings.

To convince him, I wound my arm through his, smiled, and said, "Yeah. Mulled wine's my new favorite."

He held his paper cup of the same up for a clinkless toast, and we both took a drink of the spiced beverage.

Normally I loved this event. I still had memories of the four of us—my mom, my dad, Ryan, and me—making our own cocoa, pouring it into a large thermos, and taking it to the town square.

These days, there were local vendors who sold cocoa,

coffee, hot toddies, hot buttered rum, mulled wine, and more to drink, plus candied apples, fudge, popcorn, and other sweets. The treats alone were enough to lure even a recluse out of the house.

I'd had no appetite for three days, so the treats weren't a factor this year. In fact, I'd considered begging off and heading to my apartment, knowing my roomies would be here on the square along with the rest of the town, and I'd have the place to myself. My family would have none of that though. Between Molly's over-the-top excitement, Cynthia's concerned gaze on me, and Ryan's determination to keep my mood up, there would be too many questions if I didn't participate.

The day hadn't been a bad one. There were admittedly a lot of positives.

Instead of attempting to cook a feast as Cynthia and I normally did—and knocking skulls repeatedly as we shared the kitchen—she and I had agreed to order a precooked dinner from Country Market. Best decision ever. The food was good, the convenience was priceless, and the admission that neither of us was up for being Rachael Ray—or Reba Yates—at the holidays was sanity saving.

After the meal, when the three youngest had left the table, I'd broken my news to Ryan, Cynthia, and my dad. Well, some of my news—that I'd decided not to go to school, after all. Though my dad tried to be supportive and positive, I could tell he was disappointed—again. I was surer than ever it was the right move for me, so I'd sat up taller and explained my plans to become a nanny. Ryan had volunteered to help me set up my official business in the coming weeks, and my dad had started to come around and support the idea.

Later, as Cynthia and I had washed dishes while everyone else watched a football game, I'd stepped out of my comfort zone in the spirit of our new agreement and confided about the personal aspects of leaving my job for Knox. I'd been stunned when she was sympathetic and even disappointed on my behalf.

Baby steps, right?

I had to admit it felt good. So much better than bickering or veiled barbs.

In spite of my supportive family, as the square filled up around the live tree whose branches were laden with large, colorful balls and bows, the physical ache in my chest tightened.

Three days had passed since I'd seen Knox or Juniper. I was staggering from the two separate losses, plus a third one —the future I'd I wanted more than anything. One day, I hoped like hell I'd get it through my head that choosing a future that relied on another person never worked out for me.

As I blindly looked out at the crowd, my thoughts veered to Knox and Junie. Without making a conscious decision, I realized I was scanning the crowd, looking for them. I doubted they were here though. Juniper's bedtime was soon, and it was cold. She was too young to remember this. Knox would likely stay in tonight, and her tree lighting debut would be next year, when she was one.

I slammed my eyes shut on the pain that thought brought. She'd be one, likely walking, maybe starting to talk, and I'd have missed out on twelve months of her life. More than half of it.

"I'm…I think I'm gonna go home—"

Ryan squeezed me to his side and kept his big-brother arm there before I could finish the sentence. "Stay with me. Please? It's starting soon. Look."

Mayor Constantine and some of the event organizers were buzzing around in the gazebo where the mic was set up. High-school band members were taking their places between the gazebo and the forty-foot-tall, decked-out pine tree.

Ryan was still watching me, giving me a weird look as if

the stakes were high instead of just the average small-town tree-lighting ceremony. I checked his cup to see if maybe he had more than a mulled wine in there, but it looked just like mine and was still half-full.

Brayden came bouncing over to us, his eyes sparkling with holiday joy I envied. I forced a smile and extended my arm for a hug.

"Can I try a sip of your wine?" he asked.

I tilted my head. "Where's your cocoa?"

"Gone."

Ryan leaned forward to size him up. "Hey, I already gave you two sips of my wine."

"It's good," Brayden insisted, all grins, as if he knew he was busted.

"Our baby brother, the lush," I said, giving him an affectionate shove in the chest. "Not on my watch."

"Y'all are mean," he said with an exaggerated drawl. His attention diverted to someone on the other side of us. "Mom, can I go hang out with Joey and Matt? They're right over there."

As Cynthia and our dad negotiated Brayden's limits and privileges for the evening, I peered up at the windows of my apartment. They were dark, promising peace. Though the din of the crowd would be audible, it would be muffled. Background noise. Which, come to think of it, would leave me way too alone with my thoughts.

I sighed, resigned, and took another sip of wine. "Y'all are mean," I muttered without conviction to Ryan as I leaned my head on his upper arm, turning my attention back to the gazebo…and promptly popped it back up straight so I could see.

Was that Knox? In the gazebo? Talking to the mayor?

"What…" I said it to myself, but Ryan was tuned in. I could feel his gaze locked on me. I kept my own eyes glued to the gazebo, waiting for a better look at the man talking to the mayor. He was tall, wearing a black winter hat that showed a hint of dark hair. Then Mayor Constantine shifted and…

That was Knox.

My heart thundered at the first glimpse of him in three and a half days. "What's he doing?"

Mayor Constantine picked up the microphone and tapped on it, the sound echoing through the crowded square as gradually people noticed him and shushed those around them.

"Good evening," he said. "Happy Thanksgiving!"

The crowd returned the greeting. It became quieter but nowhere close to silent as he spoke. "Before we get started, I'm going to hand over the mic to one of our own. He says he'd like to clear some things up."

As I tried to puzzle out what was going on, Ryan stood up next to me. Knox took the microphone.

"Hello, everyone." Knox was so intimately familiar that my heart ached.

The crowd broke out into a collective chatter as people wondered out loud what was going on.

When he said, "My name is Knox Breckenridge," everyone went silent, their attention locked on him.

"I'm relatively new here, but you might've seen my name mentioned a few hundred times if you follow the Tattler." He paused as laughter filtered through the crowd.

"I'll only take a couple of minutes of your time, I promise. Since I've become a regular subject on the town app, I'm hoping to clarify some things," Knox continued. "I came to Dragonfly Lake a few months ago for a vacation, fell in love with this small town, bought a house, and never left."

I didn't blink, waiting to see where he was going.

"That's the short version," he continued, then let out an endearing nervous laugh. "I left out a few minor details…"

There was more laughter from the masses, the warm, inclusive, laughing-with-him type.

"For example, you might have heard I crashed into the

beloved, reputable Henry family. Yep, I'm that guy. I appeared out of nowhere, looking to connect with the father I never knew and the half-brothers and -sisters I'd only just found out about. Way to make an entrance to my new hometown, huh?"

More laughter rang out, and I found myself enthralled by everything he said, smiling even though my heart was still cracked wide open.

"Lucky for me, the Henrys are some incredible, open-minded people, and they welcomed me with open arms. Well"—he looked to the side of the gazebo, brows raised, smile crawling across his face, and I spotted Cash, Seth, Holden, and Ava, who was holding a bundled-up Juniper in her arms—"it took a blood test and some heated discussions, but *then* they welcomed me with open arms."

The three Henry brothers grinned and nodded as if to say, "Damn straight."

"In hindsight, maybe that wasn't the best way to introduce myself to you all," Knox said, indicating the crowd as a whole. He shrugged. "That was small potatoes though, because then, before a single full day could pass, I found myself in the plot of a different movie. Ever heard of an old one called *Three Men and a Baby*? That was suddenly my life, except there was only one man and a baby, and that man was me." He turned and looked over at Juniper, the smile on his face so full of adoration and love that I could see it from my spot fifty feet away.

"The day my ex left the baby girl I didn't know about in my SUV turned out to be the luckiest day of my life. And yes, for those keeping track, we're now on the second paternity test of this short story."

He lowered the microphone and shook his head, laughing to himself as everyone laughed with him again—myself included, though my laughter came through tear-filled eyes.

"Juniper wasn't the only reason that Wednesday in

October was the best day of my life," he said, his tone going serious.

Knox peered out at the crowd, zeroing in on our area in front of the flower bed to the left of the Christmas tree. Movement from Ryan, next to me, caught my eye, and I realized he was still standing, his phone flashlight on, and was waving it from side to side. Knox noticed him too and nodded.

I shot a confused look up at my brother, but he very deliberately did not look at me as he lowered his arm, sat back down, and kept his attention on Knox.

"You see, that day, not only did I meet my daughter but I met a girl."

My heart skipped at least three beats as I stared at him across the distance, afraid to move, afraid to breathe.

"When Quincy entered the scene and showed me how to care for my daughter, I went on sheer instinct and did the only thing I could think to do. I begged her to stay and be a nanny for the baby." Knox stood at the edge of the gazebo, his attention focused on me, our gazes locked in spite of the hundreds of people in between us. "Here's where it gets controversial—again." He emphasized the last word.

I laughed with everyone else, and several tears plunged over my lids and dripped down my cheeks. I swiped them away and felt my brother's supportive arm around me.

"I fell in love with my daughter's nanny."

I gasped, and my hands flew to my face, emotion pouring out of me in a mix of laughter and tears. I realized I'd stood, not caring about the hushed comments around me, barely registering Cynthia's heartfelt, "Aww."

Still staring at me, Knox continued, "That's right, people. She's more than a decade younger than me. My former employee. I know you might be thinking I'm a terrible person. Or I'm a spotlight-loving attention hog. Or I don't have the sense God gave a goose."

Instead of laughter, the crowd was quiet, as if waiting to

hear what he'd say next—just like me. He studied the ground in front of him for a few seconds before going on.

"You'd be right about that last part. I might be book smart, but I'm here to admit, in front of God and all you people of this amazing town, I was dumber than a box of rocks when it came to Quincy. I was worried about what people would say. Worried I was too old for her, that I'd hold her back if we were together." He let out a self-effacing laugh. Let several more seconds pass. Then he straightened and looked at me again. "Quincy, I'm sorry I screwed up. I hope you'll accept this as the heartfelt groveling you deserve and that you'll give me another chance."

I was already on my way toward him, across the throng of people, weaving my way, not seeing anyone else as I went, completely zeroed in on the man I loved. The man standing in that lit-up gazebo, baring his heart and soul. For me.

It seemed like forever before he met me just outside of the gazebo, having handed the mic back to the mayor, who made a comment about how hard it was to follow that scene. I barely noticed any of it as I rushed to get to Knox.

As soon as I made it through the crowd, I ran the last few steps to him and jumped into his waiting arms. I never doubted for a second that he'd catch me. Wrapping my legs around him, I kissed him as if my life and my happiness depended on it. On him.

A couple of seconds later, I noticed the applause, the whistles, the cheers coming from the entirety of my little town. *Our* little town.

Overcome, with tears streaming down my face, I pulled back enough to look in his beautiful, love-filled blue eyes.

"Knox," I breathed out, grinning bigger than I'd ever grinned in my life.

He stared down at me, so familiar, so good-looking, so perfect for me that my toes curled in my boots. "I love you, Quincy."

"I love you too. So much."

We kissed again as the mayor launched into the tree-lighting ceremony, diverting attention from us, introducing the band and the resident of honor who had the privilege of hitting the big switch to turn on the lights. I didn't pay attention to any of it.

Eventually I noticed someone hovering close by: Ava. With Juniper.

"Oh," I said, tearing up again. "Come here, Junie Bee."

I took the subdued baby girl from Ava, who beamed at me. "Another stubborn male pulls his head out," she joked. "I'm so happy for you two."

"Three," I said, then kissed Juniper's cheek and pulled her into Knox and me.

"Thanks for keeping her, Ava," Knox said.

"Anytime. You guys have a memorable night," she said, then hurried off to Cash's waiting arms.

Juniper leaned her tired head on my shoulder as Knox took my free hand.

"Come home with us," he said. "We don't need a nanny. We just need you."

"Hmm." I pretended to turn over my options. "Will I have my own bedroom?"

"Not a chance," he said, his voice going low, sexy, irresistible.

As the crowd counted down to zero and the tree's thousands of lights twinkled on, I leaned into him, soaking in the feelings. For so many years, I'd been searching for a place that felt like home. I finally found it just when I'd least expected it.

It was here. *This* was it. Knox and Juniper were it for me.

EPILOGUE

QUINCY

Christmas Eve had arrived, and my heart was full.

I'd never understood that saying before. Now I knew it was a legit physical sensation where you had so much joy inside of you your heart felt as if it was bursting with sparkles and overflowing with gratitude.

The best news was that Knox's ex had signed a voluntary surrender of parental rights. This little girl in my arms was his, and we no longer had to worry about Gina surfacing and demanding time with her. It was the best Christmas present in the history of Christmas presents. I would never understand the woman who gave birth to this beautiful girl, and maybe her mental health diagnoses were to blame, but I was grateful that Knox had closure.

Even before that news, Knox and I had planned a Christmas Eve party and invited everyone we loved. Now we just had extra to celebrate.

We'd decorated the house until it brimmed with holiday beauty, with evergreen garland, silver bows, white bulbs, and twinkle lights everywhere. The tree was fourteen feet tall, reaching to the ceiling at that end of the living room, and we'd loaded its branches down with ornaments. Underneath the evergreen was a bounty of wrapped packages, a good half of them for the baby girl who likely wouldn't remember them anyway. We couldn't help ourselves.

I was standing by the tree at Juniper's insistence—she was obsessed with the reflections of the lights in the glass bulbs and loved watching them blink slowly on then off.

"Hey, honey." My dad came up beside me. "Hi, Junie Bee." His voice got ridiculously adorable when he spoke to Juniper.

"Hi, Dad. Having fun?"

"It's been a great night, hasn't it? All three of your younger siblings have behaved, gotten along even. Cynthia and Faye hit it off as if they've known each other for years. Your friends are a pleasure to talk to. Thanks for inviting us."

"Of course," I said. "But be honest. What you like most is the food."

"Truth? The olive balls and the spiral-cut glazed ham are the best things I've eaten in recent memory. I could live on them alone."

"If there were leftovers, I'd give you some," I said, laughing. "Wouldn't we, Junie?"

"We're getting ready to leave, but I saw you and this cutie pie alone and wanted to tell you how proud I am of you."

"Um, thanks, but we had the food catered in. I can't take any credit other than the extensive tasting we had to do."

"You poor girl." He laughed. "I meant in general. This." He looked around us, becoming entirely serious. "The life you're making for yourself."

"Thanks, Dad." I wasn't sure if you could call it that since Knox and I had only been together a little over a month, but whatever it was, I'd never been happier.

Grasping my upper arm gently and pulling me to face him more fully, he said, "Cynthia pointed out that, all these years,

I might've made you feel pressured to go back to school, and I suppose she's right."

I nodded, surprised by the seriousness of the topic in the middle of the festivities.

"All I've ever wanted for you, Quincy, is a happy, fulfilling life. Maybe I thought school could help you find that." He shook his head. "What's important is that you find *your* path. The Quincy path. Only you can say what that is, but from where I'm standing, it looks an awful lot like you've found it, daughter of mine."

I smiled, a little choked up. "Knox makes me happy, Dad. Juniper makes me happy."

"It's obvious. And that makes *me* happy." He kissed the top of my head and squeezed my shoulder. "Good going, Quincy."

I laughed, elated...at his long-awaited credit as much as with my current life situation. "Thanks."

"I love you, dear girl."

"Love you too, Dad."

He hugged Juniper and me. "We'll see you tomorrow for dinner, right?"

"Absolutely." We planned to spend Christmas morning with the Norths and Henrys, then head to my parents' in the late afternoon. It'd be a busy but full holiday for us, in the best possible way.

With June still in my arms, I got my family's coats, met them at the door, and hugged Cynthia, Hannah, Molly, and Brayden. Knox joined us, sliding his arm around me.

"Thanks for coming," he told my family as he hugged them too.

"Thank you for having us. This has been a delight," Cynthia said as she wove her arm through my dad's.

"You two have a good night." My dad sent Knox a weighty look that didn't make sense to me, but then he and

Knox had spent time out on the deck together earlier, monitoring the snow that had begun coming down lightly.

Knox's reply was a smile and a nervous nod.

In the past month, we'd had dinner with my family three times, allowing them to get to know Knox and vice versa. Cynthia and I had truly managed to smooth things out. Though we weren't best friends, the tension had dissipated, and we were gradually getting to know each other on a deeper level.

Brayden and Molly adored Knox. Hannah doted on Juniper. And my dad seemed content to have us all get along. Their acceptance of the man I loved, plus my improving relationship with my stepmom, made me feel like I finally fit into the family.

Once we shut the door, Knox put his arm around me again, kissed my temple, and said, "A little over an hour till I get you alone."

I laughed, noting the way my body responded to his suggestiveness. "This is our party and our friends. You're supposed to enjoy every second of it."

"Then you shouldn't have worn that dress." He breathed the words into my ear.

The sensation and the words were so hot that I wondered if there was a way to empty the house in the next thirty seconds so he could peel said dress off me. It was a simple dark green sequined thing that ended at my upper thighs and hugged my body just enough.

"A little over an hour," I said. "In the meantime, this one is ready for her bedtime bottle." Juniper was resting her head on my shoulder, her thumb in her mouth, lids starting to droop.

"I'll get her ready for bed. I promised Faye she could give her the bottle."

As if she had baby-bedtime radar, Faye scrambled happily over to us. "Is it time for bed for this princess?"

Laughing, I kissed the baby and handed her over and watched Faye and Knox head down the hall toward Junie's room.

Piper, Hayden, Taylor, and Jewel were huddled together on one side of the sectional, engrossed in whatever they were discussing. Based on the way Hayden's gaze ping-ponged between Piper and Jewel, my curiosity was piqued. I headed over to them and sat on the ottoman next to Hayden.

"What's going on?" I asked.

Jewel's eyebrows rose as she said, "Alex is coming home."

My mind needed a few seconds to catch up. Alex... One glance at Taylor's face filled in the blanks. "Worth?"

"The one and only," Jewel said.

Piper, who sat between Jewel and Taylor, laced her hand with Taylor's. Taylor's creamy skin looked paler than usual, and she chewed on her lower lip.

"Are you...okay with that?" I asked Taylor.

Her gaze bounced up to mine. "Of course."

Alex Worth was the same age as Jewel, the same age Taylor's brother would be if he hadn't been killed in combat several months ago. Tragically, Alex had been piloting the army helicopter when it came under attack. From what I'd heard, Alex had managed to heroically land it, but his best friend, Vance Elliott, had lost his life.

Hayden patted Taylor's knee sympathetically, and we all sat there without saying anything.

"I'm going to get a glass of water," Taylor said. She flashed us a smile that was forced, closer to a grimace, as she stood and rushed off to the kitchen.

Eyeing her sympathetically, Hayden said, "Me too. I'll make sure she's okay." She went after Taylor, leaving the three of us there, stumbling for what to say.

"That's going to bring everything back for her, right?" I asked.

Piper and Jewel exchanged a meaningful glance. "I suspect it's a whole lot messier than that," Jewel said.

Piper leaned forward. "Years ago, Taylor admitted she had a crush on him." Her voice was barely audible with the party going on around us.

"On Alex?" I tried to wrap my head around that when both of my friends nodded.

Alex Worth was a jock, outgoing, good-looking, popular. Taylor's brother's best friend. Taylor was a certified genius, shy, and quiet. She seemed like the type who'd choose brains over looks every day. Not to say Alex wasn't smart, but no one was smart on Taylor's level.

"Do you think she's still crushing?" I asked.

"No idea," Piper said. "I mean, Alex is a hero—that's absolutely not in question—but her brother… How do you even process something like that? I'm still trying to accept that Vance is gone and he's only my cousin."

Jewel was leaning forward too as we all tried to imagine how Alex's return would affect their cousin.

"You guys can stop talking about me now." Taylor leaned her head between Piper and Jewel from behind the sectional, startling all three of us.

"We're just worried about you," Piper said.

"I'll be fine." Taylor flashed another attempt at a smile. "But I'm going to go home now. This has been fun. Thank you for inviting me, Quincy."

"Of course. I'm so glad you made it." I stood to hug her and held on a couple of extra seconds, knowing she must be going through so much. "Merry Christmas."

"Merry Christmas."

Jewel and Piper both hugged her as well and made sure she didn't want company. She assured them she didn't.

We'd barely sat down again when a familiar voice rang out from the door.

"Hey, Seth," my brother Ryan said as he came inside.

"Cash."

I stood again, grinning.

"I'm going out for some fresh air," Jewel said. Something about her tone caught my attention. It wasn't friendly.

I glanced at Piper, who shrugged. "Too many people?"

"Maybe that's it." I doubted that was it. Jewel was medium extroverted and worked in crowds of people every weekend. I glanced over my shoulder toward the door to the deck just as she reached it. She shot a look toward the kitchen, toward my brother, that I couldn't quite read. It wasn't friendly.

I tried to think back to whether there'd been tension between them before, but I couldn't even remember the last time they'd seen each other. It'd been years, as far as I knew. Weird. Maybe I was imagining it.

Instead of puzzling over it for another second, I went to greet my brother, who was shaking Knox's hand.

"Quincy," Ryan said as I came up beside him, tripping over my own feet and laughing at myself. "Have you been over-served at your own party?"

I laughed and threw my arms around him. "Not even close. Thank you for coming."

Now that he was here, my evening was complete. All the people we cared about most had shown up: Knox's dad and Faye, Knox's half-siblings and their significant others, my closest friends, a couple of the single dads from Knox's group, everyone in my family.

I didn't know how the night could get any better.

KNOX

Quincy was everything I could ever want.

Not only was she the best mother a child could have, but

it turned out she could host a heck of a party. I'd never been much of a party-throwing type, but with her in my life, I suspected I'd want to live differently, be more social, celebrate the little things more often. And the big things.

My pulse sped up at that thought.

As I turned out all the lights except the tree and the twinklers, casting the living room and kitchen in a cozy warmth, I added to the list of things I loved about Quincy. She was full of joy and sunshine, loved to laugh, didn't take herself too seriously, and the way she'd worn that little dress tonight… A low growl rumbled out of me at the memory. What the holy hell had I done to have such a gorgeous woman fall in love with me?

If I didn't have detailed plans for the rest of the night, I'd be in the bedroom with her, peeling that dress off and loving the body beneath it. The loving-her-body part would have to wait just a little longer.

I'd shed my khakis and button-down and pulled on my flannel pj pants and a sweatshirt, then checked on Juniper, who was sleeping soundly.

The last of our guests—Seth, Everly, Cash, and Ava—had gone home nearly an hour ago after insisting on helping us clean. My dad, Faye, Hayden, Zane, and Harrison had left earlier so they could make the drive back to Nashville before the snowfall became heavier.

There'd been no tension tonight, not with Cash or anyone else in my new family. There'd been only love, teasing, laughter, and goodwill. Everyone we'd invited mixed well, from Max and Chance to Quincy's younger siblings to everyone in between. The holiday spirit had been a tangible presence in our home. I couldn't remember ever feeling so blessed.

I wasn't done with this night yet, not even close. I had plans, but as I peered out the door to the deck, I was mentally pivoting.

The snow was coming down in large, beautiful flakes now.

The ground was covered, though it wasn't yet sticking to the deck. The night sky was lightened by the white reflection and the strings of lights along the deck railing.

In light of my altered plans, I shoved my feet into my boots, went out onto the deck, and moved the welcome mat out by the railing. As I glanced up to the sky, the effect of billions of flakes coming at me was mesmerizing. Magical. Just as I'd hoped.

I hurried back inside and found Quincy's boot slippers and puffy jacket. When she emerged from our room, she wore a thermal pajama set with polar bears wearing Santa hats. There was supposed to be nothing sexy about them, but her wearing them? My blood was stirred.

"I thought we were going to cuddle on the couch and look at the tree?" she said when I held up her jacket.

"Change of plans. You have to see this snow. It's magical."

Without questioning, she spun her back to me and let me slide her coat on. I pointed at her boots, and she stuffed her feet in, then faced me with a "what now?" look.

I picked her up bridal style, carried her out to the mat, and set her down.

With her pretty eyes looking up at the heavens, she let out an awed gasp.

"It's breathtaking," she said, holding her hands out to her sides as if trying to catch all the flakes. "Like a snow globe."

Instead of looking upward, I couldn't take my gaze off Quincy. As she did a slow half circle, her neck craned back to take it all in, I laced both our hands together. Her pretty blue-green eyes sparkled. Her expression was full of wonder, childlike, and that was just one of the two billion things I loved about her.

"I love you, Quincy." The words burst out of me in a cloud of steam.

She lowered her gaze to meet mine. "I love you too. And you were right. This is absolutely magical."

"Good." Still holding her hands, I lowered myself to one knee, then dug in my pocket for the box. My hands shook as I opened the top, removed the cushion-cut diamond engagement ring, and held it up among the falling snowflakes.

Quincy's eyes went wide, and her smile morphed to a gape. A few strands of her blond hair blew in the breeze as her cheeks pinkened from the cold. All the love in me gathered in my chest like a physical explosion waiting to happen. I had to work to swallow.

"Quincy Yates, will you marry me?"

With a squealing giggle, she rushed into me, throwing her arms around me, nearly knocking me backward onto the wet deck. I wrapped my arms around her and held on for all I was worth, not caring that my pants were already getting wet in the knee.

"Oh, my God," she said into the side of my head. "Yes. Yes! Yes, I'll marry you, Knox. I'll marry you right now if you want."

I stood, afraid I'd drop the ring.

Bouncing up and down on her feet, she turned her attention to the ring and held out her left hand.

Still shaking, I grasped her hand and slid the ring on her finger. As soon as it was all the way on, a rightness, a contentment washed over me unlike anything I'd ever experienced.

"It's perfect," she whispered. "I love it. I love you."

When she looked back up at me, tears filled her eyes, happy tears.

"I love you more," I said, grinning hard.

"Prove it." This was what we'd started saying to each other the past few weeks, like a game. Our usual way to resolve it was to take it to the bedroom and set about proving ourselves. Proving our love. "But not out here."

We both laughed, then our lips found each other's for a soul-connecting kiss. Not breaking contact, I lifted her off the deck until her legs wrapped around me. My hands slid down to her ass to hold her, and, still kissing her, I turned to rest the backs of my fingers against the railing, shielding her from the wet surface.

When we paused for air, I said, "One more question for you. Will you become Juniper's mom? Make it official by adopting her?"

Quincy's tears spilled over the rims of her eyes. "Yes! Of course I will. In a heartbeat. I love that baby girl as if I gave birth to her myself."

"I know you do."

"How soon can we do that?"

"I'm not sure, but having Gina's forms will help. I had an idea in the meantime though."

"Yeah?"

"How would you feel if we started making more babies right away?"

"You want more babies?" she asked, her teary eyes sparkling as I'd hoped.

"With you I do."

With an audible outburst of happiness, she lunged into me for another kiss. When she pulled away, she asked, "And you want to start right now?"

"Hell yes. This 'old dude' isn't getting any younger, you know."

She laughed. "Neither am I. I am, however, getting wetter, and I mean that in an urgent, nondirty way. My butt is soaking wet and cold."

I lifted her away from the railing, pulling her softness against my erection. "Let's go in and get those wet pants off. I'm just the guy to warm you up from the inside out. Tonight and every night after, baby making or not."

"Tonight and every night after," she repeated. "I can't wait for you to prove it. For the rest of our lives."

BONUS EPILOGUE

Two years later, Thanksgiving Day

KNOX

"Come here, baby girl," Quincy said as she helped two-and-a-half-year-old Juniper out of her car seat.

"I not a baby, mama."

"You'll still be my baby even when you're twenty."

I grinned at the familiar exchange between the two as I grabbed the gear and our contribution to the meal and Quincy hoisted our daughter up into her arms, but I was preoccupied.

Today would be a memorable one. My father, Simon, and his wife, Faye, were hosting the entire Henry-North clan for Thanksgiving in their brand-spanking-new lake house.

In the two years since I'd moved to Dragonfly Lake, we'd all become a close-knit family who gathered at least one Sunday a month for dinner at Faye and my dad's in Nashville. So there would be teasing, bullshitting, and sharing a holiday meal, all with an underlying love and respect for each other that surpassed even my wildest dreams of what a big family could be like.

But…

There would be babies.

So many babies, including Cole and Sierra's newborn daughter, Oakley.

Quincy and I had been trying to get pregnant since our wedding night a year and a half ago. Giving it our all, if I did say so myself.

At the one-year mark, nervous that maybe my age was the problem, I'd had testing done. To my relief, everything had come back okay, but we still weren't knocked up.

Quincy had an appointment in two weeks to see if there was a physical reason for our struggles on her side. I knew she was nervous, afraid of what might be discovered.

With all the babies the Henrys and Norths had popped out, today would be like salt in the wound.

We walked toward the front door of the sprawling house on the shore, apparently among the first to arrive judging by the lack of cars—not a surprise at all since Quincy insisted on getting here early, as usual. I put an arm around her to steady her and her thirty-pound Juniper load as we ascended the three steps to the front door.

"You doing okay?" I asked my wife, knowing full well what her answer would be.

"Of course. This place is so Faye, isn't it?"

The house was a farmhouse-style two-story with six bedrooms, the largest dining room I'd ever seen, and an expansive patio on the lakeside. We'd visited last weekend, when they'd officially taken possession of the newly constructed home.

Neither Faye nor my father was the showy type, but they'd decided they wanted a second home on Dragonfly Lake so they'd have headquarters near their North grandchildren in Nashville and their Henry ones here. Though this one would be used more in summer, Faye had insisted on hosting Thanksgiving to break it in.

"Mimi," Juniper said at the mention of Faye, her eyes lit up as the door opened to us. "Mimiii! Papaaa!"

My dad greeted us warmly while Faye took June and showered her with kisses, making me smile as it always did.

Cash, Ava, and their eight-month-old daughter, Bronte, were in the open kitchen, the chef having volunteered to assist with the meal as he frequently did. He and Faye worked well together in the kitchen, with him bowing to her matriarch status and her respecting his food expertise in turn.

"Hey, you three," Ava said, fatigue dulling her eyes. I knew Bronte still wasn't sleeping through the night, and Ava and I had just come off a book release a few days ago and all the work that had entailed.

Quincy hugged Ava and kissed Bronte, then Ava carried Bronte to a playpen in the adjacent great room and lowered her into it. She whirled around and looked at me expectantly. "Did you see?"

"See what?" I asked as I set two bottles of wine on the counter.

"Our highest rankings yet on every one of the stores," she said, beaming.

"The new book?" I asked, realizing I hadn't thought to stalk the rankings since last night. We'd had Thanksgiving brunch with Quincy's family this morning, and my mind had been on anything but work. When Ava nodded enthusiastically and recited some of our book's numbers, I let out a whoop.

Quincy hugged me, then Ava, then my dad high-fived me, and Cash paused to give me a fist bump.

"Well deserved," Faye said as she pulled something out of the oven.

Behind us, the door opened to a bluster of people. I

glanced nervously at Quincy. She plastered on a big, happy smile as Drake hollered, "We're here. Party can start now."

He ushered in Mackenzie, who was six months pregnant with twin boys and looked like walking was uncomfortable. "Hey, everyone," Mackenzie said, managing a grin that looked genuine.

Greetings were returned, and then Seth and Everly entered, with three-month-old Beckham in Everly's arms, his eyes wide as he took in what was verging on a crowd.

Another glance at my wife revealed nothing except a smile, but I knew underneath that pretty smile there was sadness that we didn't have a sibling for Juniper yet.

"Heavens," Faye said as she deserted her post in the kitchen and rushed to hug the four adults, patted Mackenzie's bulging belly, and then extended her arms toward her youngest grandson.

"Forget the food," my dad said jovially. "The grandbaby parade is in full force."

With Beckham in her arms, Faye turned toward the kitchen with an apologetic expression.

Cash waved her off. "I got this. Love on your babies."

Holden and Chloe and their almost-two-year-old daughter, Sutton, were next, along with Hayden, Zane, and Harrison, who was three. The noise level increased at least tenfold when the littles who could walk screeched toward their Mimi and Papa and aunts and uncles.

My wife, bless her gorgeous heart, soldiered on and put herself in the middle of all of it, doling out hugs and kisses and high fives to everyone, and I joined in. It'd been a long time since I'd felt like an outsider, but I still relished being a part of this.

There was a lull in the arrivals, but that was the only kind of lull, as the great room, kitchen, and dining rooms filled with people and noise. Juniper had followed Harrison and

Sutton to the toy bin in the corner of the great room. The trio was already pulling out books, cars, and stuffed animals.

The adults were helping themselves to beverages and the appetizers Hayden had set out on the island.

Over the next ten minutes, Gabe, Lexie, and three-year-old Wyatt showed up, and then Mason, Eliza, and their kids—Calvin, who was seven, Jasper, three, and Emery Rose, nine months old—made their not-so-quiet entrance. There were more hugs and greetings and squeals to add to the crazy but incredible chaos.

I happened to be standing next to Zane and watching my wife across the room when the door opened again. I knew who it was without looking, since Sierra, Cole, and their newborn were the only ones who hadn't arrived yet.

I was certain everyone in the room missed it except me: when Cole stepped inside with their daughter, Quincy's lids lowered for a second longer than a blink, as if she was steeling herself.

My gut tightened into a knot as I wondered futilely yet again why we hadn't been blessed with our own pregnancy. As much as I wanted another child, I knew Quincy's yearning was even stronger. As she'd confided to me a week and a half ago after another appearance of her period, having a baby was her number one goal in life. But it seemed to be the one thing she couldn't have.

I wanted more than anything to give her that, to put a baby in her womb. I'd never felt so fucking powerless in my life.

Joining her at Cole's side to admire his and Sierra's daughter, I wrapped an arm around Quincy. Once she'd fawned over Oakley, she looked up at me and flashed a smile that didn't quite hide her sadness. All I could do was hold on to her, so that's what I did.

————

QUINCY

I had no reason to feel melancholy. None.

I was surrounded by so many people I loved and who loved me. This extra-large double family truly was a blessing I sometimes couldn't believe I'd lucked my way into.

And my own family… Cynthia and I had fully buried the hatchet, and I could even say I enjoyed spending time with her now. Brunch earlier at Ryan's, with the Yates side, had been the best holiday I'd had with my immediate family since losing my mom.

Then there was Knox and Juniper, the loves of my life. My God, I was so stinking lucky to have them. How could I be sad about not having more children? How selfish was I?

But sitting here after a gigantic, plentiful, delicious meal, with Knox's arm around me, Juniper in one of the bedrooms napping, and the rest of the family in clusters around the television, I couldn't help it. My heart hurt so much I felt a little light-headed and sick at my stomach.

We were all focused on the TV, watching the holiday special episode of *Historical Homes*, the cable show Sierra had been a part of for several years. This was her last episode, as she'd resigned from the weekly show once she'd become pregnant. Her producer had convinced her to come back as soon as Oakley was born to film the idea that had been tossed around for the past couple of years—a holiday special that showcased some of Sierra's residential remodeling projects that Hayden had decorated for the season.

The two made an unbeatable team. Everyone had oohed and aahed and complimented Sierra and Hayden throughout the show, which had just concluded.

As I glanced around, I couldn't help noting all the babies. So many babies. Most of them tucked in tight with their parents, creating clusters of three and four, but a couple upstairs, napping in cribs that Faye had ensured were in place and assembled first thing. Drake was adorable and super attentive to pregnant Mackenzie, jumping up and retrieving whatever she needed, just like I knew Knox would if my abdomen were ever to be bulging with a baby.

Chloe came up beside the sofa I was sitting on and whispered in my ear to come with her. I had no idea where she was leading me, but with a squeeze of Knox's leg, I followed her.

She wound her arm through mine and led me away from the masses and up the stairs to the second floor, where Juniper and Sutton were sleeping in separate rooms. At first I thought she wanted to peek in on the kids, but she led me to the bathroom, tugged me inside, and closed the door.

"What…?" I asked.

She took something out of her pocket and handed it to me.

As soon as I saw what it was, I shook my head. "I'm not taking a pregnancy test, Chloe. I had a period almost two weeks ago."

About to say something, she stopped and frowned. "You did?"

"I did."

"But you threw up a few mornings ago when I dropped Sutton off."

I took care of her daughter and Bronte alongside Juniper on weekdays. Soon we'd be adding little Beckham to the mix. I loved it even more than nannying, because these little ones were family.

"Pretty sure it was the sausage I had for breakfast," I told Chloe.

"You're so tired you drifted off during Sierra's show."

I cringed. "Only for a few seconds," I said. I'd hoped no one noticed. The show had been interesting, but I was so worn out and… "That's from overeating. Post-meal coma."

Chloe tilted her head and stared at me as if puzzling something out. "Was your period normal?"

With a little laugh, I said, "I don't have normal periods, but it was enough for me to know it was there. That a baby was *not* there."

Her brows went up. "So, like, a short one?"

"Like a day. Chloe…I love you, but I'm not pregnant."

"Sometimes there's bleeding when a fertilized egg implants."

"And sometimes there's just no pregnancy and a girl gets her period."

"A very light period. With multiple other signs of pregnancy. Quincy, I don't want to get your hopes up falsely, but I've been watching you for the past two weeks. You've been more tired than usual."

"I have a two-year-old."

With a half laugh, she said, "Amen to that. Will you do the test just to shut me up? Please? Then I swear I'll butt out."

I studied her, not wanting to pee on a stick for anything. I'd peed on so many sticks, had so many hopes dashed in the past year plus. It was getting too hard on my heart.

"Why are you pushing this?" I asked.

She pressed her lips together. "I just…really want you to be pregnant, Quincy."

With a laugh I didn't feel, I said, "I want to be pregnant too— Oh, my God. You're knocked up again, aren't you?" It hit me like a wrecking ball to the head. "You didn't have wine. You've been peeing all afternoon. Chloe!" In spite of myself, I was excited for her. I'd wrestle with my jealousy later.

"Don't tell anyone yet, but yes. But dammit, I didn't bring you up here to tell you that. The last thing I want to do is upset you."

"You being pregnant doesn't upset me. Well, mostly not. Taking another test will upset me."

"Unless there's a reason you threw up and you're exhausted and your boobs look bigger."

"You've been looking at my boobs?" My boobs weren't bigger that I knew of.

"Forgive me," she said. "They're very nice boobs." She held out the test again. "Humor me, please? Then I promise I'll never bring it up again."

I closed my eyes and bit my lip, wondering if I could hide my feelings for the rest of the day when the test came back negative.

"What if I'm right, Quincy?"

And there was that microscopic kernel of hope I'd tried to get better at crushing.

Dammit.

"Fine." I took the test. "Are you going to watch me pee?"

She shook her head. "I'll be right outside the door, waiting to hug you either way." She pressed a kiss to my forehead. "For luck."

I attempted a smile because she was being sweet, then closed the door once she was out of the room.

There were no instructions with the test as she'd plucked a single out of a multi-pack. I knew this because I'd become an expert on the product. I was familiar with this brand. Knew it required two minutes for results. Knew a double line signified a yes.

Squeezing my eyes shut as I sat on the toilet and tried to force Chloe's secret news out of my mind, I followed the steps. Peed on the stick. Finished up and washed my hands. Gulped in a shaky breath to brace myself.

As I dried my hands, my gaze shot to the test on the counter. Two minutes hadn't passed yet, not even one, so it wasn't face-the-facts time yet. Nevertheless, when I laid eyes on the little plastic stick, I couldn't help it. I broke down and started weeping.

———

KNOX

Quincy and Chloe had been upstairs for more than ten minutes. My curiosity was morphing into concern, and then Chloe came back by herself.

I waited to see if she'd explain where my wife was, but she didn't meet my gaze as she went straight to Holden's side, kissed his cheek, and acted like nothing was amiss as she settled in to watch the football game we'd switched to after Sierra and Hayden's show.

Before I could ask, Sierra perched next to her and started in on the topic of breastfeeding.

I decided to find out for myself what was keeping Quincy. My guess was that Juniper had woken up early.

I took the stairs two at a time, paused at the top, and strained to hear any sound that wasn't from the main floor. The adults were loud, and the door where Juniper slept was closed tight, but I noticed the bathroom door was open a crack, and light poured out. I headed that way.

When I was about to knock, I froze, listening. Quincy was…crying?

"Quince?" I pushed the door open a few inches at first to poke my head in. When I saw her sitting on the closed toilet, head in her hands, shoulders shaking, I burst the rest of the way in and bent down by her side. "What's wrong, sweetheart?"

When she didn't immediately answer but threw her arms around me and pressed her face into my shoulder, I was afraid I knew. The baby parade had finally gotten to her.

"I'm so sorry, Quincy," I said, holding on to her awkwardly.

She shook her head but kept her face buried.

I stood and pulled her up with me so I could hold her better, closer. When she looked up at me, anguish wasn't what I read on her face. Her eyes were…filled with joy? Red-rimmed for sure, but there was an undeniable spark.

"What's going on?" I asked, thoroughly confused. "Are you upset?"

Her shoulders still vibrated with sobs, but she shook her head.

"Talk to me, Quince," I said.

She used my shirt to wipe her eyes, but as she peered up at me, they refilled instantly.

"We're…we're gonna have a baby, Knox," she said in a high-pitched, incredulous voice.

I stared down at her, stunned stupid. "We're… What did you say?"

"Pregnant." She laughed as she bounced up and down, then threw her arms around my neck.

Her words wound their way to my brain at the speed of molasses, but after a few seconds, I got it. I didn't understand why she was sobbing alone in the bathroom but…

The white stick on the countertop caught my eye. I could see the double line from here, and we'd been through this enough times to know we wanted a double line.

The truth finally sank all the way in.

After all this time, all these months of trying, Quincy was pregnant.

I squeezed her to me, lifting her off the floor as I howled loudly with joy.

Quincy laughed. "Can you believe it?"

"Wooo-hoo-hoo-hoo." I spun her around the roomy bathroom, lifting my head to the heavens in gratitude.

"What the hell's going on?" Holden said in the doorway, looking concerned. "You're gonna wake up the kids."

Most days I'd do anything in my power to keep the kids sleeping, but today my sheer, utter happiness overruled practicality. Throwing my head back again, I yelled, "We're gonna have a baby!"

"Holy shit. For real?" Holden asked.

"What's going on up there?" Cash called up from the main floor.

Holden let out a whoop, then hollered, "Quincy's Knoxed up!"

I laughed at the idiotic pun. Actually it might've been the best pun ever.

"What?" Faye's voice came from the bottom of the stairs, and then I heard Chloe confirming the news to everyone down in the living room.

"Oh, my God. Finally!" Hayden came tearing up the stairs and burst right into the bathroom. She threw her arms around Quincy and me, then Ava joined, then Everly and Lexie.

Gabe and Seth loomed in the doorway. I spotted Cash behind them, and Sierra and Cole, holding a sleepy Oakley. Before I knew it, the bathroom was full of our family, hugging us, shouting congrats, high-fiving.

Everyone knew we'd been trying for more than a year. Everyone knew how heartbroken we'd been each month that passed with no pregnancy.

"Why don't we all go downstairs and celebrate instead of cramming into the spare bathroom?" Faye said from the doorway in her no-nonsense voice.

"Grand idea," Holden said. "Can't have a party in the john."

Laughing and joking, everyone filed back out and headed down the stairs.

Quincy and I stayed and held on to each other, my chin resting on top of her head, until we were alone.

I pulled back enough to look her in the eyes, her swollen, pink, never more beautiful eyes.

"It's really early to tell people, isn't it?" she asked, not looking remorseful at all.

I exhaled heavily at that truth. "These people are our

support, whatever happens. I choose to believe we'll have a healthy baby in nine months."

"Me too." Her broad smile told me she wasn't upset. "You're happy."

"I'm so fucking happy, Quince."

"Me too. Stunned and happy. I was so scared there was something wrong with me."

"You're perfect," I told her.

She laughed. "So far from perfect."

"You're perfect for me."

"I love you."

"Love you more."

Running her hands up my chest, she said, "Prove it."

With a growl, I pressed her against the wall with my body. I kissed her, infusing all of my love into it.

Before I could get too serious, there was a knock on the doorframe a foot away from us, startling us both.

"I got voted to be the spokesperson," Drake said. "Your dad said to tell you to get your rears downstairs so we can drink a toast. My wife said, and I quote, 'I'm not going up that flight of stairs for anything, and I need to squeeze Quincy and squeal with her, so tell them to get their butts down here.' Little tip for you," he said directly to me, "when a woman is six months pregnant with twins, you do whatever she says."

"Amen," Quincy said, laughing.

I stepped back, and she took my hand. We followed Drake out of the bathroom, toward the stairs, as I tried to adjust my pants enough to walk normal. My wife could still turn me on in half a heartbeat.

Downstairs, Faye was making the rounds with champagne and sparkling apple juice. I picked up two flutes while Quincy went over to Mackenzie for the squeezing, squealing thing.

When she came back to me and snuggled into my side, taking the juice flute from me, she looked up into my eyes.

There was so much love radiating at me it nearly brought me to my knees.

"Okay," Faye said. "Everyone have a glass?" She handed off the bottles to my dad, who set them aside then put his arm around her. "I'm so, so overjoyed for you, Quincy and Knox. I know it's been a bumpy road, and that makes today all the sweeter." Murmurs of agreement sounded around the room. Faye lifted her glass. "Congratulations, and here's to one more grandbaby!"

There were clinks and *hear hears* from all corners. I took a swallow, then pulled Quincy even closer, soaking in this moment.

"Uh," Holden said above the din. He glanced at Chloe, sitting next to him. Her grin widened and she gave a barely discernible nod. "Make that two. Two more grandbabies. We're due in July."

Faye gasped with happiness, my dad, grinning widely, held on to her, and everyone else cheered, congratulated, laughed, and drank another sip.

The commotion started to die down when Hayden stepped forward. "I've been competing with my older brother my entire life, and this time, Holden, I win again. Zane and I are having a baby in June!"

The uproar was even louder. Glasses were set aside in favor of hugs and congratulations and, yes, squeals. The house hadn't been quiet for a second all day, but now it was at its loudest, its happiest.

"Sierra, when are you going back to work?" my dad asked. She was still on maternity leave from her remodeling company. "We might need to add on to this place sooner than we ever planned."

With a laugh, Sierra said, "Call me anytime. At this rate we'll need a multi-phase ten-year plan."

The ruckus woke up the kids who'd still been napping, and soon all thirty of us were crowded into the great room.

Thirty that would be thirty-five by this time next year. And one of those extras would be mine and Quincy's.

With Juniper in one arm, her head resting against mine, and Quincy standing in front of me, comparing early pregnancy symptoms with Hayden and Chloe, I pulled my wife against me and our daughter, content. Thankful.

This—the huge, noisy, chaotic extended family and these two girls who were the most precious beings in the world—was what life was meant to be.

NOTE FROM THE AUTHOR

Thanks for reading *Unexpected*! I hope you loved Knox and Quincy.

Next up is the Single Dads of Dragonfly Lake. Watch for the first book in early 2024!

If you missed the North Brothers series, you can dive into book one, *True North*! Find out what happens when Mr. Socially Awkward spontaneously volunteers to be his beautiful boss's fake date.

Find it in ebook, audiobook, and paperback in my author store at amyknuppbooks.com!

———

If you liked *Unexpected*, I hope you'll consider leaving a review for it. Reviews help other readers find books and can be as short (or long) as you feel comfortable with. Just a couple sentences is all it takes. I appreciate all honest reviews.

———

Unexpected is part of the Henry Brothers series, which includes:

- Untold (prequel)
- Unraveled
- Unsung
- Undone
- Unexpected

The Henry Brothers series is a spin-off of the North Brothers series, which includes these stand-alone stories:

- True North
- True Colors
- True Blue
- True Harmony
- True Hero

ALSO BY AMY KNUPP

Coming Home

Musicians

Second Chance

Workplace Romance

North Brothers Audiobooks

ABOUT THE AUTHOR

Amy Knupp is a *USA Today* Best-Selling author of contemporary romance. She loves words and grammar and meaty, engrossing stories with complex characters.

Amy lives in Wisconsin with her husband and has two adult children, three cats, and a box turtle. She graduated from the University of Kansas with degrees in French and journalism. In her spare time, she enjoys traveling, breaking up cat fights, watching college hoops, and annoying her family by correcting their grammar.

For more information:
https://www.amyknuppbooks.com

Printed in Great Britain
by Amazon